THE VOICE OF AMERICA: STORIES

Also by Rick DeMarinis

The Voice of America: Stories

Rick DeMarinis

W.W. NORTON & COMPANY

New York   *London*

The text of this book is composed in 12/13½ Bodoni Book,

with the display set in Corvinus Skyline.

Composition and manufacturing by the Haddon Craftsmen, Inc.

First Edition.

Library of Congress Cataloging-in-Publication Data

DeMarinis, Rick, 1934–

   The voice of America: stories/Rick DeMarinis.

     p. cm.

   I. Title.

PS3554.E4554V65 1991

813′.54—dc20   90–46671

ISBN 0–393–02967–0

W.W. Norton & Company, Inc.

500 Fifth Avenue, New York, N.Y. 10110

W.W. Norton & Company, Ltd.

10 Coptic Street, London WC1A 1PU

1 2 3 4 5 6 7 8 9 0

Acknowledgments

Harper's for "Insulation" and "Rudderless Fiction: Lesson 1 (A Correspondence Course)"; *Epoch* for "Desert Places"; *Cutbank* for "The Voice of America"; *Story* for "Safe Forever" and "Horizontal Snow"; *The Georgia Review* for "Paraiso: An Elegy"; *Vox* for "The Whitened Man"; *The Paris Review* for "An Airman's Goodbye"; *Antioch Review* for "Aliens"; *Epoc* for "Wilderness."

Contents

THE VOICE
OF AMERICA:
STORIES

Safe Forever

MORE PEOPLE HAD been blown up or burned to death in 1945 than ever before in history thanks to aerial bombardment. I was eleven years old and in love with aerial bombardment. What could be more elegant than a squadron of B-29s unloading five-hundred-pound bombs or clusters of incendiaries on Tokyo, Nagoya, or Yokohama? My nightly prayer to Jesus included a plea that the war last at least until 1952 so that I could join it. I wanted to be a pilot or bombardier aboard a stratosphere-skimming Superfortress, our first true strategic bomber. So, when VJ Day came on August 14, all my dreams were vaporized in mushroom clouds of despair.

I was out on my ice-cream route in the Oakland suburb of Sobrante Park when victory was declared. My pushcart was full of 7-11 ice-milk bars, fudgesicles, and orange sherbet push-ups but sales were slow. I rang the bells that were wired to the handle of the pushcart hard and loud, but the streets remained empty. Then, as if they had been given a signal, people rushed out of their houses. I gave credit to my energetic bell-ringing. I felt the power of my bells. But they didn't approach me. They gathered on their lawns and in their driveways, drinking liquor directly out of bottles. Some were singing and cheering. Men and women kissed each other wildly and children, infected by the frenzy of the adults, ran in circles, screaming. It was a warm afternoon and there was no reason these people shouldn't have wanted ice cream. I rang my bells at them. I yelled, "Seven-eleven bars! Fudgesicles! Push-ups!" My ears rang from my own clamor.

Two men approached my cart and yanked open the heavy, insulated lid. They reached into the smoking cold box and helped themselves to boxes of my stock. They started passing out handfuls of fudgesicles, 7-11 bars, and push-ups to the cluster of children that had followed them. I held out my hand for payment, but they ignored me. They reached past my outstretched arm and helped themselves to more of my stock. "Wait!" I said. "You have to pay me!"

"The war's over, buster," one of them said. "The Japs said 'uncle.' "

I tried to grab back a carton of fudgesicles, but he held it over his head. Women and children began to reach into my cart as if it were their right. "Don't!" I said. "You can't do that!"

"What are you, some kind of war profiteer?" one of the men said. "I got news for you, the war's *over.* " He was about twenty-five years old and healthy-looking. Though I was panicky now, wondering how I was going to explain the loss of my stock to my boss and stepfather, Dan Sneed, a calmer part of my mind wondered why this man wasn't in uniform. Why weren't *all* these men in uniform? Dan Sneed was 4-F. What excused them?

I guess the question was visible in my eyes. It made him nasty. "Put a smile on your kisser," he said. "This is the happiest day of your life. Or maybe you're a Jap-lover."

He took my pushcart and wheeled it away from me at a fast trot. When he made a severe turn, he dumped it. The rest of my stock, along with several steaming blocks of dry ice, shot into the street. The children swarmed on it, screaming happily. Then someone came up behind me and untied the strings of my change apron. All my quarters, dimes, and nickels fell around my feet. I dropped to my hands and knees to retrieve them, but I had to compete with other children and a few adults.

I was paralyzed by defeat. I sat on the curb. After the money and ice cream were gone, the crowd moved away from me. I righted my cart and wheeled it back the way I came, my bells hanging silent.

An elderly woman who lived a few houses from ours tried to buy a 7-11 from me. I told her I was sold out. She put her dime back into her change purse. "You be *sure* to pray thanks for our atom bombers," she said, as if scolding me for taking victory over Japan for granted.

"I will, ma'am," I lied. I felt no gratitude. God had not granted my prayer that the war go on for another seven years. Why should I be thankful for early victory?

"Many won't have to go now," the woman said. "Many will be safe forever."

She looked at the closed lid of my pushcart and sniffed. "Sold out already?" she said. "That seems unlikely."

I pushed my cart away from her.

"You remember to pray thanks," she said. "Your mother might have lost you to the war, save for our bomb."

"I know," I said, gloomily.

The house was empty. Mother and Dan Sneed were still at work. I fixed myself a bacon and American cheese sandwich and listened to my radio programs. Terry and the Pirates were still fighting Japs somewhere in Burma. Jungle Jim was still tracking Nazi agents in a South American rain forest. Superman had located Hitler's secret weapon that would have guaranteed a German victory and was carrying it into outer space where it could be disarmed safely. It was all anticlimactic. The war was a dead issue.

I switched off the radio and carried my plate back into the kitchen. That's when I saw Mother's note, taped to the icebox.

"Charlie, put the roast in the oven at 3:30. 300°. Boil ten spuds. Wash some lettuce. Shell peas. Set up the bar. Company tonight." It was almost four. I'd been doing all the cooking since Mother had been hired as a welder at the Kaiser shipyards up in Richmond. Dan Sneed worked until dark, managing twelve pushcart boys as well as operating his own ice-cream truck in the Piedmont and Emeryville areas. He wore an all-white uniform. The jacket had a "Mr. 7-11!" patch stitched over the left breast pocket. I put the bloody rolled rib roast into the oven and turned on the gas. After I rinsed the lettuce and shelled the peas, I carried the card table out into the living room and covered it with a white tablecloth. I took Dan Sneed's stock of liquor out of a kitchen cabinet and set the bottles in a neat row on the card table. I set a row of drink glasses in front of the bottles. Later, I would chip enough ice from the twenty-five-pound block in the icebox to fill the pewter bucket. I rechecked Mother's instructions to make sure I hadn't forgotten anything, then went back to the bar and poured myself enough sloe gin to darken my tongue. A thread of fire tickled my throat. "Banzai!" I yelled, holding my glass high. "Take that, Jap!" I yelled, making ack-ack sounds between my teeth.

I went out to the garage, light-headed, to visit my B-25. It was spread out on the workbench, half finished. It had been the hardest model I'd ever attempted to build. I knew I would not finish it now. A freewheeling sense of despair overcame me. The B-25 Mitchell was the first bomber to strike at the heart of Japan, back in 1942. But now it was ancient history, just as the war itself would soon be. Next to the B-29 and its atomic bomb, the Mitchell was as dated as the Wright brothers' "flyer."

The two Olson gasoline engines that would have powered my B-25 sat in their mounts, bolted to the workbench. I primed one of them with a little gas, connected the spark-plug wire to the big Eveready dry-cell battery, and spun the prop.

The little engine sputtered, then caught, instantly filling the garage and neighborhood with a high-pitched roar. I opened the needle-valve throttle all the way, my mind happily saturated with noise. A haze of pale smoke hung in the garage in layers. I filled my lungs with it. Burning gasoline was one of my favorite aromas. I bent down to the exhaust port, mindful of the invisible propeller, and sucked fumes up my nose. A climbing tide of vertigo rocked me back.

The concrete floor of the garage felt like rubber. So did the driveway and sidewalk. I knelt down and ran my hands through the dry August lawn to see if the grass felt rubbery too, but it felt like the weak legs of docile insects. I pulled a gray tuft out of the dry ground and tossed it across the street. Then I went next door to see Darwin Duncan, not my best friend, but convenient.

"You want to go to Hayward?" I asked him.

Darwin was a small boy with an unhealthy yellow glow. His mother was a registered nurse. She kept a bookcase full of medical texts. Darwin and I would often study the *Human Anatomy for Nurses* text when no one was home.

"What for?" Darwin asked suspiciously. He was wearing heavily padded earphones. There was a soldering iron in his hand.

"What do you mean, what for? To go swimming, why else go to Hayward?"

Darwin and I went to the Hayward Plunge at least once a week during the summer. It was a big indoor pool. I'd learned how to swim there, and how to dive. My favorite dive was illegal, but the lifeguard didn't stop you unless you were bothering people with it. You'd sprint along the edge of the pool, then dive with a kind of spinning, corkscrew twist. The motion caused your body to auger its way to the bottom. It was frightening because you didn't have control. Hydraulic pressure seized you, applying an uncancelable torque that you had to ride out. You had to see the corkscrew dive to its end.

Then, when you hit bottom you had to figure out which way was up, even though it was obvious. You were disoriented.

But Darwin didn't want to go swimming. He was working on his radios. He was a radio nut. His room looked like a repair shop. Every flat surface, even his bed, was littered with the scavenged parts of old radios. His current project was a nine-tube, four-band superheterodyne. He was a genius, but his parents worried about him. They wanted him to be normal, like me. "Why don't you play baseball, like Charlie?" they'd ask him, in my presence. "Charlie, why don't you teach Darwin how to throw a football?" But they were wrong about Darwin. He was probably a better athlete than me. I knew he could beat me in a footrace, at least. He just preferred to work out technical problems in the privacy of his cluttered bedroom.

His room was hazy with solder smoke. I liked the smell of solder smoke, too. Not as much as the smell of exhaust fumes, but the nose-pinching, acrid taste of hot solder had its appeal. It was like sour incense. I cleared a spot on Darwin's bed and sat down to watch him work. He slid a thin screwdriver into a tangle of multicolored wires to make an adjustment of some kind. "I'm aligning the intermediate frequency amplifiers," he said. Darwin was a year older than me and had skipped the fifth grade.

Human Anatomy for Nurses was shoved under his night table. I picked it up and thumbed it open to the section on Human Reproduction. The illustration of a woman lying on her back with her legs up and thighs held wide always made my heart lurch. This reaction was instantaneous and reliable. Then my mouth would go dry, and if I swallowed my throat would click. All her parts, interior and exterior, were flagged with Latin labels. In my bed at night, after my routine prayers, I would whisper the forbidden Latin names as if I were preparing myself for some dark, subterranean priesthood. The pages of this section of the book were greasy with use. I thumbed ahead to the cutaway view of a tumescent penis fully encased by a vagina. My throat clicked loud enough to be heard, but Darwin didn't look up from his delicate adjustments. I'd seen this drawing a thousand times, but the red machinery that allowed human beings to repeat themselves endlessly down the centuries made my palms sweat.

Darwin handed me the earphones. "This is London, England," he said casually. "Loud and clear, with some selective fading."

I put the earphones on. Behind a roar that sounded like a waterfall, I heard two comedians exchange quips about Adolf Hitler as if he were still alive and subject to the sting of ridicule. They were hanging on to the war, too.

When I went home, Mother had dinner on the table. "Where have you been, Charlie?" she asked.

"Darwin's," I said.

"Dan's not too thrilled with you."

I went into the front room. Dan Sneed and a lanky WAVE were drinking highballs. I started to tell him that the loss of my stock wasn't my fault, but he spoke first. "You didn't chip any ice, Charlie. How am I supposed to make drinks for our guest if there isn't any ice?"

"I'm sorry, Dan," I said. "I forgot."

"You forgot," he said. He leaned down to get a good look at me. "Your blackheads are coming back again," he said. He was a tall, narrow-shouldered man with thin brown hair combed straight back. "Use the washcloth on your face, Charlie."

"Don't be too hard on him, Dan," said the WAVE. "He's got beautiful manners. He's got the manners of an officer and gentleman." She touched my cheek with her open hand. Her hand was damp and chilly. She had a long, melancholy face but her eyes were bright and fun-loving. I decided to tell Dan later about what had happened on my route. Nothing could be done about it now anyway.

I went to sleep that night trying to picture the secret Latin parts of the WAVE, but I had trouble getting past her crisp blue uniform, which I admired extravagantly. The next morning, I found that uniform strewn down the length of the hallway, as if she had undressed on the run. Mother and Dan's bedroom door was not completely shut. I pushed it open an inch. The lanky WAVE was in bed with them. She saw me. She sat up and stretched, the sheet falling away from her breasts. I ducked, as if from a wild pitch. "Wait up, Charlie," she said. She made a halfhearted effort to pull the sheet up. *Ampulla, areola, adipose tissue, epithelium,* I thought. "How about starting the coffee, kiddo?"

"Yes, ma'am," I whispered. Mother and Dan Sneed were still asleep on either side of the tall WAVE.

I made the coffee, then started some bacon frying. I broke six eggs into a bowl and whipped them until they were foamy. Then I collected the full ashtrays and drink glasses from the living room and brought them into the kitchen. I dumped the ashtrays into the garbage, then put the glasses in soapy water to soak. I laid six slices of bread on a cookie sheet and put them under the broiler. When she came out, all made up and in her uniform, breakfast was ready.

"You run a tight ship, Charlie," she said. "But I don't know if I can deal with all this." She lit a cigarette and blew smoke out one side of her mouth, away from the food. "We drank a bit last night." She sipped her coffee, but did not touch the food.

While she smoked cigarettes and drank coffee, I ate. Her breasts were large and slung low. I made myself see them through the fabric of her uniform, the dark pink *areolae,* the abrupt nipples.

She shoved her plate across the table. "Here," she said. "You're a growing boy. You've got room for this." when she yawned the low breasts rose, straining the buttons of her tunic.

I walked her to the bus stop on East 14th Street. She worked at the Alameda Naval Air Station. She said she was two hours late. "Not that it matters," she added. "Nobody but the fanatics are going to report on time today. Ask your folks."

We waited together for the bus. She sat like a man, her legs stretched out in front of her, crossed at the ankles, her arms resting on the back of the bench. A cigarette dangled from her full lips. "I'm from Iowa, Charlie," she said. She stared into the distance as if she could see cornfields. "Christ. Iowa. If they think I'm coming back to Dubuque after working in the Bay Area for two years they've got another think coming. This is paradise, for my money."

The bus came. We stood up together. She straightened her uniform and crushed her cigarette out on the pavement. She shook my hand. "You're a solid citizen, Chas," she said. She pulled me close and hugged me, her chest pillowing my face.

On my way home I bought a twenty-five-pound block of ice from Mr. Salas, who ran the ice dispenser. Mr. Salas didn't speak English but he was in a joyful mood. He cupped his hands in front of him, then threw them upward. "Boom!" he said, shaping the air between us into a mushroom cloud. I smiled because he expected me to, and he patted and tousled my hair.

It was the job I hated most—carrying a block of ice home. Mr. Salas had tied twine around it so that I could carry it, but the twine cut into my fingers and I had to set the block down on the sidewalk every so often, and its awkward weight made the muscles in my arms burn. Now that the war was over, we would be able to get a refrigerator. The atom bomb had made that possible. The first time I saw a photo of that mushroom cloud, I thought of Aladdin's lamp and the genie that rose out of it as smoke. Because of that cloud of magical smoke, we would have all the things that were impossible to have during the war. I realized I should be thankful, and I prayed my thanks that night, just as the old woman had suggested, but my heart wasn't in it. Mid-prayer I lost the drift and wandered into dreams of combat: P-47 Thunderbolts strafing German supply trucks, airborne troops engaged in door-to-door combat in French villages, destroyers dumping depth charges on Jap subs. When all my combat scenarios had been exhausted, I watched the lanky WAVE sit up in bed and stretch, her long breasts reaching upward. I fell asleep with the incomplete prayer on my lips and dreamed of refrigerators. I opened one of three that sat in our kitchen and took out a heavy roast. Blood from the roast splashed my feet. I didn't have any clothes on. The WAVE said, "You're an officer and a gentleman, kiddo." She sat at the kitchen table sipping coffee. I asked her what time it was. "It doesn't make any difference," she said. "Yes it does," I said. "No it doesn't," she said. "Not anymore, Chas." The natural melancholy of her face seemed a thing apart, something that could live on, long after she was gone. I ducked away from it.

I felt like I had been asleep for days, but when I woke up it was only half past midnight. I got dressed and went out to the backyard. There was a short fence between our yard and the Duncans'. I hopped the fence and rapped on Darwin's bedroom window. He opened it and I climbed in. I knew he'd be working on his radio, and he was. His room was hazy with accumulated smoke. His eyes were red. "I'm adding a two-stage RF amplifier," he said. "It'll triple the sensitivity."

I nodded. I couldn't think of anything more boring than working on radios. "Can I get the book?" I asked. He was bent over the upside-down chassis, soldering iron probing the tangle of wires, threads of white smoke curling past his ears. He shrugged.

I tiptoed down the hall. Darwin's parents were asleep in their bedroom. They were both snoring—almost in harmony. I didn't need to turn on the living-room lights. I knew exactly what shelf the book was on and where it was on that shelf. I drew it out of its place slowly with my already damp fingers. It's familiar weight and texture excited me.

I cleared a spot on Darwin's bed and the book fell open to

the well-visited pages on Human Reproduction. Even though I had seen those illustrations a hundred times, the sexual architecture of human beings retained its power over me. The scrupulously detailed perineum, the seat of mystery, the dark valley between the columnar cliffs of the thighs, always made me catch my breath. In the same way, years later, the Grand Canyon would make me dizzy with the belief that surprise and whim ruled the visible world.

The clicking of my throat exasperated Darwin. He unplugged his soldering iron and sat on the bed next to me. "Why don't you look at something else for a change?" he said.

"What for?" I asked.

He took the book and thumbed through it. "The side view of the skull looks like Africa," he said, holding up a red, white, and blue illustration. "The mandible goes from the Congo River to Cape Town. The parietal bones are the Sahara desert." He turned pages. "The heart looks like Africa, too," he said. "The bulge of the left atrium looks like Egypt."

Darwin could be as boring as his radios. I grabbed the book away from him. It fell open to the posterior view of the external genitalia of the female. We studied the layers of complexity in silence.

"It looks like a church," I said.

Darwin often boasted about being an atheist, but his parents were religious. He hit me on the shoulder. I dropped the book and it walloped the floor. We held our breaths but the harmonious snoring from his parents' bedroom didn't pause. "You want to see Vicki Zebard?" I said.

He shrugged. "Sure," he said indifferently, as if I'd asked him if he wanted to go to Hayward.

The Zebards lived on the last street of the development. The field behind their house was staked for a hundred new homes. With commando stealth, we crept up to the dark house. "Maybe it's too late," I said, my cowardice beginning to assert itself.

"It doesn't matter what time it is, stupid," Darwin said.

I knew that, of course. All we had to do was tap on her window. It made no difference that it was nearly 2:00 A.M. I groped in the dirt for a small stone. I heard my blood billow past my ears. I was breathing hard but not hard enough to keep up with my accelerating heart. I felt dizzy. Darwin took the stone from me. He lobbed it against Vicki's window. The light came on after the third stone almost cracked the pane. The blind rose slowly, and there was Vicki Zebard. She peered out at us. She held a hand up to her eyes, as if to shade them from the dark. Then she yawned, or pretended to yawn. She sat down on her bed and lit a cigarette, legs crossed, nightgown hiked up to her thighs. She seemed oblivious of us, lost in her own thoughts. We hopped around in the dirt below her window without making a sound. "Do it, do it," Darwin hissed. She enjoyed torturing us. Finally she stood up. She raised her nightgown over her head, very slowly, in one-inch increments. Vicki had just turned thirteen. She was a heavy girl no one really liked. She walked to school alone, and she was always alone on the playground, unless someone wanted to torment her a little. She picked up her cigarette and paced back and forth in front of the window, her large, flaccid breasts opulent in the dull light from her bed lamp. To enhance the idea that she was unconscious of us, she talked to herself. She poked a finger into her cheek thoughtfully, as if stumped about something. She'd cock her head to the left and then to the right. Her pubic hair was dark and powerful, fully adult, rising almost to her navel. Darwin was still hopping silently, but I was partially paralyzed. When she pulled down her shade, Darwin jumped on me. We rolled around in the dirt for a while, in a kind of celebration. Then we had a footrace home, Darwin beating me by a full block.

The darkened neighborhood seemed strange to me. Did I actually live here? Did anyone actually live here? Bats flitted around the streetlights, eating millers. How strange the world was, how beautiful. I didn't feel so bad about the war being over. But I wondered, what's going to happen next, and could I bear to wait for it?

"Pudenda!" Darwin yelled.

"Mammaries!" I responded.

"Infrapubic ramus!" Darwin screamed.

"Sphincter ani externus!" I yodeled.

Like medieval monks gone berserk, we screamed the Latin names of the lower anatomy until lights began to come on in the dark little houses.

The next day was the hottest day of the year. I sold out early and came home, my change apron bulging with silver. I went to my room and stacked and counted my gross earnings, then subtracted my profit. I rolled the nickels, dimes, and quarters into paper wrappers. Dan Sneed was in Emeryville and wouldn't be back for several hours to restock my pushcart. I had an afternoon to kill. My mother was still working at Kaiser, but now that the war was over there was no need for Liberty ships. She expected her layoff notice any day now. Then she'd be a normal housewife again, she said. The world was going to be normal again. I didn't remember what normal was since I was only five or six when the war began to change everything.

The elation I felt the night before didn't have staying power. I made a pitcher of Kool-Aid and filled it with chipped ice. I carried the pitcher and a glass out to the garage. I picked up the skeletal wings and the half-finished fuselage of the B-25 and crushed them into a soft wad of balsa wood and tissue paper. Then I started one of the Olsons and breathed exhaust fumes until my depression was gradually replaced by a brain-spinning giddiness.

Darwin came over, attracted by the screaming Olson. "Let's go swimming!" he yelled.

I took one last lung-sweetening breath of burned gas and pulled the spark-plug wire loose. "Okay," I said.

"Not the Plunge, though," Darwin said. "The bay."

The Hayward Plunge in hot weather was like a greenhouse. It sapped your energy. After swimming across the pool a few times you felt dead. You felt like you were sweating even under water. And afterward you felt waterlogged.

We walked to San Leandro Bay. It was a place forbidden to swimmers because raw sewage from south Oakland and San Leandro was pumped directly into the water. Parents tried to keep their kids away from all swimming areas in that big polio year of 1945, believing that the virus was carried and spread by water. San Leandro Bay was especially feared. But the fear of parents was an abstract thing, an irrelevancy, like the rusted BB-pocked signs that warned against trespass or dumping, or commanded, "No Swimming."

The beach was lumpy with seaweed and garbage. Broken bottles gleamed in the oily sand. Small waves lapped at a mossy mattress someone had tried to launch. None of this seemed ugly or inappropriate to us. It was San Leandro Bay.

There was no one else around, so we stripped. Darwin sprinted into the halfhearted waves screaming. I followed him. The water was warm and thick, like soup. It stank, but it was not like the eye-burning chlorine stink of the Plunge. I loved swimming here, in salt water, because you could not sink. The heavy water made you buoyant and you felt you would stay afloat even if you dozed off.

Darwin was floating on his back, his small erection periscoping the brown water. "Penile distension," he yelled.

"Corpus spongiosum!" I screamed, sending up a periscope of my own.

We swam for hours, then walked home sunburned, salt-crusted, and weak. I sat on a curb next to an idling delivery van and breathed its exhaust. Darwin sat next to me. He wasn't a habitual sniffer of exhaust fumes like me, but he didn't mind them. School would begin in three weeks. Darwin had already graduated from Stonehurst elementary school and was attending junior high, and he hated it. He looked like a fifth-grader. The big eighth- and ninth-graders picked on him mercilessly. I hated the idea of going back to Stonehurst, even though I'd be a sixth-grader, loaded with seniority. I had squandered summer. And now that the war was over, school was bound to be more boring than ever.

The last Saturday before school started, Darwin and I went to Emeryville, where the Oakland baseball stadium was, to watch the Oaks play the hated San Francisco Seals. We bought tickets for the right-field bleachers, the cheapest seats in the park. We wanted to be out there in right, where the left-handed sluggers would hit their homers. I brought two gloves—one for Darwin—anticipating free baseballs.

It was a dull game for seven innings. The Oaks hadn't hit a ball out of the infield. My personal hero, Les Scarsella, the aging slugger who had hit .300 for the Boston Braves back in 1940, had struck out once and had popped out to shortstop. He was closing in on another forty-home-run season, so my hopes were high. Gene Bearden, ace of the Oakland pitching staff, had held the Seals to four hits and one run, a line-drive homer by their powerful first baseman, Ferris Fain. Then, in the bottom of the seventh, Scarsella slapped at a three-and-oh pitch and drove it over the center-field scoreboard, with Wally Westlake on second. Darwin and I went crazy, pounding each other with our gloves and screaming out the Latin names for the sexual apparatus. In the top of the ninth, though, Ferris Fain, with Hugh Luby on first, caught a hanging curveball and drove it deep to right. It was a line drive all the way, still climbing as it passed over our heads and out of the park. We'd been calling him names at the top of our lungs—mons pubis! ductus deferens! labium majorum!—and, as if he'd heard and understood and wanted sweet revenge, he straightened out Bearden's sloppy curveball and laced it into the streets of Emeryville.

The weak end of the lineup came up in the bottom of the

ninth and the game ended on three dribbling ground balls, all to Hugh Luby, the Seals' great second baseman.

We rode the bus home depressed. We both felt a little queasy from all the hot dogs we'd eaten. Darwin looked more sallow than usual. A glaze of sweat made his face shine. He complained of a sore neck. "I'm going to puke," he said.

"Wait till you get home," I said.

He stepped between two parked cars and vomited. Hearing someone vomit always made me want to vomit, too, and so I kept walking until I couldn't hear him. When he caught up to me, he said, "I don't feel so hot."

"It was all those hot dogs," I said.

"No, I think it's the flu."

We walked the rest of the way without talking. When I opened the front door of our house, I heard arguing. There was a man I didn't know sitting at the kitchen table. He was short and nearly bald, but he had thick, muscular wrists and forearms. His forearms were tattooed with American flags. He was sipping from a bottle of beer. Mother and this man had been drinking for a while. "I'm going to celebrate!" Mother said, smiling viciously at Dan.

"Celebrate *what?*" Dan said. "Unemployment?"

"Look here," said the man at the table. "I don't think I want to get into this."

"Shut up, Weldon," Mother said. "You're an invited guest. I'm going to make you supper. I invited Weldon for supper. He was laid off today, too. I don't see why he can't have supper. We're going to enjoy ourselves."

"Looks like you've already been enjoying yourself," Dan said. Dan, still in his whites, had just returned from his Piedmont route.

Mother threw a dishrag at him. It hit the window, then draped itself over the curtain rod. Dan lit a cigarette and blew smoke thoughtfully at the seated man. Then he saw me in the doorway. "I need to look at your books, Charlie," he said.

"You're running short. What are you doing, giving away ice cream?"

I hadn't told him about my VJ Day disaster yet. I shrugged and went to my room. He followed me. "I think you owe me thirty dollars, Charlie," he said. I had a mason jar full of dollar bills and another one full of change on a shelf in my closet. I took the bills down and counted out the money I owed him. He took the bills and stuffed them into his wallet. But that wasn't the end of it. He looked at me for a while, studying my face. "Stay put," he said. He went out. When he came back he had his Vacutex. "I told you a thousand times to use a washcloth on your face. You can't be meeting the public with blackheads all over your face. Blackheads and ice cream don't mix." He'd ordered the Vacutex from an ad he saw in *Popular Science.* It was a syringe that sucked blackheads into it. I hated the thing. It was painful and it didn't work.

Dan pushed me into my chair. He cupped the back of my head in his left hand and applied the Vacutex to my face. The tip of the Vacutex was hollow. He pressed it on a blackhead, then drew back on the syringe. Supposedly the blackhead was lifted out of my face and sucked into the body of the syringe. It didn't work, but Dan Sneed believed in it anyway. He believed that if he pushed it harder into my face, the black-head would eventually loosen its grip. When he gave up, my blackheads were haloed with bright red circles.

I washed my face in cold water, then went out to the kitchen to see if Mother was really going to make supper. She was sitting on Weldon's lap. Dan Sneed was leaning against the sink counter, looking forlorn. "We're going to San Francisco," Mother said. "We're going to the Top of the Mark to celebrate. Vaughn Monroe is playing there." She gave Weldon a sloppy kiss. Weldon turned bright red and tried to show Dan Sneed a "no harm done" smile, but Dan was staring at the wallpaper.

I went back to my room and took a few dollars out of my

money jar. There was an Abbott and Costello movie playing at the Del Mar Theater in San Leandro. I went next door to see if Darwin was feeling good enough to go with me, but his mother said he was running a temperature. She looked at me suspiciously, as if I had something to do with Darwin's illness. "Did you boys go swimming in the bay?" she asked. She was a huge woman, tall and thick.

"No, ma'am," I said. "Just the Hayward Plunge."

She squinted at me. "Do you have the measles?"

I touched my still-smarting face. "No, ma'am. My stepfather squeezed some blackheads."

"You shouldn't squeeze them. All you need to do wash twice a day with soap and water."

I went to the movie alone. I loved the Del Mar Theater. It had a huge photograph of Harold Peary on the billboard. Harold Peary was a Portuguese actor who played the Great Gildersleeve on the radio. He was from San Leandro and the entire town was proud of his success.

Darwin had polio. I visited him once in the Oakland Children's Hospital. He was in a long white room that had a dozen iron lungs in it. The breathing sound of the twelve iron lungs was eerie. The lungs were silver canisters about seven feet long. The paralyzed children were lying on their backs inside the canisters. Only their heads were outside the lungs. I sat next to Darwin and looked at his face in the mirror that was placed at an angle directly above him. The mirror allowed you to sit down and talk face-to-face to the person in the lung. The trouble was, the person in the iron lung could only talk when the machine had allowed his paralyzed lungs to draw enough air, but the machine was slow. I asked Darwin how he was feeling, and the machine would click and sigh and then Darwin answered, "Not too good." I wanted to cheer him up, but it didn't seem possible.

"How's your transversus perinei profundus?" I said.

A nurse making an adjustment on the iron lung next to Darwin's turned to look at me.

Darwin's machine clicked and sighed. His face in the mirror was expressionless. "How's your clitoris?" Darwin asked. The nurse raised an eyebrow and shook her head at us. Darwin closed his eyes and when I spoke to him again he didn't answer. He'd fallen asleep.

Shortly after school started, Dan Sneed left home for a job in Fort Worth, Texas. I wasn't sure if Mother and I were supposed to join him later or not. Mother found a job in an Oakland department store demonstrating yo-yos, which had become a postwar fad. It didn't pay nearly as much as her welding job, but it was all she could get. The job market, now that the defense plants were idle, was depressed. A man moved in with us. His name was Mel Sprinkle. He'd worked at the Kaiser shipyard, too, and had yet to find another job that suited him. He made me nervous. He hung around the house most of the day, reading the newspaper and making phone calls. "There's not much work for a man like me," he'd say. I took that to mean either that he was overqualified for most of the jobs he saw advertised or that his skills were rare and generally unappreciated. He was muscular and athletic-looking and he ate everything I cooked, but he didn't seem to have much energy. He wore one of Dan Sneed's old bathrobes around the house while he drank coffee and studied the want ads.

Now that Dan Sneed was gone, I was out of work, too. I hated hanging around the house with Mel Sprinkle, and so I spent afternoons and weekends out in the garage or wandering through the neighborhood, watching work crews frame new houses in the bare fields next to Sobrante Park.

On the Sunday before Thanksgiving, I went to an air show at the Oakland airport. The Army Air Corps's first jet fighter, the Bell P-59 Air Comet, was the star of the show. It flew circles around the heavy, slow-moving fighter planes of World War Two. It was a point on the horizon, coming at you, making no sound. Then it was right in your face, fifty feet over the field, a silent flash of silver followed by its own slow thunder. One by one, the outclassed piston-powered fighters landed, clearing the sky for the future. They taxied to their hangars in an embarrassing flourish of waddling turns as they exercised their obsolete maneuverability. Quaint propwash made skirts billow and hats fly while the Air Comet stood on the fire-belching nozzles of its twin jet turbines and climbed vertically into complete invisibility. The crowd, faces painfully up-turned to the zenith, made no sound.

The week Darwin came home from the hospital—on crutches with steel braces holding his useless legs rigid—I broke my arm in two places. I jumped a curb on my way home from school and lost control of my bike. I came down hard in the middle of a busy lane of traffic. A woman screeched her brakes to avoid running over me, then pulled her car over to the curb. She saw my bent arm and told me to get into the car. She picked up my bike and put it into the backseat. It was a bad break, a compound fracture. A shaggy tip of bone peeked through the ripped skin. I gave the woman directions to my house, while marveling at the fragile architecture of human anatomy.

"You're a calm one, aren't you?" she said. "Are you in pain?"

I looked at my wrecked arm. It fell away from itself midway between wrist and elbow, making a perfect Z. *Ulna, radius,* I thought. "No, ma'am," I said. I was insulated from pain by shock. I felt light-headed, as if I'd been breathing gas fumes in the garage. I let my face rest against the cool glass of the window. She drove slowly, in second gear, trying to avoid bumps that might jar my arm. She talked to me as she drove, her soothing voice rich with motherly concern, as I imagined myself in the Plexiglas nose of a B-29, on the one-way mission that would carry me into the rest of my life.

Desert Places

FRED OCEAN WROTE to his wife, Sara, twice a week—amusing, energetic letters meant as much to cheer himself up as to entertain her. He made the stark Arizona landscape bloom with Disneyesque exaggerations: "It's so desolate out here the red ants look up at me beseechingly when I walk to the post office. They want me to kill them." He described with good-natured cruelty the geriatric midwesterners who came here to Casa del Sol to retire among the scorpions, lizards, and black widows. He assembled the details of the daily skirmishes between their sixteen-year-old daughter, Renata, and his mother. "So far it's a bitchy little war of hit-and-run raids and long-range sniping," he wrote. "But it's going to escalate into a full-scale nuclear exchange if we don't get out of here pretty soon." He didn't tell her that his panic attacks had returned full-blown since he and Renata had arrived in Casa del Sol, or that because of them, he'd started drinking again. Nor did he mention the woman in Tucson, Germaine Folger, who had become his de factor drinking partner.

The high spirits he mustered for his letters home did not extend to his daily life. He was exhausted from being on edge most of the time, anticipating the inevitable snide remark from his mother, Mimi Ocean, and the wild mood swings of his daughter. He felt like a tightrope walker, his mother and daughter sitting on opposite ends of his balancing pole.

Renata hated the desert retirement community and begged at least once a day to return to Seattle. "I need *green,*" she said. "Nothing's green here. I've got to see a green tree, green grass, green water. I feel like I'm stuck in a million square miles of kitty litter." But he had promised Sara to keep Renata here for at least a month. What had been a close mother-daughter relationship had become a contest of wills, beginning about the time Renata started high school. Renata hated high school and wanted to quit. Both Sara and Fred believed that a month of exile would give Renata the perspective she needed to take stock of her life and to reconsider.

So far the strategy was a failure. The hoped-for tranquilizing effect of the remote desert community did not materialize. The opposite happened. Renata had become more hostile, more headstrong in her poorly thought-out plan for total independence. She wanted to go to work as a gofer for a rock band, eventually breaking into the management side of concert tours—all this on the basis of having talked to one of the Eurythmics for three minutes in a Portland hotel lobby. They had tried to force her back into school, but neither Fred nor Sara—aware of what went on in big-city high schools these days—had the necessary belief in the quality of the education Renata was receiving to give their efforts moral authority. In any case, they would have had to tie her hand and foot and deliver her to the school grounds, but even then she'd eventually walk away, refuse to do the work, or find some other way to defeat them.

Fred's mother hadn't seen Renata for three years. In that time, Renata had grown to adult size. She was five feet ten inches tall, with a strong, wide-shouldered build. Her only interest in high school had been the swim team, but that hadn't been sufficient to hold her. Her punk costume and hairstyle—a collection of colored spikes that made her look like an old representation of Miss Liberty—put Mimi Ocean off immediately. "Good Christ, what in the hell did you let her do *that* for?" she asked Fred at the airport in Tucson, well within Renata's hearing. "She looks like she's on leave from some halfway house for mental cases." His mother, who had just had cataract surgery, inspected Renata at close range through special eyeglasses that looked like goggles.

"Luckily," Fred wrote, "Rennie finds the wild life around here interesting. For example, there's a swallow's nest in the entryway to my mother's house. It's tucked up in a corner and has three or four baby swallows in it. Rennie checks on them every morning, fattening them up with toast crumbs. There's a big aggressive roadrunner that passes through the backyard every afternoon. He pokes around for a while before moving on. Rennie calls him Big Bopper."

It struck him that his letters to Sara were a kind of espionage, treasonous to both his mother and daughter. For that reason, he had to write them late at night in the privacy of his bedroom, or at the local cemetery where his father was buried. Needing an afternoon escape, he'd drive his mother's white Cadillac convertible out to the local "boot hill," the grassless, hardpan graveyard that had once served the adjacent nineteenth-century mining community of Doloroso. Doloroso had been partially restored into a certified "ghost town," the owners of which had their cash registers primed for the permanent tourists of Casa del Sol. "I like this cemetery," Fred wrote. "It's filled with the bones of miners, gunfighters, and Civil War deserters—a worthy cast for a big-budget western. I think of Dad and the other retirees who are buried here as sort of underground tourists, mingling with the local color." He wrote his letter seated on a bench-high stone next to the flat concrete slab that marked his father's grave. His father's slab looked—appropriately, Fred thought—like a section of prestressed concrete used in bridge construction. It was more of a barrier against burrowing animals than a memorial.

Renata hated the cemetery and would not accompany him there, even though it meant that she'd be in the house alone with her grandmother. She liked Doloroso, though, because it had a café, and this was where Renata took most of her meals. She couldn't bear her grandmother's cooking. "Mother is essentially blind," Fred wrote. "All kinds of debris winds up in the food—hairpins, buttons, even animals. Last night—I swear to God—something crawled out of the paella. It was cricket-size. Rennie and I watched it drag itself across the table trailing a saffron slick. It moved badly, as though it had left a couple of legs back in the casserole pan. Rennie retched, excused herself, plunked down in front of the TV with a can of cashews and a Pepsi."

The stone Fred sat on marked the grave of one Henry Phelps, a man killed in something called "The Arrowhead Mine Disaster of 1912," according to the inscription on the brass plate attached to the front of the stone. He imagined that Phelps and his father would have had common interests—Ivan Ocean had started out as an iron-ore miner in northern Michigan back in the 1920s. The notion that the two men were somehow compatible satisfied a relic curiosity in Fred. Perhaps they were sharing a mild and unharried eternity, trading memories in the closeted earth. Why not? If the Mormons could give their honored dead entire *planets* to rule, why not this simple and unembroidered afterlife for the honorable bones of Henry Phelps and Ivan Ocean?

When Fred wrote his letters in the cemetery, he felt as if he were addressing both his wife and his father. He whispered each word out loud before committing it to paper, even though he knew his father wouldn't appreciate his humor, or, more accurately, the whimsical melancholy in which it was couched. He remembered how his father would sit behind his no-nonsense steel desk, his barrel-like torso erect, glancing at his watch impatiently, only half listening, picking out a phrase now and then to single out as evidence of his son's faulty and perilous grasp of reality. "Life makes no apologies, son," he once said. "And self-pity is the *worst* reaction to hard knocks."

The mottoes of rust-belt capitalism had always been easy to make fun of, but Fred had come to understand that, hokey as they were, these mottoes aptly represented his father's honest strength, his untethered spirit. Ivan Ocean had risen out of the iron-ore mines of northern Michigan to become the owner-manager of Decatur Metal Fasteners, Inc. "Rennie is Dad all over again," Fred wrote, "just as stubborn, just as impatient, hating all forms of dependence, waiting for her chance to cut the ties. No wonder she wants out of high school. Yesterday she called it a 'day-care center with team sports.' Dad quit school when he was fifteen—did you know that? Ran off to Escanaba, lied about his age, got a job in a Negaunee mine, worked his way through Michigan Tech, bought his ticket for the capitalist gravy train. He doesn't know it—" Fred scratched that out and rewrote: "He didn't know it but he was never able to accept discipline, either. He was a wild mustang with frontal lobes. They say character traits leapfrog the generations. Think of the Fords. Henry was the mustang, his son Edsel a sweet old plug—nice guy, but he went swayback under the saddle—but Henry the Second, the grandson, was the mustang reborn. So it is with Rennie, me, and Dad. (Hey, am I leaving you out of this formula, darling? But you've always said that Rennie is one-hundred percent Ocean.) Mother can't see the similarities, but I can, and they are real, even to the physiognomy—the big, peasant build, the tough jaw, the unblinking eyes that both you and I have trouble meeting head-on. I'm the Edsel of the clan, honey, the rage-less caretaker, the nice guy with a music box tinkling where there ought to be a snarling dynamo. I'm just the conduit for the genetic fire."

Whoa, he told himself, dropping his writing pad and pocketing his pen. He didn't like the drift of this letter. He didn't like the metaphors, the deft but unconscious switch from witty reportage to dark confession. (He could almost hear his father coax, "Don't stop now, Freddy, you're on the right track. You're headed for a solid dose of reality. Go for it, boy.") "Reality is overrated, Dad," he said out loud. A sudden gust of wind, a dust devil, sucked a plastic rose from the grave of another retiree, carrying it high in a violent spiral. He watched the dust devil vandalize the old graveyard, scattering the unwilted artificial bouquets. It rocked the Cadillac as it crossed the road that paralleled the cemetery and moved toward Doloroso, where it seemed to lose interest, allowing its hoard of fake roses and bits of twigs and litter to settle back to earth.

That night he dreamed of dust devils, grown to tornado size. They were coming for him. He drove the Cadillac into the desert, trying to escape, but the engine gradually lost power and finally quit. He put the top up, rolled up the windows, turned on the air conditioner, the tape deck, the radio, but nothing worked for long and the wind chuckled insanely against the pitching car. He woke up sweating, sick to his stomach. He reached for the Rolaids on the night table, then realized that the nausea was from adrenaline and that he wasn't sick but frightened, the fear coming to him disguised as an idea that could be worked out or ignored. He rolled over, pulling the covers up, hoping to slow down his accelerating mind in the bogs of sleep, but the adrenaline kept coming and he began to shake. He got up, moved down the dark hall toward the living room, switched on the lights. His mother kept a stock of gin and tequila in a cabinet against the wall. He took down the gin from the top shelf, poured himself a quiet glassful, drank half of it down. He went out then into the patio, under a night sky that seemed blistered by a million stars. He sat in a deck chair and took small gulps of gin. "Jesus, Jesus," he said, rocking back and forth.

When he went back into the house it was nearly dawn. His mother was already up, making coffee. He tried to slip back into his bedroom unnoticed but she saw him and called him into the kitchen. "You're drinking," she said.

"Medicinally," he said, not wanting a lecture or an argument or even permission, but she was a drinker herself, well into her cups early every evening, and did not press it.

"When are you leaving, Freddie?" she said.

"Eleven days," he said—too quickly—and he realized that he'd been marking time.

Without her goggles his mother's eyes seemed unnaturally dark and liquid—nocturnal eyes capable of absorbing more of him than ordinary sight would permit. "Eleven days won't change anything," she said. "Eleven hundred days won't be enough."

"Oh, Mother, come on," he said. "Rennie's not that—"

"Rennie's not the problem, Freddie. *You* are. You're afraid of your own daughter."

"Brilliant," he said, turning away from the black, unfocused eyes.

"Say what you want, it's true. You're afraid of her, afraid she won't love you. But you're fooling yourself, Freddie. Rennie's a whole lot tougher than you are. She's a steam roller and she knows it. As long as you treat her with kid gloves, she's going to walk right over you."

"Fine," he said. "I'll take the belt to her."

His mother sighed. "No you won't. You couldn't. And even if you could, it's far too late. Let her do what she wants. She will anyway." The coffee finished perking and she poured out two cups. After taking a small, hissing sip, she said, "Freddie, I'd like the two of you to leave. I'd like you to go back to Seattle as soon as you can."

He almost took advantage of this remark. It was an old habit. He put on a wounded look, the phrase he wanted was on his lips, but he saw a tear start out of an old ruined eye and he held back.

"You miss Dad a lot," he said.

"I do," she said. "I really do."

When he went back to his room, Renata was sitting on his bed. "I want to burn down this house," she said.

"You can't," he said. "It's made out of clay. Adobe."

"Then I'll turn the hose on it and dissolve it. Ashes to ashes, mud to mud."

She was actually smiling. She smiled so seldom these days it almost broke his heart. "Brat," he said, slapping her lightly on the thigh.

"I want to go home, Daddy," she said, her voice small, like a remnant of childhood.

"So do I, baby," he said.

He sat next to her on the bed. Renata put her arm around his shoulder. "Daddy," she said. "You're out of your envelope, you know that, don't you?"

"What?" It was hard to keep up with teenage jargon. He wasn't even sure it was jargon, since Rennie tended to invent her own.

"You're over the edge, out of your element," she translated. "You're red-lining, Pop."

"Look, Rennie—"

"I heard you talking to Grandpa yesterday. You were in the bathroom, shaving. I think you're weirding out. Daddy, I want to go home for your sake, too."

"I am surrounded by Wise Women," he wrote, later that morning in the cemetery. "I guess I'm either lucky or cursed." He started to cross that sentence out but dropped the pen. Sara had been after him lately to "rethink his situation." He was in a dead-end job, but it was secure and he liked it. He'd been a technical editor for Boeing for twelve years and he'd reached the ceiling as far as promotions and big salary jumps were concerned. He didn't mind—he liked the job well enough to excuse himself from the lures of ambition. He had no desire to climb the corporate ladder. He was paid decently, he got an annual cost-of-living raise, he was well liked, and he had managed to make himself as indispensable to his unit as the man he worked for, maybe more so. He had what all reasonable men wanted: job security—and this long leave of absence bothered him. Sara thought the time off would make his boss realize just how important he was to his unit, but Fred was uneasy. His work would pile up or be done poorly by someone else. But more than that, he missed the job itself. He actually relished cleaning up the strangled prose of engineers, who, left to their own narrative devices, could make the operation of a pencil sharpener seem as arcane and as potentially dangerous as the operation of a breeder reactor. His was a small job in the great world of jobs, but it was what he wanted. He was content. At forty-two, life had become pleasantly fixed and unchanging for Fred Ocean.

"You're an old man already," he heard his father say. He could see how his father must have appeared to the other retirees of Casa del Sol: the big, sturdy, peasant features, battered but unhurtable. Ivan Ocean: even the name was strong, suggesting both the Russian masses and the sea. Ocean was a retooling of a difficult Russian name, Ozhogin, which was a bit too slushy for the parochial phonetics of American rust-belt English. Ivan Ozhogin, son of Vladimir. Born in the U.S.A., in post-frontier North Dakota, moved out of his home after knocking his father and older brother down a flight of stairs, rode the rods to Escanaba, buried himself in the red rock of iron country, emerged as a man with a slashing, take-no-prisoners vision of America. He was a happy man, but not a content one. Never content. The content do not contend. The happy people of this earth are the fighters, the conquerors, the risk-takers. Fred, lovingly, put a Mexican wedding shirt on his father, white slacks to match, huaraches on his big wide feet. He saw him tanned Apache brown, saw his white teeth flashing as he shouted, "You think you've got it made. Let me tell you, you don't deserve what you have. You don't deserve Rennie or a wife like Sara who only wants you to do your best. You're going to lose all of it. You'd let the world go to hell and not blink an eye as long as you were content. Men like you, my boy, can't hold on to anything except by luck." Even in death his father was full of instructions and warnings. The trouble with such advice was that it only made sense to those who gave it. Crazy mustangs did not travel with dollar-a-ride ponies. Advice from his father, he always believed, was like clothes handed down: you could wear them only if they fit. His father's instructions fit him like a shroud. "Back off, Dad," he said gently. He watched his father, as if on a freight elevator, sink down into the hard ground to resume his reminiscing chats with Henry Phelps, a man more to his liking. Fred picked up his pen and pocketed it.

He drove into Tucson, ostensibly to make reservations for weekend tickets to Seattle. But he didn't drive out to the airport. Instead, he stopped at the Conch, where Germaine Folger would be waiting for him.

"Well, gracious," she said. "Look at you, tiger."

He glanced at himself in the smoky mirror behind the bar. He'd driven in at high speed with the top of the Caddy down. His hair was wild and his eyes were spooky—wide and wind-whipped red. His heart was tripping along at highway speed, and he was very thirsty.

"What's been chasing you, honey?" Germaine said. "A ghost?"

Judging from her cozy slur, Fred knew that she'd been here for a couple of hours already. Germaine was older than he was by at least ten years. She was a tall woman with a doughy but still pretty face. She had a small mouth. Her lips were thin and pouty, like the lips of a child. He liked her looks. He liked the wet brown eyes that seemed to have been evolved specifically for barroom light. And he liked the way an old torch song would send her gaze into the middle distance as if she were revisiting scenes from a bittersweet past. He'd never seen her in sunlight, and he could not imagine her squinting her way across a sun-bright parking lot. She was a barfly. He smiled at the old-fashioned word. She was half ruined but not destitute. She dressed well, her credit was good enough to allow her to run a tab, and the stones in her rings looked genuine. Her husband sold real estate in Scottsdale. He'd made a fine art of keeping his distance from her.

"It's been a hard week, Germaine," he said.

"Could be a trend, baby," she said, patting his hand.

Fred ordered a bourbon and soda. The jukebox in the Conch specialized in ballads from the 1940s. Dick Haymes was singing "All or Nothing at All," saturating the dim air with a dangerous nostalgia. Everyone in the Conch looked on the verge of making a serious, life-upsetting error.

"Maybe you ought to start thinking about heading back to Seattle," Germaine said. "This country can be tough on you webfeet."

"That's for sure," he said. "In fact, that's why I'm in town. To make reservations."

"But you came here first."

"I didn't say I was in a hurry," he said, clinking her glass with his.

She smiled—bravely, he thought, because her eyes seemed resigned to a future measured in hours. She still had the power of her former beauty, and though the reason he was attracted to her was not that simple, he didn't try to find a deeper motive. He'd wanted her strictly as a drinking partner. That was safe; anything beyond that could be avoided.

"Hell, webfoot," she said, recklessly. "Maybe we should say goodbye in style."

He sipped his drink, as if thinking it over.

"I've got to get to the airport," he said.

"The *air*port isn't going anywhere," she said. "Besides, there's a travel agency around the corner from me." She put her hand on his, a proprietary gesture that took away his right of withdrawal. "Listen, Freddie," she said. "We're friends, aren't we? My apartment's a minute away. I think I know what you like."

Fred believed her. He believed that she possibly knew what he liked better than he did himself. She was a student of the small variations that made one man different from another. It accounted for her wrecked life.

"My dad says what I like isn't good for me," he said.

"Then it's time your dad minded his own business, I'd say."

They went outside, where the sunlight instantly betrayed her face. Her eyes tightened to leaky slits, and her chalky skin, blasted by the desert sun, became mottled and rough. In the darkness of the bar she had seemed melancholy and wise, but out here in the harsh light she only looked mournful and perplexed, as if the pain of old abuses was still alive.

He walked her to the parking lot. "I'll follow you," he said, and he did—for five blocks, where they were separated by a traffic light. He saw her pull over on the other side of the intersection to wait for him, but when the light turned green he made a hard right and headed for the airport.

"Well, say it, Pop," he said, as he eased the Cadillac onto the freeway.

"There's nothing to say, Freddie. I would have done the same thing. You have to weigh the consequences of your actions, since only you can be responsible for them."

He gave his father a diction and vocabulary in death that he hadn't had in life. It was easier to talk to him that way. The blunt homilies and warnings needed a good technical editor if they were to be taken seriously.

"Did you ever play around, Pop? Did you ever find a woman who knew what you liked?"

It was the sort of personal question ghosts can't answer. Fred found one of Renata's tapes in the glove compartment and plugged it into the deck. The flogging beat, the tortured guitars, and the brainless lyrics eliminated the possibility of further conversation.

At the cemetery the next morning, Fred added a paragraph to the letter he'd been working on the last few days. "You'll probably get this after we're home," he wrote. "But these communiqués from desert places are habit-forming. I'll probably continue writing to you twice a week for the rest of my life. Proximity is our most deceptive enemy, I think. Distance is more than simple geography. Ask Rennie. I'm closer to Dad now than I've ever been, and he's somewhere across the universe. He thinks I'm incorrigible. It's true. But so is he. So is Rennie. We all are. Just like the tarantulas. We've got them, you know, big across as tortillas. Early this morning I escorted one off the premises. He'd done an incorrigibly tarantula thing. You know that nest of cute swallow chicks Rennie's been monitoring? Well, Nature's got no use for cute. The tarantula got them. I found him, after noticing the empty nest, sitting fat as a cat among a litter of darling little feathers. I eased him out of the entryway with a broom. He was so bloated on infant swallow meat he could barely waddle out of there. Then I dutifully swept up all the feathers. I pinned a cute note to the nest: 'Bye-bye, Rennie. We've flown away to become rock-star swallows. Thanks for everything. Wish us luck.' Dad would say, 'No one was ever hurt by a light dose of reality.' My answer to that would make him slap his forehead in disgust. Reality, Dad, is public enemy number one, truth be known."

When Fred got back to the house it was still early. Rennie was asleep and his mother was sipping warm gin in the bathtub—her arthritis was acting up again—and his father was whispering sharp warnings in his ear. As a concession to all of them, he took the note off the empty swallow's nest and threw it away.

Paraiso: An Elegy

HART IS DEAD. Cancer got him. He died well. What I mean is, he died pretty much as he lived, without fear or dread, and he died without the sort of high-torque pain or mind-gumming drugs that would have blunted his ability to find interest in the process of dying. We still talk about him in the present tense. "Hart has presence of mind," we say, and "Hart can't tolerate French movies," and "Hart likes his beer freezer-cold." His gray stare, somewhat quizzical due to the tumors thriving near the occipital region of his brain, asks you to be honest: Never say what you don't mean. If in doubt, remember, silence is incorruptible. You can spend half a day with Hart and maybe trade three opinions. But he likes his jokes. He likes the sharp observation that punctures the gassy balloons of hypocrisy, pomp, and self-importance. As a photographer and poet, that's what he's about. And so he can get you in trouble. He's a little guy with a proud chest. His camera bag, always slung on his shoulder, makes him list ten degrees to port. It makes him walk with a limp.

It began with an omen. We were in Juárez, Christmas 1988, fending off a gang of seasonal pickpockets who had moved into the border town from somewhere in the interior. They circled us like a half-dozen bantamweight boxers, nodding and shrugging, feinting in and dancing back, bumping us, confusing us with large, friendly smiles. Hart pulled out his little Zeiss and started to spend film while our wives, Rocky and Joyce, dealt with the footloose thieves. These wives are tough, friendly women from the bedrock towns of Butte and Anaconda, Montana, respectively. When a quick brown hand slipped into the throat of Rocky's purse, she slapped it away, brisk as a frontier schoolmarm, and my tall, strong-jawed Joyce yanked her purse clear with enough force to start a chain saw. The thieves tap-danced away from the white-knuckled determination of these good-looking *güeras*, with no hard feelings, no need to get righteous. The phrase *No me chinguen, pendejos* was ready on my lips, and I whispered it in rehearsal since I am fluent with set phrases only. And Joyce, who *is* fluent, hissed, "Don't you *ever* say that in this town unless you want to take your gringo whizzer back across the bridge in segments."

Joyce works in a Juárez industrial park, teaching idiomatic, rust-belt American to executives of the *maquiladora* industry who need to travel north. Her company assembles computer components for GM, and pays its workers an average of five dollars a day, which is a full dollar above the Mexican minimum wage. Joyce gets eighteen dollars an hour because she insists on being paid what the job's worth, having come from Anaconda, a town so unionized you can't pour tar on your leaky shed without getting hard stares from the organized roofers. It troubles her that the Tarahumara Indian beggar women on Avenida Diez y Seis de Septiembre can make twice as much on a good day as a worker in a *maquiladora*. That's why she didn't get hysterical over the pickpockets. Their mostly seasonal earnings are on a puny scale compared to what the foreign-owned *maquiladoras* siphon into their profit margins. If anyone was close to hysteria it was me (the gringo instinct to protect and prevail knocking at my heart), not the iron-willed women from Montana. My fists were balled up, and my mind was knotted, too, with such off-the-subject ir-relevancies as my honor, my male pride. *¡Lárguense a la chin-gada!* I felt like saying, but I also knew that if I did things would get serious in a hurry because these thieves from Chihuahua or wherever have a more commanding sense of honor than I do. We gringos might have a more commanding sense of *fair play*, but honor is too abstract to touch off instantaneous grass fires in our blood. It applies to flag and parents and, at one time, to a young man's conduct in the vicinity of decent girls, but it has never functioned as a duty, uncompromising as the survival instinct, to oneself.

And if I did get lucky and scatter them with a few wild punches, then what? The streets were dense with locals who do not think the world of these pale, camera-toting, wisecracking, uninhibited laughers from a thousand miles north of the Río Bravo. And when a nearby *tránsito*—a black-and-tan-uniformed traffic cop, the local version of the *guardia civil*—strolled by to see what was what, speaking the same street Spanish as the purse-snatchers, whose story did I think would be heard? Who did I think would go to jail? This was before Hart's diagnosis, when we were all planning a succession of trips starting with the thrill-a-minute train ride from Ciudad Chihuahua to Creel and on to the Barranca de Cobre, and later in the year, to Puebla and Vera Cruz. *"Que le vaya bien,"* Joyce called to the retreating pickpockets. And a smiling thief replied, his Spanish courtly and dignified, "And may it also go equally well for you, lady." Rocky, a former parachute journalist who now teaches Bullshit Detection 101, rolled her black Irish eyes and muttered, "Jesus. Joyce must be campaigning for sainthood. The Bleeding Virgin of the Cutpurse. They wanted to take your MasterCard, honey, not test your Spanish."

We stopped in the Kentucky Club on Avenida Juárez for a round of self-congratulatory margaritas, then crossed back into Texas, purses and wallets intact. We felt generally upbeat. But in the river, on the north bank, we saw a decapitated mule. We hung over the rail, staring at the mud-colored carcass bloating in the silty river, as if this had been the planned high point and ultimate purpose of our tour. Hart said,

"Omen, troops." We looked at him. This was one of those moments in life when things get too slippery to catch in a net of words. We looked at each other. An innocence rising up from childhood struck us dumb as Hart attached a long lens to his Zeiss and photographed the headless mule.

2

Joyce and I are on this trip with Hart and Rocky, looking for something in the desert. A kind of comradely spitefulness has made us rowdy and solemnly amused by turns. I guess it is Death we are spiting, though no one comes out and says so. We like each other because we know we are misfits who have found our niche in the friendly halls of universities.

We are western by chance, and remain so by choice. We love cars and rock and roll more than we love fine art and baroque music. We wear this preference on our pearl-buttoned sleeves. We've been antsy from birth: The verb "to go" was the first one we learned to conjugate. We've got Cowboy Junkies in the tape deck and a six-pack of Lone Star balanced on the console between the seats. Drinking and driving is a western birthright. This is Texas, where it's legal to have opened containers in a moving car. This law (known affectionately as the Bubba Law) may be repealed soon, but we're not in a mood to worry about it: the lab report on the biopsies is in and now we all know the worst. Hart has six months, if he's lucky—six months, that is, if the tumors crowding his vertebrae don't break in and vandalize the spinal cord tomorrow or the next day.

Hart has the perfect vehicle for this type of travel. A 1972 Chevy Blazer with the big 350 long-block V-8 throbbing under the hood. The Blazer is a two-ton intimidator. Hart is not into intimidation, but the slender Celicas, Maximas, and Integras that pull into our slipstream don't know that. They tend to keep their distance from the big, rust-brown, generously dented Chevy. Hart and I sit up front, Rocky and Joyce sit in back—a western arrangement not meant to signify the relative status of the sexes. A traveler from New Haven, say, might look into the Blazer and see Hart and me up front in straw hats with beer cans on the dash, and the women eating coffee chews in back, perhaps catch a strain of the Cowboy Junkie's visionary wailing, and think *highway buckaroos and the little women, tsk, tsk.* This is unfair to the Yankees, of course. You might find the same arrangement in a dented Blazer in New Haven. Only in New Haven, I suspect, the highway buckaroo remark might be justified. Two couples riding this way back there *would* be making a statement, whether they wanted to or not. Turning ourselves into an illustrated idea is the last thing in the world the four of us would do.

We're heading in our roundabout way for Tucson, normally a five-hour trek from El Paso, where we live. The sandstorms have raised cubic miles of desert, turning it into coastal fog. Our running lights are on and we've slowed to forty and the wind is making the big Blazer rock and roll. Hart is feeling the strain, having just undergone his first series of radiation treatments, which he found entertaining. ("Star Wars, troops. They levitate you into the center of a big dome where smart machines that know your body better than you do sniff out and then zap the intruders.") I have offered to drive, but no one drives the Blazer except Hart. He loves this truck as a settler might have loved his big-bore buffalo gun, his horse, or his quarter section of homestead bottomland. And so it's decided: We'll turn off at exit 331, get on U.S. 666, and head for my widowed mother's adobe hacienda in Paraiso, Arizona, where Death has left his stain and dull gloom not long ago.

It is late afternoon when we pull into her driveway, and Mom—Sada—is already in her cups. She's been working all morning on *Storm over the Dragoons,* a six-by-three-foot oil painting, and now is drinking ruby port to unwind. Painting

has helped fill in the gaps left by the removal of Lenny Bur-
bek, her husband for the last twenty-six years. Cancer got
him, too.

Sada pours wine for us at her kitchen table. The house
smells of oil paint, even though her studio is out in the attached garage. "Hart, you look fer shit," she says. Sada, at
eighty-two, has dispensed with all the social delicacies.

"Fer shit is an improvement over yesterday," Hart says,
holding the cup of ruby port but not drinking. The road beers
have already given him grief. Alcohol, mixed with the tumor-
poisoning chemicals circulating in his system, makes him
sick. He's got a tumor in his liver, too, and his liver won't
forgive and forget. Hart puts the wine down and takes a picture of Sada. She is a mask of fierce wrinkles and looks more
like an old Navajo or Apache squaw than the immigrant Scan-
dinavian that she is. Hart has this theory: The land eventually
has its way with us. Live in this desert long enough and sun,
wind, sand, and thirsty air will eventually give a native shape
to your clay, just as thirty years in Oslo will fade, elasticize,
and plump up the austere skin of an Apache. The land works
us like a craftsman works maple or oak. Ultimately, the tools
and strategies of the craftsman overcome the proud immuta-
bility of any hardwood. The land owns us, not vice versa, the
current triumph of the capitalist zeitgeist notwithstanding.
This is Hart's pet idea. The land owns us and we had better
treat it with the proper deference. You can see it in his prints.
It is often the text and always the subtext of his poems. "We
all need a pet idea," Hart says, "even if it's a stupid one. Even
a stupid idea, pursued long enough with enough dedication,
so that all its dead ends are discovered, will lead you to the
same place as a nifty one." We don't ask Hart what or where
that place is. We act like we know, and maybe we almost do.
"Besides," Hart says, "*ideas* are ultimately wrong anyway."

Sada fixes her favorite dish that night, linguini with clam
sauce, along with big prawns from Puerto Peñasco, down on
the Sea of Cortez. Tyrell Lofton, Sada's boyfriend, eats with

us. Tyrell is a West Virginia mountain man bent on turning
his piece of Paraiso into mountaineer country. He's planted
black walnut trees, tulip trees, and a variety of conifers, and
has a fecund greenhouse that produces several tons of winter
tomatoes. He dreams of building a small still—a genetic man-
date. And his house, made of scrap wood, has been half built
for twenty years. He's a lean, hard-knuckled seventy-five-
year-old widower who also has the weathered Apache look. As
we eat, I can tell Hart is planning photography sessions with
Tyrell and Sada, for no one we know proves his pet idea better
than these two.

After dinner, Sada begins to fidget around. She wants to go
dancing. "Have you kids been to the Duck Inn?" she asks
coyly. The Duck Inn is a little geezer saloon that caters to the
population of Paraiso. "They've got a terrific little band there.
The ex-sheriff of Tombstone owns the place. He's also the
bandleader."

Sada was a dancer in the Ziegfeld Follies and there is no
quit in her. Her bottle-blond hair is startling above her brown,
massively grooved, big-cheeked, purse-leather face. "I think
we'll pass, Mom," I say.

She scoffs. "Don't be an old fart, sonny, you're not even
fifty yet. Come on, we'll have a few laughs."

Tyrell, who always has a twinkle in his faded blue eyes,
says, "Goodness me, I don't think they ever had *four* professors in the Duck Inn all at once." Tyrell is quick to spot the
potential fun in a given situation, but his remarks are never
mean or sour. According to Tyrell, it's okay to take the light
view of humanity, since only trees have honest-to-God dignity. It's his pet idea.

"Hart doesn't feel up to it," I say.

"The hell I don't," Hart says, his face drawn, his jaw tight
enough to reflect light.

And so we all walk to the bar, surrounded by black night
and the thousand unblinking stars of this high desert. Hart
amazes me, plodding along, one painful step after another,

Rocky hanging on his arm. What amazes me is his placid indifference to the Big Change coming his way, his refusal to let it become the major dramatic event of the season. And then I think of his pet idea, and how the desert might shape a body for pain, too. The Apaches took pain in stride, even sought it out as a measuring stick of their individual worth. The deserts of the Near East have produced prophetic pain-seekers for thousands of years. Jesus, destined for pain, did not pile up annuities or build Alpine retreats to hide himself from it. Blood and sand are the primary colors of the desert. The agonies of crucifixion are storming in Hart's bones and guts, but he won't let us in on this internal secret. I am reminded of Sada's third and last husband, Lenny (another de facto Apache), settling into his easy chair gingerly, as if some wickedness had turned his burly, ex-ironworker's frame into crystal stemware. Lenny and his pal from down the street, also dying of cancer, would sit in their bathrobes and watch the Playboy channel for hours at a time, sampling each other's painkillers. There they were—two old men, all the vigor of their lives sucked into the unappeasable black hole of cancer—denying the sex-hating Intruder by watching the rosy, pile-driving rumps of fornicating youths hour after hour, snacking on chips and *queso,* washing down opiates and tranks with beer, giving a thin cheer now and then to the gymnastic skills of the actors. Lenny died in bed pushing himself up to a sitting position while insisting that he felt much, *much* better.

Paraiso is not exactly a retirement village, though most of the residents are retired. There are a few younger people who commute the ninety miles to Tucson to work. They live here because real estate costs half as much and because the air is about as clean as late-twentieth-century American air can get. A few of these people are in the Duck Inn, dancing and carrying on. Sada knows them all and shouts their names. She backs her straight shots of vodka with draft beer and she has a what-the-hell look in her eyes. Soon she is up on her feet, dancing alone among the younger folk, holding her peasant skirts up over her old hardscrabble knees and yelling, "Yippee, son of a bitch, yippee!" while her carpet slippers flap. Then Tyrell leaps up, his wide pale eyes almost glassy, and does a solo mountaineer buckdance which no one challenges. Rocky is laughing her choppy, nicotine-stained laugh, and Hart, though he's got a white-knuckled grip on his untouched mug of beer, is smiling. Joyce nudges me under the table, whispering, "Hope you feel strong. You and Tyrell are going to have to carry Sada home." And the fiddlers chop down feverishly into their fiddles as if everything now depended on this crazed music.

Later that night, as the coyotes howl and the screech owls make their eerie electronic screams, Joyce and I hear Rocky crying softly through the wall that separates our bedrooms, and under the crying, Hart's laboring snores. Unable to sleep, I get up and prowl the house. It is 3:00 A.M., the hour of the wolf, dead center of night when all of us are naked in our small separate selves. At this hour all the technological wonders and powers of America seem like a feeble dream: the optimistic cities of glass and steel, the superhighways, the elaborate networks of instant communication, and the medical colossus that, for all its precise weapons and collective strategic genius, cannot discourage the barbarous imperialism of a wretched horde of mindless tumors.

The garage light is on. Sada is up, too, working on her big landscape. She doesn't hear me come in, and I watch her drag a broad, paint-fat brush across the base of the Dragoons, the range of mountains where Cochise and his band of righteous Chiricahua warriors held off the U.S. Army for ten years. The mountains are blue-black under the angry flex of muscular storm clouds. All the rage of Sada's eighty-two years is in this canvas, which, the longer I look at it, seems more like a thunderous shout than a painting. "Some painting, Ma," I say.

She whirls around, her leaky Apache eyes burning with a

warrior's need to run a spear into the dark gut of the beast. "It's all I can do now," she says.

3

As we head south toward Douglas and Agua Prieta, I am thinking of the strange girl who lives across the street from Sada. She is sixteen and suffering the pain of boredom and the deeper pain of her own oddness, which will isolate her more than geography ever could. Joyce and Rocky found her lying in the middle of the street, her hair chopped close to her scalp, as if by a hunting knife. Thunderclouds sat on the Dragoons. Joyce thought at first that the girl had been run over, but she was only waiting. I am waiting for something to happen to me, is what she said. Joyce and Rocky left her there, spread-eagled in the road, as the tall clouds moved closer and God's original voice began to rumble with its old no-nonsense authority. Red-tailed hawks lofty as archangels swept down out of the dark sky, choosing among opportunities. Joyce and Rocky decided: Maybe the odd girl was right and was playing her aces now, while she still had them. Maybe we are all waiting for something to happen to us— death or life—but for the girl lying in the street the issue was unclouded by career, marriage, property, and all the other trump cards that must be deferred to before we can clear the slate and move on.

Hart's Blazer pitches and yaws over a rough highway that will take us into the mountains. We have turned onto a narrow, shoulderless road that cuts west into the southern foothills of the Dragoons, as we head now for Bisbee instead of Douglas and Agua Prieta. "I've always wanted to see the Lavender Pit," Hart says.

Traveling by whim is touring at its best.

The old houses of Bisbee cling to the sides of the mountains, prayerfully as exhausted climbers. And the streets, angled like derailed trains, work their way up to the highest ledge of dwellings. We walk these steep streets, finding level ground in a doorway now and then to catch our breath. Hart's been taking painkillers and tends to stagger against the unexpectedly oblique tugs of gravity that have made the older buildings lean into each other like amiable drunks. He stops now and then to photograph the odd geometry of a ruined hotel, the grit-pocked face of an old miner, the bands of Japanese tourists who photograph everything in their path as if making a visual record of what will one day be all theirs. The four of us often agree that World War Two is still being fought, that the atomic bombings of Japan merely forced a change in weaponry. After Hiroshima and Nagasaki, the tide turned, and now Japanese samurai in three-piece suits, portfolios in hand, are succeeding where Tojo's fanatic armies failed. Choice Hawaiian beachfront and Rockefeller Center are theirs, the great evergreen forests of Oregon are theirs, and lately, giant cattle ranches in Montana. "I could settle down here," Rocky says. "In one of those shacks on the side of the mountain. This place is like Butte, without Butte's winters."

Rocky prides herself for being realistic. She knows we all understand that she is imagining her life without Hart. The terms are hard, but they always have been. We are alone, we have nothing to sustain us but a few pet ideas fueled by a dram of courage. The rest is a pipe dream. Not that pipe dreams are not necessary, we've just got to know the differences. This is Rocky's pet idea, and it's one that she's earned. Ten years ago she survived the removal, from her brain, of a benign plum-sized tumor that made her trade her career in parachute journalism for an academic one.

We are required to be brave. Another pet idea. Also Rocky's.

The Lavender Pit is really two pits, big enough to drop a pair of medium size cities into. On the way out of Bisbee, after getting half-drunk in the Copper Queen Hotel (Hart managing this with a carefully sipped double shot of mescal), we stop with the tourists to gape at this man-made Grand Canyon. Rocky, who has seen her town, Butte, more or less consumed by such a pit, says, "Sucks, don't it?" to a tourist lady from Arkansas. The tourist lady smiles stiffly and turns her camera on her husband and daughter, who backstep dutifully toward the Cyclone fence that guards the lip of the pit and the thousand-foot drop beyond. The red gouge in the earth looks like a fresh wound, the god-size tumor removed, the lake of blood vacuumed out. A lifeless pond at the bottom of the pit glows like iridescent pus. Oh yes, the planet here is dead. It is deader than the moon, because it was once alive.

"I'm losing my buzz, campers," Rocky says. "Let's clear the fuck out." The lady with the camera gives Rocky a murderous look, protecting the innocence of her child. Rocky grins good-naturedly. "Too late for Miss Manners, hon," she says cryptically, swinging her arm out to indicate the pit, the precarious town, the silent witness of the elderly mountains.

4

We skip Tucson and head back, but the Blazer heats up outside of Deming, New Mexico. We were headed for Palomas, the little Mexican town where General Pershing launched his failed attempt to bring a taste of gringo justice to Pancho Villa, but are now stalled in a gas station where two head-scratching mechanics decide the problem is in the fan clutch and that it will take about an hour and a hundred dollars to fix it. It's hot, over a hundred degrees, and we sit inside the crankcase smell of the garage drinking lukewarm Cokes and watching a TV that seems to have only one color: puce. One of the advertising industry's truly horrifying commercials comes on: "Your marriage will never end. Your children will never grow old. Your pets will never die." It's an ad for a video camcorder, showing a family watching their dead past captured and preserved forever. Whatever unhappiness lies ahead, it cannot touch these moments of joy. Mom kissing Dad in the kitchen; Junior chasing a ball; Rover begging for table scraps—immortal, immutable. Old age, sickness, alienation, divorce: all our little hells defeated by videotape. Paradise secure in a cassette, the grim episodes edited out.

We step back into the heat and stroll up the desert road. To the east, the gray humps of the Florida Mountains wobble in the corrugated air. A man, ragged and barefoot, approaches us. He's so far beyond the liberal dream of salvage and social recycling that he almost seems happy. His weak hair and crosshatched sunburned skin make him look sixty but his clear blue eyes put him closer to thirty. He is hashed with small cuts, as if he's been climbing through barbed-wire fences all morning. Hart greets him with the head-on nod of equals. Hart and the ragged man are down to common denominators, and they recognize this in each other. The man asks for a cigarette and Hart gives him one, then lights it for him. As the rest of us stroll on, Hart reaches into his camera bag. When Hart has his camera ready, the man begins to shift his weight from left foot to right and back again. The asphalt road is burning hot and I assume the man is moving oddly because his bare feet are giving him trouble, but then he raises his stick-figure arms as if they were big sunny wings and begins to turn in half-circles, first one way, then the other, his cigarette held delicately in his fingertips. He lifts his face up to the sky to let God see him better, and chants a broken-throated nonsense. It's an Indian dance, or his idea of one. "He didn't want any money," Hart says when he rejoins us. "He said all he needs now is smokes. He gave me permission to take his picture, but only while he was doing his atonement dance."

We continue our stroll; the man, who doesn't need an audience, continues his dance. The sun has baked curiosity out of our thoughts. Curiosity is a luxury of the temperate zone. When a shoeless man in a parched land tells you he's doing an atonement dance, you more or less have to accept him at his word. Besides, there's enough to atone for to keep half of humanity dancing shoeless in the desert for a century while the other half lights cigarettes for them.

A few months later I will think of this moment while looking at Hart's photographs matted and framed on our apartment walls, and it will seem as if all of us are moving to the drumbeat of some privately realized dance—the ducking pickpockets with large incongruous smiles under their stony eyes; Sada and Tyrell holding hands shyly but glaring like unyielding Apaches from their mountain stronghold, determined to make their stand; Rocky tugging defiantly on her cigarette as she fixes something at infinity with wide-open eyes that won't blink; even the headless mule floating near the concrete bank of the Rio Grande like an offering to the indifferent northern gods. And Joyce and me, caught looking at each other with slightly shocked expressions, as if on that very day, before the small white church in Palomas, we grasped for the first time that love is possible only because it must end.

—for Zena Beth McGlashan

God Bless America

I AM WITH Dunkie in the Bali Hai Café. He is nervous today and speaks with gravity, in full paragraphs, complete with long punctuational sighs and grimly significant glances. He moves his finger like a baton, directing my flawed attention. If I don't recognize a paragraph-ending sigh for what it is and interrupt him, his finger stops and he scowls at me for several seconds. Then, when my voice trails off, he continues. He's been washing down bennies with decaffeinated coffee all morning and by noon his mainspring is explosively tight. Dunkie is wired.

He tells me his novel is almost finished. *Tumults and Insurrections* is in its final rewrite, all eleven hundred pages of it, and he assures me it is possibly the Great American Novel the world has been waiting a century and a half for. "I'm out there with Mr. Melville, Gregory," he says, his voice knotting up before the naked wonder of his achievement. "In fact it's possible that I've blown Mr. Herman Fucking Melville out of the North fucking Atlantic."

The Bali Hai is a thatched-roof bar and eatery with large windows that overlook a nice but undramatic strand of San Diego Bay. He stares with grave melancholy at the water as he watches the listing *Pequod* shudder and go down. Then he catches me glancing up at the ceiling, my yawn suppressed. No one talks about the Great American Novel anymore, but

Dunkie is an untutored throwback who doesn't know we are living in the Great Age of Criticism and that fiction itself has taken a backseat to theories of fiction. He doesn't know that the critics, armed with the Rosetta stone of deconstruction that unmasks all texts, are technically capable now of reducing contemporary fiction to a cultural twitch, and will soon create hypothetical fictions—"prop" novels and stories—that will exist only as authorless, *a priori* propositions that verify and sanction their far more useful cipherings. So Dunkie sees my yawn as simple inattention, not a mask for the skeptical reflex. This makes him instantly bitter at the prospect of not being appreciated by his contemporaries. "But I guess it's up to posterity to call the balls and strikes," he concludes stoically.

Dunkie dictates his novel into the telephone while his typist, Florence Halley, takes it down. Florence charges him two dollars a page, and so she is richer—on paper—by twenty-two hundred bucks, excluding rewrites. Dunkie lives on credit sustained by a possibly large inheritance. Many wait in line for payment; each day the line grows longer.

Florence is my present girlfriend. She's a thirty-nine-year-old eccentric and a distant relative of the astronomer who discovered the comet that bears his name and hers. She has been on her own since her ex-husband, another throwback writer, decided she smothered his talent, discouraged his muse, and was a slave to bourgeois materialism. Six months after leaving her, he put a .25 caliber derringer bullet into his brain.

Dunkie also despises the middle classes. "I hate consumerism, Gregory," he tells me, adopting the aggressive, visionary pose of a kitchen-sink socialist of the 1930s. "Things beget more things. Middle-class life blankets your creative spirit with accumulation." Marxism, populism, socialism, labor unions, the intelligentsia's flirtation with the blue-collar world, the radical chic of the sixties: All remote as Halley's Comet, but Dunkie's stylus is stuck in a groove—he's got one refrain, a handful of notes.

And though I nod in agreement I avoid his glance. It's a glance that asks too much: It wants you to not only understand the burden of genius but the more pedestrian problems that make the life of a man of destiny a hell of small distractions. He doesn't want to hear that everyone else is plagued by the same bothersome demands. I once told him I gave up my magazine subscriptions and sold my big TV set because I was trying to reduce the number of distractions that took me away from my work. He paused theatrically, gazing down on me from sheer Olympian altitude. "Your *work?*" he said, his generous lips drawn into an elaborate, operatic sneer. It was his only comment.

Dunkie is unique. Not many people are unique. Most of us have a horde of approximate selves slipping easily or stumbling fitfully through some quarter of the world. My father could have doubled for Vincent Price of B horror film fame. My mother looks like a loose-living Betty Furness gone to hard drink. People tell me I look like a slightly worn-out Edward R. Murrow, which flatters me in a way but scares me too, since Murrow, as I remember him, seemed about as worn out as you can safely get this side of intensive care. Dunkie, though, is truly unique. He's six feet eight inches tall and weighs one hundred and ninety pounds. He has wide, blade-thin shoulders and a precariously thin neck that serves as a dangerous pedestal for his long-skulled head, from which hangs the wild shoulder-length hair of a nineteenth-century anarchist. He was a college basketball star, one of the few white players of the mid-sixties who had a thirty-inch vertical jump and who could slam dunk—thus his nickname. But he gave up his scholarship when a politically radical but safely tenured professor revealed to him the exploitative nature of collegiate athletics.

Dunkie is a compulsive talker and a shockingly sloppy

eater, and is casually insulting. "Gregory," he tells me, "this detritus you write, this so-called romance slop. I think it's destroying your soul. A man can't expend his life energy producing brain-rotting flotsam and not expect to be slimed over by it."

The waitress brings our lunch. Dunkie picks up his utensils and goes to work, filling his mouth several times before speaking again. Then he taps the air between us with a fork full of pasta primavera. Bits of cream-coated herbs and spices pelt my unprotected hands. "Words, my dear friend," he says, his jaws rotating meditatively, a Benzedrine sweat beading his forehead, "words are not to be taken, nor issued, lightly. In the beginning was the Word. You'd better think about *that*, Gregory. This world, the heavens, the very gods, owe their existence to the Word."

"It's a meal ticket, Dunkie," I mutter. I don't point out that the money I earn with my soul-sliming romance novels is paying not only for his lunch, but also for his car. He had it repossessed—a 1989 Saab Turbo—and had become almost suicidal without it. I paid the three missing back installments and prepaid another one—advances against Dunkie's inheritance. His father, a retired Army general, died two years ago, leaving an estate worth upward of six hundred thousand dollars. Unfortunately for Dunkie, he left no will, and Dunkie's three sisters are conspiring to split the estate among themselves, convinced that their eccentric brother has wasted his life pretending to be an Important American Writer and will only squander his one-quarter share. The sisters are probably justified in this belief, but Dunkie has engaged legal counsel, and the matter has been in probate court now for two years.

I have my own problems. I write my Candelabra Romances under the nom de plume Veronica LaMonica. I have a three-book-per-year contract, and am suffering what is commonly known as writer's block. I don't think of it so much as a block as a lapse of will. Essentially, I write the same story over and over—you don't mess with success. If the phrase "If it works don't fix it" did not originate in the romance-novel industry, it might as well have.

I think of my novels as the linguistic equivalent of a gigolo making love to a shy but eager housewife who is somewhat uptight and not quite convinced his illicit attentions won't degrade her but is nonetheless willing to give him the benefit of the doubt, hoping to be led gently into volcanic release through a cleverly orchestrated breakdown of constraint. It's a simple formula: You establish the heroine's Frustration, you introduce her to Alternate Possibilities, you give her titillating glimpses of the Golden Stud, you choreograph the Dance of Yes, No, and Maybe, and you end in Multiple, Phosphorescent, but Stainless Orgasms followed by the required nod to Domestic Equilibrium: the Exchange of Vows. It's a living; a good living. And, for all its calculated playing to libidinous hausfrau daydreams, it is an honest living. I work hard, my books give moderate pleasure, the critics ignore me, and I earn profits for my bosses. Next to dirt farming, this business is as rooted in the good old American sweat-of-the-brow, dollar-paid-for-dollar-earned ethic as you can get. I am not ashamed. I serve a purpose. God bless America.

"Goddammit, are you listening to me, Gregory?"

"I've got to go, Dunkie. I'm meeting Florence at General Cinema. We're going to the half-price matinee."

"Words, Gregory! The human modulation of ordinary air! This is what I'm getting at. When you emit language, whose *voice* do you think you're listening to? The air that tinkles your wind chime also passes over the vibrating meat of your vocal cords—that very same innocuous air produces the *Word.*"

"Ah. I see what you're getting at, Dunkie. But, really, I've got to . . ."

He hammers the table with his fist, making the ice in our water glasses jump. Bits of pasta hang on threads of cream from his beard like luminous albino silkworms. "No, you do *not* see what I am getting at. If you did you would give up your

whoring!" Amphetamine sweat gathers on his pale brow.
His eyes are adrenalized—round and tattered. The nervous
waitress brings him pie—he always has a dessert—hot straw-
berry-rhubarb pie with a gob of ice cream on top. The bennies—diet pills—have a paradoxical effect on his appetite. He
eats enough for five men but stays anorexically thin. "Ah ha!"
Dunkie says, his eyes moving over the treat with impish anticipation. He mops his forehead with his napkin, then tucks it
into his shirt. He leans down to the pie and sniffs it, his thin,
magnificently arched nose hooking down as if to spear the pie
itself, the nostrils flared and hissing like bellows.

I recognize my chance to bail out. I stand, scoop up the
check, button my coat. "See you later, Dunkie," I say.

Unlike Dunkie, I respect the unashamed materialism of the
American Worker and the God-fearing closet eroticism of his
Good Wife. This refusal to join the corps of sneering elite is
the secret of my success. So why do I put up with Dunkie?
Why does anyone put up with anyone? It's my flaw: I put up
with people. Another example: I also put up with Florence
Halley. She smokes in bed and dresses like a bag lady. Because of her famous name she fakes scientific insight but she
thinks TV programs come into her house through the electrical outlets. When I explain the radiant properties of high-
frequency electromagnetic waves, she scoffs with disbelief.
"Where do you *get* such creepy ideas?" she asked. "The
National Enquirer? I suppose you believe in UFOs, too?"

And, to be fair, Florence puts up with me. She hints for
commitment, but I give her none. She is my typist as well as
Dunkie's. But I am a tyrant for perfection, where Dunkie will
let the typos and misspellings go. "Anal-retentive nit-pick-
ing," Dunkie once called my refusal to accept a blemished
page. I have reduced Florence to ugly sobbing rages by my
demand for competence. And, for the record, I *do* believe in
UFOs. I've seen one.

Jasmine McDougal, my ex-wife, would not put up with me. Those were my neurotic years, when I was still wallowing in self-delusion. I spoke with an English accent and drove a blue Morgan. I believed I had an incandescent talent. My light would be *seen*. I didn't expect to sink the *Pequod*, but I thought I had a chance of making the world forget Jacqueline Susanne.

My son, Carlo, *has* to put up with me, though we tend to give each other a wide berth these days. He's a high school senior who also thinks my novels are as socially redeeming as the sales pitch of a streetwalker. On the other hand, he doesn't feel the things I buy him are therefore *tainted*. He's got himself mixed up with a bad crowd—Jesus groupies. I find the occasional edifying pamphlet on my desk: The When and Where of Christ's Return. What the Babylonians Knew. Set Your Watch to Celestial Standard Time. *Were* the Jews Blameless? But there's hope: He loves the Toyota sports car I bought him, and arranges himself behind the wheel with a distinct James Dean narcissism as he guns it out of the driveway.

I would like Carlo, and others, to appreciate me for what I do and for what the doing of it has accomplished. Is this whining? Yes. The hearty, self-righteous whine has more integrity than the stoic shrug. Quote me. You can't turn on the Sports Channel these days without seeing a twenty-four-year-old million-dollar athlete whining about his contract, the insensitivity of his team's owner, or the appalling, cultureless city he has to play in. I love it how they whine *without shame* before the millions of unexceptional Americans of humble income. But, this *is* America. You've got to love it, shameless whiners and all.

I saw the UFO when I was in the Air Force. I was stationed at an early-warning radar base on the Canadian border in north-central Montana, the 778th AC&W Squadron, part of a multitiered line of defense against the airborne Russian hordes. We were on practice alert, and I was pulling guard duty down by the sewage lagoon, fighting off wasp-size mosquitoes. It was hot, and the relentless Hi-line wind had quit blowing. Then, in an eyeblink, I found myself in pleasant shade. I looked up and saw a disk the size of a parking lot drifting silently overhead. I pointed my unloaded M-1 at it. Sal Russo, guarding the other side of the lagoon, saw it too—we were the only ones who saw it. Sal ran back to the squadron area screaming "UFO! UFO!" and of course was met with cynical laughter that lasted the rest of his enlistment. Whenever Russo walked through the squadron area, you could hear the distant falsetto calls "UFO! UFO!" following him like the high mutterings of scavenger birds. I kept my mouth shut about it, which was the only reasonable thing to do. Russo wanted to reenlist but because of this incident they wouldn't let him.

Sal wouldn't forgive my silence and once challenged me to a fight over it. I declined, but he attacked anyway. We were drinking in the VFW Club in Havre, and wound up in the dark back alley throwing blind punches. Why do I mention it now? For this reason: The UFO changed my life. It made me realize that I, Gregory Woodrow Pastori, was not the crowning glory of biological evolution. I gradually learned to take myself less seriously. It didn't happen overnight. For years I couldn't accept a diminished status. I deliberately put aside the impact of the incident. I got married, maintained my lofty literary intentions, and made everyone around me miserable. Jasmine left, leaving Carlo with me. Shortly afterward, I got back to basics.

Live as happily as you can, take care of your loved ones, stay as sane as conveniently possible, and don't try to sink the *Pequod* or any other literary vessel you think is sailing off with cargoes of High Significance that would be more ably delivered by you. The white whale lives. The white whale owns us. All *Pequods* sink. Oh yes, we are as insignificant, dense, small-minded, petty, hopeless, and unredeemable as we appear to be. We are blind pupfish in a mighty ocean. This is, of course, not exactly a prime-time bulletin.

But, for fish, we are pretty good at entertaining each other. Maybe that's what we're best at. My Candelabra Romances aren't going to launch neo-transcendentalism or any other neoism. They're just going to let some bored hausfraus kill a little time. That's America's major industrial contribution to the world: new and wonderful ways to kill time. God bless us. For time is the enemy. Murder it blissfully and live.

Florence Halley has a shoddy sense of time. It's one of the things I like about her, though it can be irritating now and then. She arrived at General Cinema fifteen minutes into the show. We skipped the movie and went to her little house on the beach. She lives twenty minutes north of town in a shack her mother owns. The house is worth a million, or rather the half-acre it sits on is, but Florence's mother won't sell. The condo builders have come after her with big guns but she and her lawyers fight a guerrilla war of delaying tactics. The property has been condemned and uncondemned four times. The greasy-jawed forces of greed against a helpless widow? Don't buy it. It's just an old woman's righteous glee in interrupting the mutations of progress. She's been offered a cool million three, she's seventy-nine years old, the house has no sentimental value since she didn't buy it until she was forty-eight and then only as a rental, and the house itself is a wreck. Beach sand sifts in through gaps around the window frames. The floor joists are spaced an illegal thirty-six inches, and so the floors sag and slant. Except for the bathroom, each room has only one working electrical outlet. The bathroom has four, so Florence keeps the toaster and blender in there.

Another thing I like about Florence is that she likes my writing. Dunkie's stuff gets by her. She doesn't understand *Tumults and Insurrections.* "This can't be true, can it Greg?" she says, holding up a page her computer has just printed. "At the same time Columbus discovers America, the Pope sets up this really gory bullfight right in front of St. Peter's, in Rome, because he's so happy that the Arabs have finally been kicked out of Spain? And this bullfight is attended by two of the Pope's mistresses and four of his children? And *five* bulls are killed? And at the same time, Columbus is hallucinating the second coming of Christ because he smoked some Indian loco weed, and Christ turns out to be this gorgeous but chaste Indian princess named Anita Forgives Enemy?"

"The world is passing strange, dear," I say. I pat the empty space beside me on the bed. (Florence works in her bedroom, since the one electrical outlet there is more reliable than the one in the living room.) "Come to bed, Flossy," I say.

She tosses Dunkie's work aside. "Wait, let me get in the mood," she says. She picks up one of my old manuscripts and reads aloud the Multiple, Phosphorescent, Stainless Orgasm part: " 'Her throbbing desire met the furious steel arc of his manhood with both surrender and triumph. The sculptor, Armand Girardeaux, turned her over in his finely carved but powerful hands, demanding her compliance, which she gave willingly. "You shock and surprise me to death, Armand," Samantha gasped. "I've never done it this way before." "There are many things you have not done that you will learn to do, *ma chère,* " Armand replied. "You devil! You wonderfully outrageous devil!" she cried out. "I am no devil, I am but an humble artiste," he breathed, his words filling her ear with forbidden fire.' "

"The furious steel arc awaits," I say, patting the empty sheet next to me.

"You devil!" Florence says, pulling off her ragged Carl Sagan T-shirt. "You wonderfully outrageous devil!"

"I am but an humble artiste," I reply.

Florence has a little brother named Ion, which is a deliberate misspelling of Ian. I mention this to illustrate the kind of family she comes from. Ion is a physicist employed by a computer firm up in Silicon Valley. Ion Halley, Ph.D. He signs his letters to Florence that way. "All my love, your brother, Ion Halley, Ph.D." The inclusion of his credential implies a criticism: Ion feels that Florence has wasted her life. Florence didn't finish college. She, too, was a physics major, but she didn't believe in electromagnetic radiation. She scoffed openly at the theories of Heinrich Hertz and claimed that his early radio experiments were faked. She is, at heart, a primitive. If she weren't delicate and a bad camper, she'd be right at home with the Bushmen of the Kalahari.

Wasn't it Melville who said that the sea and meditation are wedded forever? Whoever said it was right. I love to stroll along the beach in front of Florence's house. I can map out an entire novel in an afternoon of beachcombing. Lately this hasn't been working for me. Walking the beach only produces a great hazy distance between me and my muse. I've asked my editor to let me try a new twist in the usual plot line—throw in a blind serial killer for a few chuckles and thrills, or give the Golden Stud a vagrant sexual fantasy life. This kind of variation might rekindle my desire, but it's against the rules. You might as well ask your banker for a fifty-thousand-dollar loan so that you can open a bookstore that deals only in the literature of ocelot worship.

After an hour of unproductive strolling I head back to Florence's shack. I make myself a tuna sandwich and take it into the bedroom. Florence is on the phone with Dunkie, taking dictation. A phone caddy propped on her shoulder keeps the receiver against her ear as her fingers fly over the keyboard of her word processor. I peek over her shoulder at the amber screen, spying on the process of creation in its rawest form. Dunkie's novel takes place over five hundred years, beginning with 1492 and ending in the present. He's now rewriting a chapter that deals with the Louisiana Purchase. The prose is awkward, redundant, and frequently ungrammatical, and yet I am envious and irritated that it comes so swiftly and with such uncritical ease. If Dunkie had some capacity for self-criticism he would be thrown into stultifying despair, but that's only wishful thinking on my part. I am being small-minded and petty, but then I am no Ahab and never knew one.

Without fully realizing what I am doing, I find myself in Florence's closet, looking at her shabby dresses. Then I fully realize what I am doing. Maybe Veronica LaMonica needs to be coaxed into existence. Maybe she needs a sign of commitment from me. Florence is as tall as I am but doesn't have my potbelly. Even so, one of her gray, bag-lady dresses fits me fine, though I look five months pregnant in it. She even has a few wigs that she used to wear when she was a full-time secretary for a now-defunct savings and loan company. I pull on a chestnut wig with luxuriant curls, find her limited supply of makeup in the bathroom, and go to work on myself. The beard shows through, but all in all I'm not too bad. Her shoes won't fit me, so I slip on a pair of sizeless thongs. Florence notices none of this, as she is fully engaged, transferring the relentless voice of American genius into her computer's binary memory.

I sit at the kitchen table with notebook and pen, and wait. By the time Florence emerges from her two-hour session with Dunkie, I have filled ten pages of a legal pad with what looks like acceptable work.

Florence looks exhausted. She pours herself a beer and sits down at the table opposite me. "So, what is this, Greg?" she says. "Something you've been meaning to tell me but couldn't find the words?"

"Call me Veronica," I say, holding up the legal pad and flipping down page after page of furious scrawl. "I'm working again."

"You'd better be careful. There's no such thing, you know, as a free lunch. You've heard about contagious magic? Your nipples might become sensitive. You might start shopping for shopping's sake. Who knows, you might get to *like* dressing up like a woman."

"Not *a* woman, Florence. *Veronica.* And so what? Veronica is me, my mainstay against an impoverished old age. I owe her."

"Then you'd better do her right," Florence says. She goes to the bathroom and returns with some bottles. She repaints my lips, applies some fuchsia eye shadow, mascaras my eyelashes. She sits on the floor and paints my toenails fluorescent tangerine, then does the same for my fingernails. She unzips the back of the dress, fits me out with a brassiere that she's stuffed with Kleenex. She stands back and examines her work.

"Not bad," she says. "But you're not going to fool anyone, Greg—"

"Veronica."

"You're not going to fool anyone, Veronica, but you could hang out at Horton Plaza at night and collect any number of fine young perverts."

"I don't want fine young—or old—perverts, Flossy. I want twenty keepable pages a day."

"Good luck," she says, her voice dusky now with a shady emotion as she slips her sinister hand up Veronica's dress.

"Looks like there's perverts galore right here at home, anyway," I say, but she doesn't laugh. And the look in her eyes is deranged enough to make my heart thump and flutter. What strangers we harbor.

"Whatever works, Dad," Carlo says, but he's clearly mortified by this unexpected appearance of Veronica. Unfortunately, he has a friend with him, a little Jesus person who looks like he's about to launch his lunch. "My dad's a writer, Billy," Carlo explains. Billy looks relieved, and then he looks forgiving, but I catch a sly third glance that has mischief in it as Carlo leads him out of my office. For Carlo's sake, I shower and change into a manly outfit, Levi's and plaid shirt, snakeskin Tony Lamas on my feet. I roll a cigarette in front of Billy and ask him about the Chargers' chances this season.

"Football is a pagan ritual," Billy says. "It is an extension of the circus games of ancient Rome. The cheerleaders are vestal virgins who are offered to the gods. We deny football, and all other games." He speaks doctrine prettily, with the beatific, argument-trumping smile of a true believer.

I try to catch Carlo's eye. *Oh, and* I'm *the weirdo?* I want my expression to say, but his gaze is fixed on the linoleum. To save the situation I change the subject. "Well, Billy. Did you know there were UFO sightings back in Biblical times?" I light the cigarette and blow dense, unfiltered smoke out my nose. Then I notice my fingernails: still fluorescent tangerine. Carlo tries to stare me into good behavior, but I know what I'm doing. Billy, Jesus person or not, is still a teenage kid with teenage-kid curiosity.

"Some people say that," Billy admits, swallowing hard. Like all good zealots, he is suspicious of information that won't fit into doctrine. Nothing is permitted Inexplicability. Billy is a nice-looking, white-haired kid with skin that appears to have been sandpapered to a high-gloss pink, then coated with clear lacquer. I have to resist the urge to tap his forehead.

"Personally, I believe in them," I say.

"We've got to go, Dad," Carlo says grimly.

"We don't believe in life on other planets and all that type of SF junk," Billy says. "God just created one earth. That's what the Bible says."

"What do you suppose he created all those extra suns for? Must be a few hundred trillion of them."

"Suns? You mean stars."

"Suns are stars, stars are suns, Billy."

"No, stars are just stars. God put them there so that the ships at sea can find true north. And for other things just as practical, like measuring distances in space."

"I saw a UFO once," I say.

Billy looks at Carlo, Carlo looks at the ceiling. "Good*bye*, Dad," Carlo says, heading for the door.

"Big as a white whale, Billy," I say. "Whoever they are, they've beaten gravity. Also the speed of light. And if they've beaten both gravity and the speed of light, then chances are they've beaten death, too. Symmetry of time beyond the quantum level, and all that. Makes you think, doesn't it, Billy?"

Billy nods. His Adam's apple, big as a fist, seems to be inching up his skinny throat. Billy is a likable kid and, in spite of the narrowly structured cosmology he's been given, he's attracted to the notion of the unindoctrinated, freewheeling imagination. And he knows, instinctively, that the attraction is dangerous. What he doesn't know is that it is America's energizing beauty. He follows Carlo out the door, gulping air.

"God bless America, Billy," I call out after the boys.

Then I put on my dress again, make up my face, and resume my life as Veroncia. Ten more steamy pages pour out of my Smith Corona, all of them keepers.

"The Passions of Meredith Flame"
by
Veronica LaMonica

Meredith knew instinctively that the man on the platform of the Amtrak station was someone she should avoid. She had come to Minneapolis to visit her sister, Bobbie. At least that was what she told her friends. But it was more complicated than that. Although her husband, Trent, had ended his affair with his secretary, Jean Parsons, Meredith needed time to herself, to sort things out. Could she go on with her life, as if nothing at all had happened, pretending to their friends that she and Trent were the same happy couple they had always known? She was in a turmoil of conflicting emotions, and now this man—tall, dark, with piercing blue eyes—was staring at her insolently as if he not only knew who she was, but understood the darkest regions of her broken heart. But then suddenly a glamorous woman moved into his arms and he kissed her hard and long, at which point Meredith knew that she had only imagined his interest in her. Obviously, she had seen in him something dangerous and yet attractive, something that might very well shatter her life *again*, yet had the magical power to restore her to herself, to make her wholly and wonderfully alive.

And, of course, that was far too much to expect from a man. Oh yes, they could shatter one's life—they were very good at that!—but very few had the ability, the tenderness and understanding, to nurture and restore. There were no Prince Charmings, and perhaps there never had been. She took a cab to Bobbie's house and prepared a face that would not alarm her sister and her wonderful husband, Hugh Morrisey.

—and so on.

This, and the two hundred and fifty or so pages that follow it, will earn fifteen thousand up front plus six percent royalties on the cover price. Do I have to *defend* this?

Yet that's exactly what I'm doing, back at the Bali Hai Café on a drizzly overcast afternoon with Dunkie. He's after me again to go straight. "You've got a life, Gregory," he says. "You were born, things happened to you, regrettable things I'm sure, but you're not dealing with any of it."

"*Your* novel deals with *your* life?" I say, fighting back a little. "Ninety pages on the injustices of the British Navigation Act comes out of your bruised and bleeding marrow, Dunkie? Columbus smoking hemp roll-your-owns on Watling Island is your idea of personal narrative?"

Dunkie fixes me with a baleful stare that makes me think I've gone too far. He starts to take a bite of his blackened haddock, then lowers the fork to his plate. "I don't think you've heard one word I've ever said to you, Gregory," he says. "I think we've gone over this before. My novel—yes, it deals with history. But it is the deep-rooted emotional history of all of us—and that very much includes me. My *life*, Gregory, my small life, as fucked up and unremarkable as it's been, is *in* this book."

Actually, I shouldn't be antagonizing him. He's had to weather some bad news. First of all, his sisters have won their court battle. His father's estate has been divided evenly among them and it is theirs to dispose of as they see fit. But they are not vengeful shrews: a trust fund has been set up for Dunkie. The interest from the fund will give him six hundred dollars a month for the rest of his life. He won't be allowed to touch the principal.

The worst news came from the William P. Villiers Publishing Company, the first place Dunkie has sent *Tumults and Insurrections.* The first reader, someone named Bridey Anne Noonan, gave it short shrift: "This is a clumsily written, sententious, historically incorrect tract, with a *highly* repugnant phallocentric slant. I give it two thumbs down and a swift kick in the ass." The second reader simply said, "I got to page twelve." The third was simplest of all: "Nay, bucko."

Dunkie is grim but not discouraged. "I write serious fiction," he says. "But that's not what they want. They want *you*, Gregory." A wedge of haddock lands on my shirt. "I'm here to tell you, my friend, that if you continue to give in to these people, you will destroy the last remaining fragment of your miserable soul."

"You keep talking about soul, Dunkie, as if you've got yours locked away in a gold box, untainted, pure. Give me a break, will you? I've got a kid to support. I've got alimony payments to make. My house needs a new roof. I need bridgework. You want me to save my *soul* and let the rest of my life go to hell? That's not how we do things here in America."

He's staring at me, immobile, fork frozen midway to his mouth. "What's *that* on your fingernails?" he says, puzzlement then outrage constricting his voice.

"Fingernail polish!" I say. "Fluorescent tangerine!"

The fork resumes its vital upward arc. Dunkie chews his

fish meditatively, his eyes studying me. *"Fingernail* polish," he says finally, nodding as if things are beginning to fall into place. "Utterly fucking remarkable, Gregory."

"I sometimes forget to take it off," I explain.

"Yes, yes," he says, lifting fish, chewing hard, bennies nipping at his heart. "You're the captain of your soul, no doubt about it, Gregory." He restrains himself from adding, "You poor fuck."

I want to tell him that I've completed a Veronica LaMonica in eleven days flat wearing Florence's baggy dresses. And I want to tell him where he's living: This is America, Dunkie! You do whatever *works.* If it doesn't work, try something else. Because anything goes. Anything is possible. This is the Land of Every Possible Thing. God bless it, while it lasts.

Out in the bay, a gigantic tanker looms out of the rolling fog. It's low in the water, heavy with North Slope crude. It seems to be sailing directly toward the Bali Hai as it makes its slow entrance into San Diego Harbor. Through the water-beaded window, I see the tall white letters of its name. Some nonsuperstitious owner has named it the *Pequod!* And then I hear its horn—a long sorrowful note I can feel vibrating my teeth.

I stop Dunkie midsentence to point out the tanker, but it takes a few seconds to redirect his attention. Annoyed, but too late, he squints out the window. Though the fog has reclaimed the *Pequod,* the hovering despair of its melancholy horn imposes a funereal hush on the patrons of the Bali Hai Café.

"Bit boat, huh?" Dunkie says.

"Too big," I answer.

An Airman's Goodbye

THE DAKEMANS WERE untidy degenerates, including their children and pets, according to Mom. "Some people make their pets and children as trashy as they are," she said, her voice hushed discreetly. "It's a well-known fact of life." She used me—in my crisp blue Air Force uniform complete with Expert Marksman medal and Good Conduct ribbon—and our dog, Pershing, as counterexamples. Pershing was a joyless yellow Labrador. We kept him tied to the mulberry tree in our front yard. He never barked or strained at his rope when cars, or people on foot, passed by. He was too intelligent, too dignified, to be ruled by the ordinary chaotic dog emotions. Several of the undisciplined Dakeman dogs would often come over to visit Pershing, and Pershing would allow himself to be sniffed, nipped, teased, and sometimes mounted, without protest, until Mom rapped the window hard enough to make the uninhibited Dakeman mongrels realize her anger. The motley gang of dogs would then chase each other back across the street to their house, which looked like it had been plucked up out of some 1930s dust-bowl state by a tornado and deposited twenty years later in our clean and tidy, middle-class, scrupulously manicured east San Diego neighborhood.

I had just gotten back home after twelve weeks of basic training at Parks Air Force Base outside of Oakland. I had caught the flu in the damp northern California climate and had lost twenty pounds. I went into the Air Force skinny—six feet tall and one hundred and sixty pounds—and now, at one hundred and forty pounds, I looked like I'd just been liberated from a Nazi concentration camp. Still dizzy and weak, I spent my evenings watching TV and listening to Mom whisper complaints, as if she wasn't in her own house and needed to be secretive. She complained about the Dakemans, about the rising price of meat, and, with tight-lipped bitterness, about Dad's boss, who kept him on the road six to eight months a year. I didn't mind listening to her. It was better than listening to a drill instructor scream a long list of your shortcomings into your face. And besides, the tedium I had to put up with was more than compensated for by her abundant, nonstop cooking.

"You need good, clean food, Miles," she said. "I'm sure they fed you nothing but filth at the training base." I ate the equivalent of six meals a day, hoping to put some bulk on my bones. My hair hadn't grown in yet, and when I looked at myself in the full-length mirror it seemed I was all nose and ears. The thought of looking up my old high school friends depressed me. They used to call me Nose-with-Legs—in just that way, like the title of a painting, as if I were a walking Picasso—and that's exactly what I looked like at one hundred and forty pounds.

Mom's specialty was meat loaf. I could eat six or seven slices of meat loaf at one sitting, along with a huge baked Idaho potato buried in sour cream, two or three steamed vegetables blanketed by a lava of yellow sauce, a quart of milk, and a hot wedge of apple or cherry pie for dessert. I was determined to get back the weight I'd lost before I had to report to Keesler Air Force Base in Biloxi for airborne radar training, and I would eat until a comfortable pain tightened my belly. Mom, a short, fat woman and a big eater herself, was delighted with my performance at the table. She liked her men beefy as lumberjacks. All her brothers had been lumberjacks in the forests of Oregon and northern California—big-

bellied, thick-wristed, hearty men with fine personal habits
and positive outlooks on life—and Dad was a two-hundred-
and-eighty-pound medical-supplies salesman who loved
Mom's food so much he'd make small whimpering sounds as
he ate. She connected my vulnerability to disease to my
scrawniness, and now I was scrawnier than ever. She also saw
evidence of a negative outlook in me, but this too, she believed, was a consequence of poor nutrition, the flu, and the
influence of the riffraff who, she believed, joined the military
only to improve their pathetic circumstances.

In the mornings, after my huge breakfast had time to settle,
I'd go down into the basement and lift weights for an hour or
so, tape-measure my arms, chest, and legs for signs of new
bulk, then come upstairs to shower. I'd watch TV until early
afternoon with a plate of meat-loaf or roast-beef sandwiches,
then, in the evening, while Mom was getting supper ready, I'd
sit out on the front porch and talk to Pershing. Pershing liked
to be talked to. He would sit attentively on his haunches and
study me with his big liquid eyes as I told him stories about
life at Parks Air Force Base.

I was telling Pershing how two DIs had beat up a half-
retarded kid for not changing his underwear often enough
when a muffled bang from across the street startled us both.
This was normal; you expected noises of all sorts from the
Dakeman house. A thud, a bang, or a scream, and a door
would pop open and dogs or children would come flying out
barking, crying, or laughing, or issuing blood threats. Mr.
Dakeman was usually out of work, but when he did work he
made good money. I think he was a welder or boilermaker,
and he would leave the family for weeks at a time to work in
such exotic places as Tulsa, Oklahoma, or Galveston, Texas.
Sometimes he was home for half the year or more, and toward
the end of one of these forced domestications, he would
become short-tempered, often relieving his frustration or
boredom with bouts of mind-numbing drinking.

This was one of those stretches of time when Mr. Dakeman

was between jobs. The soft explosion I'd heard had to do with Nola Dakeman, his teenaged daughter. Nola came flying out of the house, slamming the door behind her and cursing tearfully. At seventeen, she was a tall, long-armed girl with crisp black hair cut Cleopatra-style, and absolutely no sign of breasts. After she calmed down, she started walking up the street backwards, her hands shoved into her pockets, muttering to herself and scowling at the house she'd left. She was barefoot, and wearing cut-off Levis and a yellow football jersey with the number 99 on it in big blue letters. It belonged to her brother, Eldon, an awkward giant of subnormal intelligence who'd played tackle on the varsity football team in his freshman year solely because of his size. He dropped out of school a few months short of graduation to join the Navy. Eldon Dakeman was the object of a lot of jokes among my friends, none of which was repeated to his face.

When Nola saw me watching her, she turned quickly and started walking normally, and then, as if seized by a better idea, she spun around and waved. I swung my arm in a casual arc. Pershing raised his sad eyebrows expectantly. Nola smiled. "Hey, *Miles,* you're back home," she said.

"Affirmative," I said, military-style.

She crossed the street. She was wearing makeup, a lot of it. The face she had painted on herself was pretty. I never thought of her as pretty—she was just a lanky Dakeman kid across the street—but three months away from home gave me a fresh perspective.

"So, are you a big jet pilot or something?" she asked, putting one long narrow foot on the first step of our porch, stretching her other leg behind her. Her calves rounded out nicely as they flexed; her haunches curved sleek as albino seals out of her skintight cutoffs.

"Negative," I said. "I just finished basic training. Im going to Mississippi in a few weeks to study at the radar school."

"Eldon's not in the Navy anymore," she said.

"How come?" I asked. All the lights were on in the Dakeman house, even though it was still light outside. I could hear Mr. Dakeman yelling at someone, probably his wife, a slender, gray woman who always seemed distracted, as if she were trying to remember something important and couldn't go on with the next thing she had to do until she recalled it. I saw Mr. Dakeman drag her across the yard once by her wrist, pulling her into the house so hard that she swung from side to side like a kite being yanked out of a windy sky by force.

"He got kicked out," Nola said. "He did something weird, I think."

That didn't surprise me. Once during a scrimmage, Eldon pulled down his pants far enough so that his gigantic, ghostly-white butt was visible to the backfield. Mooning his own backfield was his idea of sophisticated humor. I was the third-string quarterback getting a chance to work with the starting backfield. We were in a T-formation set, and I was too busy staring over the center at a pair of growling linebackers to notice Eldon at his left-tackle spot. When I turned to hand the ball off to Joey Butterfield, the fullback, Joey wasn't there. I got creamed and fumbled the ball. Joey was on his back, laughing hysterically. I was facedown and writhing in the grass, taking late hits even though the wind was knocked out of me and Coach Stuckey was blowing his whistle so hard it hurt my ears even under the insulating pile of bodies. Coach Stuckey made the entire football team take ten laps after scrimmaging for two more hours because of our attitude problem. We wanted to kill Eldon, but at six feet six inches and two hundred and twenty-nine pounds, he was easy to forgive. It was hard to believe all this had happened just the previous fall. High school seemed like a century ago.

"What did he do?" I asked.

"I don't know. He won't say. I think he *wanted* to get kicked out, though. He hated it." She sat down on the first step of the porch, the back of her head level with my knee.

"Too bad," I said, trying to imagine hulking Eldon in a tight-fitting sailor's uniform.

Nola nudged Pershing's flank with her naked toes. "Hi Pershing," she said. "Hi you silly old zombie." She put her hand out, and Pershing leaned toward it an inch, his eyes melancholy in the waning light. Then Mom cleared her throat. She'd been at the screen door for a while, listening. "Miles," she said, in that soft, confiding voice. "I have your pork chops ready, dear." I left Nola on the porch talking to Pershing and went inside to eat.

Mom gave me free use of her car, a bright yellow 1950 Hudson Hornet. I loved its low-cut lines and power. When you got into it, you stepped down, as if into a private basement apartment. The upholstery was a dark beige plush and the dashboard held big, generous instruments and a chrome-plated push-button radio. Mom vacuumed it out once a week, as if it were part of her house. The car was clean and it still had a showroom smell to it, even though it was over five years old. Sometimes I'd have her pack a lunch—four sandwiches, pie, thermos full of milk—and I'd drive out to the beach. The surf at LaJolla Shores was perfect for body-surfing, and I'd spend an entire morning swimming out to where the big waves were breaking and then riding them in. I worked up a terrific appetite doing this, and by noon I was ready to eat my four-sandwich lunch. Then I'd drive around town for a while, looking at the sights, taking the long way home—through Balboa Park, past the zoo and Navy hospital, and then out onto the highway that ran through Mission Valley, where I'd open the big Hudson up and watch the red speed indicator dance on 90.

About two weeks before I was scheduled to take the train to Biloxi, Nola Dakeman asked if she could come to the beach with me. In spite of myself, I glanced quickly at the kitchen window of our house, knowing that Mom would be squinting out at us and wondering what Nola Dakeman wanted from her clean-cut airman. I told Nola she was welcome to come, but would she meet me on El Cajon Boulevard—four blocks away—in fifteen minutes. She shrugged—probably guessing what was behind my strategy—and said, "Sure."

In the car, she said, "What's the matter, don't you want your Ma to know you're taking me to the beach?"

I glanced over at her, a nervous twitch of a smile trying to sabotage the cool, regulation military expression on my face. She sat close to me, and I realized that she smelled. It was a strong, domestic smell, a mixture of sweat and kitchen odors—the Dakemans were known to fry everything in deep fat: a haze of grease fogged their kitchen day and night—but under this was a rich, tropical smell that was as exotic to me as the air of an equatorial seaport.

By late afternoon I was in love with Nola Dakeman. I didn't realize it until a few days later, but thinking back on our day at the beach I saw that was when it started. After we swam and body-surfed for a few hours, we came back to the blanket to have some lunch. But I couldn't eat more than one sandwich, and even several hours later the undigested sandwich felt like a twelve-pound shot in my stomach as I saw again, in my imagination, her water-beaded face, the long strands of her wet black hair pasted to her neck and shoulders, and her electrifying eyes that seemed able to transfer some of their blue voltage into mine.

I lost my appetite. I began to meet Nola out in the street after dark, and the anticipation of these meetings was so intense that I had a hard time swallowing my supper. Mom thought I was having a relapse of whatever it was I'd caught in basic training. She wanted to call a doctor, but I begged her not to. "I'll be all right, Mom," I said. "All I need is to rest my stomach a little. I think I've been eating too much. Maybe I have a little indigestion."

She regarded me with a wounded look. Cold tears glazed her eyes. "My food does not cause indigestion," she said gravely.

I'd go outside when it was dark and give Pershing some leftovers, and then Nola would come out and stroll across the street. We'd talk casually until Mom left her vigil at the kitchen window to watch one of her favorite TV shows. When she was gone, Nola and I would slip around to the side of the house and kiss each other to exhaustion, each grinding kiss lasting minutes.

I loved her smell and would dream about it at night, and the dreams eventually became erotically specific. Mom began to regard me with a kind of shy disgust when she changed my bedding. I'd never been in love before. I'd gone steady twice in high school, but that was part of an expected routine. Nola and I met every evening at the same time and would wind up necking heavily either in our side yard, between the house and the garage, or in her backyard.

The Dakeman backyard looked like a graveyard for the Industrial Revolution. The shrubless, grassless yard was strewn with the massive hulks of old arc-welding generators, compressors frozen with rust, and gutted prewar cars waiting patiently to be repaired or further cannibalized. Unidentifiable fragments of machines grew out of the sterile soil like exotic rust-colored wildflowers.

We made love for the first time in the rotting, mushroom-sprouting backseat of a prewar Buick that sat wheelless in a far corner of the Dakeman yard. It was a passionate, flailing, short-lived attempt, charged with the sort of desperation people who leap from the windows of burning buildings have, but it was the real thing: sex. "I love you! Oh dammit, I think I love you!" I said, joyous and amazed. I hugged her hard and rocked her from side to side against the mildewed mohair as disturbed moths banged into my face and neck.

She drew back, putting some distance between us. "It'll be way better next time," she said. It was a thin-lipped declaration of superior knowledge. It was my first time, but it was not Nola's. "It won't be such a great big deal for you next time, Miles."

We took a walk through the neighborhood. The nearly full moon transformed lawns and sidewalks into pewter, and the sparse fronds of the date palms that lined the streets seemed like the motionless wings of astonished angels. As we passed the dark windows of my house, I sensed Mom's unhappy, vigilant eyes watching us. I put my arm around Nola's bony shoulders. "You're really kind of okay," Nola said, as if she had heard strong arguments to the contrary. "You remind me of some movie actor."

"I do?" I was thrilled, because just that morning, while studying myself in the bathroom mirror, I'd thought that I had something of Rory Calhoun's looks—a blade-thin but muscular body; sharp, crafty face with a handsome, hawklike nose tilting out of it.

"Who?" I asked. "What actor?"

"Jack Webb," she said.

I tried to hide my disappointment. I laughed. "Dum-da-da-*dum*," I sang, thinking that the stupid *Dragnet* theme would haunt me for the rest of my life.

"You remind *me* of a movie star, too," I said.

This seemed to startle her. "Really?" she said eagerly. "Who? Tell me."

I almost said, because I was still smarting from the Jack Webb comparison, *Lassie!* But then my devotion to her overcame my anger and I quickly blurted out, "Debra Paget." And it was true, she did look like Debra Paget, the beautiful actress who played Indian princesses almost exclusively, except that Debra Paget had a magnificent body with powerful, coppery breasts that looked like they could punch holes into sheet metal. Nola had no breasts at all.

"Oh, you're *crazy*," she said, obviously pleased.

We returned to the prewar Buick after a while and did it again. When we finished, Nola said, "See? That was a thousand percent better than the first time, Miles, wasn't it?" She patted the back of my head. I'd seen her pat Pershing, whom she regarded as an emotional cripple, in this same encouraging way.

"Affirmative," I said.

I began to think that I could not bear to go to Biloxi, Mississippi, and leave Nola Dakeman behind. Life without Nola seemed like no life at all; it seemed like death. Nothing that would happen from now on could excite or motivate me if Nola was not at my side sharing every detail of the experience. I'd be no better than a zombie, sleepwalking through the world. Mom knew something was wrong, and she probably knew what it was, but she couldn't bring herself to discuss it. At best she would whisper abstract complaints, to no particular sympathizer, about the endless housecleaning, laundering, and cooking she had to do for little or no thanks.

In my lovesickness, I had become a slob. My hair was growing back unevenly in scruffy patches, but I wouldn't go to a barber shop. I didn't shave for days at a time. In the mirror, to my disgust—despite my general lack of grooming and military neatness—I began to look more and more like Jack Webb. I twisted what forelocks I had into curls, greasing them and making them hang on my forehead, hoping for a dashing, Rory Calhoun effect, but I only looked like a Picasso caricature of Sergeant Joe Friday. I even started smoking, because I had never seen Jack Webb with a cigarette in his mouth.

"I won't have you leaving filthy cigarettes around my house," Mom said, a new coldness in her voice.

"Roger, wilco," I said, stubbing out my Chesterfield in the kitchen sink.

"My car is full of beach sand," she said.

"Sorry about that," I said.

"Don't sorry-about-that *me,* young man. I want you to clean it out or not use it again. Do you understand me?"

I rolled my eyes toward the ceiling in the now universal James Dean manner. "Affirmative," I said.

And later, adopting a more conciliatory tone, she said, "Miles, I know you're seeing that . . . that *skinny* girl. I really don't understand it, not that it's any of my business, but why can't you look up your old high school friends? Why are you avoiding them?"

My old high school friends had their own lives. They had jobs now, or were in the military. We were all light-years removed from the kind of shoulder-punching, smart-mouth, street-loitering way of life we never once saw as limited, shallow, or futureless. I thought of them now, at Mom's insistence, and could not clearly remember their faces.

We were sitting at the kitchen table. Mom slid a wedge of peach pie in front of me. She pressed a scoop of vanilla ice cream into it, and then another. The fatty pink flesh hanging from her arms jiggled with the effort.

"No thanks," I said, pushing it away.

It's hard for pale blue eyes to look tragic, but when they do it takes your breath away. Tears in unreal abundance flooded down her face. She turned and stumbled out of the kitchen making warbling, wet moans. I was too shocked, for a moment, to move.

Inexplicably, my reaction to Mom's outburst was *rage.* I dumped the pie and ice cream into the sink and stormed out of the house, slamming the door so hard that something inside fell off a wall. I crossed the street to the Dakeman house and knocked on the door. I'd never gone up to the Dakeman front door once in all the years we'd lived across from each other. After at least two minutes, Mr. Dakeman himself answered. He squinted at me through an alcoholic mist. "She's out," he said. Then he grinned a little. "Come on in and wait, Captain."

We went into the living room, where Mr. Dakeman had

been watching the wrestling matches on TV and drinking Seagram's 7. An angry crackle of frying meat came from the kitchen. I could almost feel beads of drifting fat settle on my face. On the TV screen, Lord Blears was stomping the throat of Antonino Rocca, the great acrobatic wrestler from Argentina.

"You want a drink, Captain?" Mr. Dakeman said.

I started to say no, but hesitated a beat too long and Mr. Dakeman filled a spare shot glass to the brim. "Down the hatch," he said, filling his own glass and lifting it to his lips with the grace and efficiency of a journeyman drinker. I raised my glass more cautiously and then leaned forward so that my puckered lips would catch the rim before any whiskey sloshed over it. Mr. Dakeman was a round-bellied, narrow-shouldered man with big, dark-knuckled hands. He smelled of sour, days-old sweat, booze, and fried meat. He had little, intelligent eyes that glinted with a mean-spirited self-satisfaction. Though he seemed to be absorbed in the wrestling match, I knew he was watching me out of the corner of his eye as I sipped from my shot glass. I swallowed all the whiskey then and set the empty glass down. My face got hot. He refilled my glass. I lit a cigarette. Antonino Rocca had recovered from getting his throat stomped and now had Lord Blears trapped in a grapevine twist. Lord Blears, monocle in place and bellowing in pain, tried to hop to the ropes. "Phony limey bastard," Mr. Dakeman said.

"Break his back, Rocca," I said, feeling the whiskey.

"Rocca could do it," Mr. Dakeman said soberly.

We spoke of wrestling and drank as the whiskey-loosened minutes got away from us and the room darkened. At one point, Mrs. Dakeman came in with steaks fried to the density of leather and covered with scorched onions. She set the plates down on the coffee table, one for Mr. Dakeman, one for me. Mr. Dakeman accepted his dinner without acknowledgment. I started to say something, but thought better of disturbing Mrs. Dakeman's perfect distraction.

"Salt," Mr. Dakeman said, his eyes fixed on the TV set, and his wife returned with a shaker of salt, again without apparent expectation of a mutter or nod of thanks from her husband. Rocca had beaten Lord Blears, two falls out of three, and now Gorgeous George was taking on Wild Red Berry in the main event.

"Red Berry's tough," Mr. Dakeman said, a wad of steak in his cheek, "but he's too small. That hairy fruitcake's got forty, fifty pounds on him."

The front door opened and Eldon Dakeman came in. He stood in the half-light of the living room, steel lunch pail dangling at the end of his long arm. He was as big as ever but there was a curvature to his back I didn't remember. He had developed an older man's stoop. Nola had told me that Eldon was now working for Ducommon Steel down in National City, making good money unloading finished steel products from railroad cars.

"Hey, Eldon," I said.

He peered into the dim room, gradually recognizing his father and me sitting on the couch. "Hey, Mike," he said.

"Miles," I said, but Eldon ignored the correction. He had finished socializing. He went into the kitchen and came out gripping a steak in his hand. Then he went off to his room, his footfalls shaking the house. I tried to imagine what Eldon looked like in a sailor uniform. The effort made me smile. He must have seemed dangerously improbable to his superior officers. They must have come to believe that the entire hierarchy of naval command would have been compromised if Eldon was allowed to wear, and distort, the uniform.

"Miles," Mr. Dakeman said, in a musing tone of voice. "Who the Jesus gave you a handle like that, Captain?"

Gorgeous George took something out of his trunks while the referee wasn't looking. He had Wild Red Berry's arms twisted into the ropes. He rubbed the stuff from his trunks into Wild Red's eyes.

"That's cayenne pepper!" Mr. Dakeman said. "That pansy

can't win without pulling a stunt like that."

"I don't know who gave it to me," I said.

"What?" Mr. Dakeman said, leaning toward the TV set. Wild Red Berry had just drop-kicked Gorgeous George into a corner post and was now working him over with flying mares. I refilled my shot glass.

"It was probably my mother," I said. "She likes dignified names like Miles and Terence. Jonathan, Carlton, Emory. Do you know what my dad's name is? It's Leland." I was sitting on the floor by then, my legs stretched out under the coffee table. I forgot myself and spit angrily into the dog-stained carpet, thinking of my name and how I hated it. The lumpish body of a big, sleeping mongrel pressed against my thigh. A smelly child in diapers stood next to me and touched my ear with a popsicle. I saw Mrs. Dakeman come and go a number of times, carrying dishes or whispering the names of children. I saw that my glass was full again and so I emptied it as Wild Red Berry defeated Gorgeous George with a punishing Boston crab, a submission hold, the inescapable hold all wrestlers feared.

A sound from the street pierced through the cheering crowd and Mr. Dakeman's rumbling snores. It sent a spasm through my drunken heart. It was the sound of Nola's wild rebellious laughter. I started to get up, then decided to stay put. I thought I should be seen sitting on the floor with a shot glass in my hand watching TV with her father, as if I were one of the family. But she didn't come in. When she laughed again, I got up and went to the door and opened it a crack.

She was leaning against a '52 Ford Victoria. It was a beautiful car—lowered, leaded, chopped, channeled, with a custom paint job, a metallic maroon so deep and liquid it looked like you could slip your arm into it straight to the elbow. The driver of the car had his head tilted out the window. A cigarette hung from his lower lip. He was a Drifter. The club's name, carved into a cast-aluminum plaque, dangled from the rear bumper of the Ford on chromium chains. He had long sideburns and his hair was sculpted into a well-greased duck's ass. He gunned the engine now and then, filling the semidark neighborhood with a window-vibrating roar. When he let it idle, I could hear the radical camshaft make the engine stutter. It was a street dragster, meant for high RPMs. It idled nervously, the timing unsure of itself. Nola, her hands shoved into the front pockets of her cutoff Levi's, leaned down to the indifferent Drifter and waited for him to remove his cigarette. He took his time, but when he finally flipped the butt into the street, she kissed him. Her head and shoulders gradually entered the narrow window. Then the upper half of her body was inside the car, lost in a well of shadow. It looked as if she were sinking into a maroon lake. Her long foot rose, slowly, and the sandal it was wearing slipped off. The toes of the foot curled tightly. Then they splayed.

I switched the porch light on and off several times, as any father might have done. Of course, Mr. Dakeman would not have stood at the door observing his daughter protectively. The dignity and responsibility of fatherhood were not high on his list of personal standards. I glanced over at him. He was awake again, staring wearily at Dick Lane, the ringside announcer, who was giving his redundant analysis of the matches we had seen and what we could expect in the future. I snapped the porch light on and off with the outrage of someone who had rights—a father, an older brother. A lover. And, of course, I immediately felt like an idiot, like a coward. The truth was, the Drifters were a legendary car club, known for their fearless run-ins with the cops, their lead-pipe-and-chain-swinging brawls with other car clubs, and for their amazing *cars,* each of which was a legitimate work of art. I was in awe of the Drifters and their cars, and couldn't have gone out in the street to claim Nola: Without a car of equal beauty and sophistication, I could not have competed.

I sat down on the couch and poured myself another shot of whiskey. I let my glass rest on my teeth and I felt, along with the burning trickle of booze, the throbs from the radical Ford as it eased away from the house.

My heart speeded up, anticipating Nola, but as minutes passed I realized that she had gone off with the Drifter again. My irate-father-at-the-light-switch act probably meant something altogether different to her than it would have meant to a girl from a decent family. She probably thought it was her mother, or a sister or brother, warning her away from the house because her father was on a blood-letting rampage.

I left Mr. Dakeman sunk into the corner of his sofa, his sagging face pale in the TV's gray flickering light. When I crossed our lawn, Pershing grazed my knee with his big sad head. I knelt beside him and hugged him until he trembled with anxiety. He wasn't accustomed to physical demonstrations of emotional need. Then I took his rope and unhooked it from his collar. "You're free, Pershing," I said. "Go piss on a tire." But Pershing just stood next to the mulberry tree and quivered.

I was very sick the next day. Physically more than emotionally, but as my strength came back, this order was reversed. I packed, halfheartedly, the things I needed to take to Keesler Air Force Base. Civilian clothes were not permitted in basic, but in technical school we would be allowed to spend weekend passes out of uniform. Not that I looked forward to weekends. I didn't look forward to anything. I had made the mistake of waiting for the Drifter to bring her back. I'd waited out on the porch, talking to Pershing, who stayed under his protecting tree, tethered to his own timidity. I waited an hour. Then the customized Ford turned the corner and rumbled down the street. The Drifter eased up to the curb in front of the

Dakeman house and turned off his lights. Then he turned off his engine. I watched the dark unmoving car. A silence, like the hush of conspirators, sealed our neighborhood from the rest of the universe. But Pershing's keen ears twitched and he glanced quickly at the Ford, then guiltily back at me.

I imagine he heard the secret friction of flesh, the fluid roar of hearts. He looked at me in alarm, his sorrowful eyes understanding, but not quite condoning, my apparent complaisance. "I don't own her, you idiot," I said.

I tried to eat breakfast and failed. After picking at a four-egg cheese omelet for a few minutes, I had to run to the bathroom. Mom seemed sympathetic, but her sympathy came from a distance. She'd lost faith in me. I was not going to be a robust eater with a positive outlook like Dad or my lumberjack uncles. I skipped lunch, went for a long walk instead. When I got home, I saw Nola sitting on her front porch. She was wearing her cutoffs, her round white thighs held wide in brave unconscious welcome.

"Hey, Miles," she said.

I didn't trust my voice, so I just waved. I was wearing my uniform. The crisp, silvery-blue sheen of it had a good effect on me. It took away some of my bitterness. The uniform reminded me that I belonged to something much larger and far more dependable than this narrow street with its tense little lawns and hedges and the Dakeman's dust-bowl eyesore. I was an airman third class, soon to be a trained specialist, destined to fly in the RC-121-C Super Connies, the radar picket planes that defended the coastlines of our nation from sneak attack. I felt sorry for Eldon, who had lost his chance with the Navy. But it was the kind of pity that gives you a warm feeling of comfortable self-regard.

"You look sharp, Miles," she said.

I stopped. I pulled my cigarettes out and lit up. "Thanks,

Nola," I said. Then, touching the bill of my cap, I added, "For *every* thing." It was a scene from a movie, an airman's good-bye to the things that would grow small and quaint as he rose higher and higher into the blue yonder. It was the right thing to say. It was exactly what Rory Calhoun would have said.

Aliens

A SALT TIDE broke through Hornbeck's antiperspirant and the high reek of the hot afternoon was on him. He parked his truck in the driveway and went into the house. Roberta met him inside the door. "Your son mutilated his new teddy bear with a steak knife," she said.

He followed her into the kitchen. The table was set. Hornbeck was hungry and dazed with fatigue. He had skipped lunch because he'd had to help Cosmo Minor take a pair of vintage Corvettes from Mexicans in Boyle Heights and things had gone from tense to freaky when the Zambrano brothers locked themselves into the cars and the tow trucks and cops had to be called in.

Hornbeck took off his jacket and sat at the table. The hot kitchen smelled of old grease and Lysol, and now, of him. A covered aluminum pot rattled on the stove, steam jetting from the lid.

"Beam me up, Scotty," he sighed.

Roberta, a thin woman with a long, angular face etched with disappointment, opened a beer and put it on the table within his reach. "Get Lance washed up before your shower, will you?" she said, adjusting the heat under the pot. "Say something to him about teddy. He thought teddy had one of those horrible creatures living in its chest, like in that movie you brought home last week."

Hornbeck carried his beer out to the backyard, where Lance and another preschooler were playing trucks. Both boys were cranky and overheated. The few rules of order they had created for their game were crumbling. Lance was using his truck as a hammer against the other boy's truck. The other boy was trying to withdraw his truck from the onslaught, but Lance followed it with relentless blows. The other boy was on the verge of tears.

"Hey, soldier," Hornbeck said. "Time to wash up for din-din."

Lance ignored his father and swung his truck with increasing savagery, rising up on his little haunches for added leverage.

"Whoa, big guy!" Hornbeck said, chuckling a bit at the boy's determination. "Time out, my man! Mommy's got our dinner almost ready." He set his beer down on the lawn and stepped into the circle of combat. He caught Lance's truck on the upswing. Lance, enraged, pulled his truck back, but Hornbeck picked up the boy and carried him toward the house. Lance kicked and punched. His round cheeks shined explosively red. He twisted away from his father's mild rebukes, arching his back and holding his breath between screams. Hornbeck, a tall, slope-shouldered, bearish man, held the boy at arm's length and gave him a light shake. "That's *enough*, son," he said, and Lance hiccupped once and was quiet. "All right, that's fine. You're safe now in a Federation Starship tractor beam. The war with the Klingons is over, okay?"

Hornbeck put his son down. As soon as his feet touched the ground, Lance ran over to the other boy, who was still on his knees making truck noises, and swung his truck into the side of the boy's head. The crack of hard plastic on flesh made Hornbeck wince. The boy ran screaming from the yard, leaving his truck behind. Lance sat down and resumed hammering the other boy's truck, all hindrances finally removed.

Hornbeck sipped his beer and waited for his son to exhaust himself. Then he called and the boy came running happily to his dad. "Okay, war's over, soldier," he said. "The Federation wins. But look, you can't be giving major headshots to your little buddies, okay?" He scooped the boy into his arms. "Let's beam up to the *Enterprise* for our pseudo-soup and miracle-meat." Hornbeck made the high-pitched hum of the transporter beam and Lance giggled with delight.

"Lance has the attitude of a Klingon warrior," Hornbeck said to Roberta later that evening. They were in bed, reading the paper.

Roberta put her section of the paper down. "The attitude of a Klingon warrior," she repeated. "And just what *is* that? Tell me, I'd honestly like to be educated about this."

Hornbeck leaned his head back into his pillows and looked at the ceiling. "Beam me up, Scotty," he sighed.

"No, I mean it. I'd like to know, really. Let me in on how you see us. I'm really curious."

"You're a Vulcan beauty," Hornbeck said, turning toward her. "I'm insane over Vulcan woman. Vulcan women drag the one-eyed nasty from Neptune out of me."

He reached for her but Roberta pushed him away and got out of bed. She lit a cigarette. "I don't think I can deal with this," she said.

"Captain Kirk won't like to hear that, Roberta," Hornbeck said. "Maybe you'd better report to Bones for attitude rehab."

Though it was often not possible, Hornbeck preferred to work alone. This, and his addiction to science fiction movies, had earned him the nickname Han Solo. Most of the repo men at the Bolton Agency liked to work in pairs. Especially when they had to go into the neighborhoods. Having gone into Boyle Heights for the vintage Corvettes with Cosmo Minor had made a difficult situation nearly impossible. Cosmo, a stocky, impatient black man, and Hornbeck, a six-foot-six-inch hulk, had created a confrontational atmosphere that eliminated any chance for calm negotiations. And while two men were needed to get the cars back to the bank that had financed them, the presence of both Cosmo and Hornbeck at the front door of the Zambrano residence lit an us-against-them fuse that couldn't be snuffed. There was the exchange of insults, the inevitable shoving match, the gathering of hostile neighbors.

Hornbeck felt far more effective in one-on-one situations. People, when he had to confront them, didn't feel threatened by him despite his size. He had a sincere, friendly manner, and a shy, boyish smile that encouraged trust. If he had to take a car or a stereo, the delinquent owner was usually will-ing to listen to Hornbeck's reasonable arguments. And he, in turn, was willing to hear their hard-luck stories. Often the delinquent owner would invite Hornbeck into his or her house for a beer or coffee. On more than one occasion, Horn-beck was so moved by their hard-luck stories that he volun-teered to make the back payments on the merchandise himself, provided the payments were small. He saved the TV set of a stroke-paralyzed widower once by paying eighteen dollars on the man's contract with the appliance store. He became deeply sympathetic to deserted women with children to support.

Bonnie DeLuca had missed four payments on her washer and dryer. She'd met him at her door in a bathrobe. "Don't tell me," she had said. "Pay the hundred-sixty now or its bye-bye Maytag, right?" She began to cry. She opened the door wide and he went in.

"I'm really sorry, ma'am," he said, pushing his hand through his hair, unable to hide his discomfort. He found the utility room and looked at the washer-dryer set. He checked the width of the machines with his tape measure, then checked the width of the utility-room door. When he went back into the living room, Bonnie DeLuca was sitting on the couch staring into her cup of coffee. A small child pestered her knees.

"I wish I could just do what I'm thinking," she said into the cup, "but God help me I'm not that type of woman."

Hornbeck pretended he didn't hear this and went out to his pickup and skidded the hand truck off the bed. He rolled it around to the back of the house and pulled it into the utility room. Bonnie DeLuca was there, her robe partially opened. "Goddammit," she said. "I *need* my machines."

"I feel rotten about this, ma'am," Hornbeck said. He knelt to detach the hoses from the washer.

"Feel rottener," Bonnie said, kneeling beside him. She was small and vulnerable next to the sweating bulk of his long torso.

He was surprised at how easy it was to let this happen. It was a first for him. Six years of faithfulness ended, easy as hanging up the phone.

Bonnie had said, "What do you think of me? I mean, what do you *really* think of me?" They were in her bed. The weak springs of the bed had made distracting hee-haw sounds, like the braying of a donkey. In another room the child had imitated those sounds in a dreamy singsong, and was now whining for its mother.

"What do I think of you," he said, scratching his chin. "I think you're a warm-blooded earth woman. Unlike your Vulcan counterpart."

After they made love again, Hornbeck said, "And what do you think of *me?*"

"To be honest, I think you're real nice but kind of geeky," Bonnie DeLuca said.

That had been three months ago. Since then, Bonnie had not made any payments on her washer-dryer combination. The payments had been made by Hornbeck.

"What are all these savings withdrawals?" Roberta asked him one morning at breakfast.

"What withdrawals?" Hornbeck said, studying the newspaper.

She tossed the bankbook onto the table. "Forty dollars, May ninth. Fifty dollars, June tenth."

"Oh that. It's a surprise, honey."

"We can't afford any surprises. I need a replacement crown on my molar, Lance needs school clothes."

"No problem," Hornbeck said.

"There's something else. I want to put Lance into Rage Reduction before he starts kindergarten."

Hornbeck's newspaper sagged gradually to the table. "I'm sorry? You want to put Lance into rage *what?*"

"Reduction. I'm very serious about this. His violence has got to be understood and dealt with."

"All healthy five-year-olds have some violence, honey. It's very normal. We begin in the jungle. They tame us, little by little. Look at me." He twisted a pair of paper napkins into cylinders and stuffed one into each nostril. He stuck out his tongue and rolled his eyes. He stood up in a half-crouch so that his knuckles dragged on the floor. He made urgent primitive noises in his throat. "Me, ten years ago," he said.

"Cut it out. I'm trying to be serious. He's destroyed most of his toys. He thinks hideous creatures live inside them. He hurts his playmates."

"Good Klingon warriors, from a very early age—"

"Stop it! You turn everything you can't face into a comic book!"

Hornbeck smiled. He thought he had an answer to this. Her mistake seemed clear to him. What, for instance, could he not face? He started to speak, then stopped. He ran his hands through his hair and shook his head, somewhat dismayed at his inability to state the obvious. "I'm a good person," he finally said.

"So is Jerry Lewis," Roberta said.

Sometimes he didn't mind taking things away from people. The Invernesses had bought a two-year-old Cadillac for nothing down and payments of over four hundred dollars a month. They were a couple in their sixties, living on pensions in Van Nuys. They weren't poor, they had a savings account, but it was convenient for them to skip payments from time to time. They had missed three in a row now and the credit union that had granted the loan engaged the services of the Bolton Agency.

"I've always wanted a Caddy," Mr. Inverness said.

"Everyone wants a Caddy," Hornbeck said.

"Do you *have* to take it?" Mrs. Inverness said. They were in the Invernesses' living room. Mrs. Inverness had made tea, but Hornbeck wasn't drinking his.

"You've missed three payments, ma'am. The fourth is due next Friday. If you can come up with seventeen hundred and eighty-four dollars, then, no, I don't have to take it. That figure includes the late-payment penalties."

"It's our only transportation," Mr. Inverness said bitterly.

Hornbeck looked at his watch. "I'll need the keys," he said.

Mr. Inverness patted his pockets. "Don't have them," he said. "You have them, Polly?"

Mrs. Inverness shook her head. They both stared at Hornbeck. Behind their bifocals, their pale eyes were big with tentative challenge.

Hornbeck looked around the medium-to-high-rent apartment. Quality furnishings. Behind the leaded-glass cabinet doors of an antique sideboard, stacks of Wedgwood dinnerware gleamed. Mr. Inverness was wearing expensive burgundy wing-tips and Mrs. Inverness's dress did not come from a Kmart rack. They were plump, florid people who were not worried about their next meal.

"I can make my regular payment," Mr. Inverness said, "but not a cent more. We are not wealthy."

"That's not acceptable," Hornbeck said.

THE VOICE OF AMERICA: STORIES

"Listen to me, you. I'm sixty-seven years old, I've put two snot-nose ingrates through college. I've worked hard all my life. I've had a little setback, but I *deserve* that car."

"Do I look like Father Christmas?" Hornbeck said.

"Don't take that tone with me, young man," Mr. Inverness said, rising.

"Now, Kenneth," his wife said. "Remember what Doctor said about temper and blood pressure." She turned bitterly toward Hornbeck. "You're *killing* him," she hissed. "Can't you see that?"

Mr. Inverness leaned toward Hornbeck, his jaw stiff with menace.

"Just give me the keys, Mr. Inverness," Hornbeck said, glancing at his watch again. "I've got other appointments this afternoon."

"More innocent people to crucify," Mr. Inverness sneered.

Hornbeck held his hand out for the keys. Mr. Inverness sprayed saliva into it.

"You've just made my job a whole bunch easier, Mr. Inverness," Hornbeck said.

Hornbeck went into the kitchen and looked on top of the refrigerator and then scanned the countertops. The table was empty. He entered the bedroom and went through the clutter on the dressers and night tables. Then he emptied the night-table drawers onto the neatly made bed. A collection of antique dolls were arranged on a shelf under the window. The tiny red lips of the dolls were puckered and their seductive, oversize eyes regarded Hornbeck coyly. While Hornbeck was looking at the dolls, Inverness came in and grabbed his arms from behind, but Hornbeck threw him off easily.

"I'm calling the police!" Mrs. Inverness said.

"Do that, ma'am," Hornbeck said. "Tell them that you and your husband are trying to steal a car from people who trusted you to pay for it."

Hornbeck found the keys in the closet, hanging on a hook that had been screwed into the doorframe. Mr. Inverness lurched at Hornbeck, trying grab the keys, but Hornbeck stiff-armed him in the breastbone, knocking him away. Mr. Inverness sat down, his shocked mouth wide open, unable to draw in air.

Hornbeck skipped lightly down the stairwell and into the parking garage, whistling. He found the Cadillac, a pearl-gray Coupe de Ville. He gave the thumbs-up to Cosmo Minor, who was reading the newspaper behind the wheel of the Agency's flatbed truck. Cosmo looked at his watch, then scowled at Hornbeck. Hornbeck grinned and waved Cosmo off. They wouldn't be needing the flatbed after all. Then he climbed into the Caddy and drove it away hard, plumes of blue smoke geysering from the tires.

He drove the car to Bonnie DeLuca's house and took her for a ride. They stopped at a bar for drinks, then drove off to a secluded area in the Santa Monica Mountains.

"Upper Crustville," Bonnie said.

"Don't count on it," Hornbeck said. "I hauled a boat out of here a few months ago with my own truck. Damn near burned up the transmission."

Hornbeck kissed Bonnie roughly and shoved his hands under her dress.

"Hey, Bonzo," she said. "Aren't we a little out in the open here?" She turned her face away from him to look at the wide houses and expensive landscaping.

"The windows are smoked. Besides, I feel kind of pumped up. I took this baby from bloodsucking life forms hatched in the outer limits, Bonnie. Earthlings one, Evil Empire zero."

"You're a geeky kind of guy, you know that, Hornbeck?"

"But I've got a good heart," he said, pressing her down into the tangerine velour.

The house was dark and no one was home. Something was wrong, but it was past eight and Hornbeck was too hungry and tired to deal with it. It had been a long day, and he reeked. He'd taken back three cars, a living-room settee, an expensive stereo system, and, of all things, a satellite dish. The man who had the dish was crazy. He hadn't been using it to receive television broadcasts, but as a device to contact aliens. He had rigged a shortwave transceiver to the dish and was transmitting his voice into space. "I am on the brink of a monumental discovery!" the man had said. When Hornbeck started unbolting the dish from its mounts, the man became frantic. He ran around his backyard making odd gestures and babbling in a language he had made up. Hornbeck felt uneasy as he unbolted the dish. He had to kneel down and duck under the supporting struts to do the job, and the man could have clobbered him from behind with a rock or garden tool. Hornbeck knew the man was capable of doing something like that. One look into the man's face and it was clear he was crazy enough to do the next thing that occurred to him. When Hornbeck got the dish into the back of his truck, the man began howling in despair. "My research is ruined! I hope you and the slime that sent you realize that!"

"Sorry, Professor," Hornbeck had said. "E-Z Pay Appliances can't afford to support research projects."

"I was about to solve their codes, you Neanderthal!" the man had yelled as Hornbeck started his truck. "I could have moved humanity forward by a thousand years!"

"A thousand won't be enough, buddy. But I'll tell Mr. Sulu when I see him. He's good at cracking codes."

Hornbeck groped his way into the kitchen and turned on the light. There was a note taped to the refrigerator: "It's pointless to think anything's going to improve. We don't make sense to each other any longer. Dr. Korda pretty much summed it up: 'The boy's father encourages a direct-line approach between desire and object. This is an extremely unproductive trend, and will most certainly cause the boy untold difficulty once he enters public school.' I guess Untold Difficulty is the name of the game, but I want to try one more time to beat the system. I hope you understand. You'll be hearing

ALIENS 107

from Stensrud, Stensrud, and Levitz. (Legal firm.) Roberta."

Hornbeck read the note again, then opened the refrigerator. He took out the makings for a pressed ham and cheese sandwich, and two bottles of beer. He took his sandwich and beer out to the living room and then noticed for the first time that most of the furniture was gone. He went through the rest of the house. It had been stripped also. He went into the bedroom and felt the top shelf of the closet. The tapes of his *Star Trek* episodes were still there. He took a large bite of his sandwich and washed it down with beer. "Looks like she's gone back to Vulcan, Mr. Spock," he said.

"You want to go up to West Covina with me tomorrow, Hornbeck?" Cosmo Minor said.

"I guess so," Hornbeck said. "I mean no. Unless you really need me."

They were in Minor's small apartment watching one of Hornbeck's *Star Trek* tapes and drinking Canadian Club highballs. Cosmo Minor's wife, Trude, was making supper.

"This yo-yo's wanting to make payments on three computers," Cosmo said, "but he's too busy playing tug-o'-war with his dick to come up with it."

"Dumb shit."

"Hey, ain't they all."

Hornbeck felt agitated. "You're sure it's okay with Trude if I stick around for dinner?" he said.

Cosmo leaned back in his chair and called over his shoulder to Trude. "Hey, peaches. It's okay with you if Hornbeck stays for supper, ain't it?"

A sound came from the kitchen that could have been a confirmation.

"See? What'd I say, Hornbeck?"

Captain Kirk had walked through a time portal and found himself in Renaissance England. The portal sealed itself instantly, leaving Kirk stranded outside a pub in a dark street.

He spoke into his communicator but the airwaves of the six-teenth century were dead. "Now what?" a bemused Kirk murmured to himself as a scornful swordsman belittled his futuristic clothes.

"Sometimes I feel like that," Hornbeck said, gesturing toward the TV set with his tumbler.

"Like what?"

"Like Kirk there. Like I was dropped into the middle of nowhere. I mean, in the middle of somewhere strange. I feel like I just materialized in L.A. thirty-nine—Jesus, *thirty-ni-ne!*—years ago."

"Thirty-nine ain't old, man," Cosmo said, fixing himself another drink.

"I don't mean that. I mean, like I never had a basic say-so in all this shit. I mean, here I *am.* You know? But it's not my fault."

"Hey, man. Do I look like the fucking Prince of Wales?"

"What?"

"The fucking Prince of Wales don't need to figure out where he is or why they do him like they do. He just *is.* That's all he needs to know about it. The rest of us are accidentals."

Hornbeck took a pull directly from the bottle. "No one's going to tell me I don't belong, Cosmo. No one's going to tell me I'm a fucking accidental scab on the fucking accidental ass of society."

"Ay-fucking-men, pardner," Cosmo said. "But how come it's *you* feeling like that? No one's saying shit to you. You look like Merlin Olsen. You look like you fucking own the company, ace. You look like you got the world buttfucked and the world asking you to stay *on.*"

Hornbeck allowed himself a small sob, but once that passed his lips the dam behind it shook loose.

"Holy cow, Hornbeck," Cosmo said. "You want some cof-fee?"

An emotion he could not master stretched Hornbeck's face into acute angles. He rolled to the floor and brought his knees up to his chest. His chest hurt, as if it held a taloned creature. Stunned with shame, and afraid Trude might come in and see him like this, he hid his face in his arms and continued to sob quietly.

"Looky there, Hornbeck," Cosmo said, gently. "Captain Kirk kicking serious ass in jolly old England."

Bonnie DeLuca's husband came home. Hornbeck found this out when he called her and Norman DeLuca answered the phone. "Who is this?" Hornbeck had said.

"Who the fuck wants to know?" DeLuca had replied, his diction elaborate with menace. Hornbeck hung up.

He drove by the DeLuca house once and spotted her in the backyard cutting back a rose bush. She was wearing shorts and a halter. The pink curves of her body made him ache. A wretched moan broke from his throat. Hornbeck parked the truck and walked up the driveway to the back fence. He opened the gate and entered the yard.

When she saw him she dropped her clippers. "You can't come around here anymore," she whispered savagely.

"I thought I'd say hello."

"Say goodbye instead. My husband's home. He's in the house right now, taking his bath."

"This is a business trip," Hornbeck said.

"What are you talking about?"

"I've decided to take the Maytags."

"You *what?* You can't take them. I'm up to date on the payments!"

Hornbeck got the hand truck and pulled it into the utility room through the back door. He unhooked the hoses from the washer and unplugged the dryer.

"You're crazy, you know that?" Bonnie said, watching him in disbelief.

Hornbeck wheeled the appliances out and loaded them into the back of his pickup. He tied down the hand truck, but not

the appliances. Norman DeLuca came out wearing a red bathrobe embroidered with fire-breathing Chinese dragons. The
robe had billowing, half-length sleeves. Beads of water glis-
tened on the dense black hair of DeLuca's forearms. "I'm
calling the cops, asshole," he said. Hornbeck got into the
truck and started it. He looked back at Bonnie. She was standing at the edge of her lawn, her grimly folded arms pressing
her breasts flat.

Hornbeck exchanged thrusting middle fingers with Norman DeLuca, then put the truck into first gear and eased out
the clutch. He drove up the street a few hundred feet,
stopped, then accelerated hard, in reverse. When he was in
front of the DeLuca house again, he stomped on the brake
pedal, sending both washer and dryer shuddering off the
truck and into the street. The machines hit with grievous
thuds and large pieces broke loose.

Later that day he was scheduled to go to Pomona to pick up a
massaging recliner. An elderly woman had bought it three
months ago but had yet to make her first payment. He imagined that she was on social security, a widow ignored by her
middle-aged children, crippled with arthritis, and fed up with
life. But not so fed up that she didn't want to retain a few
creature comforts. He imagined himself having coffee in her
kitchen, her shaky, knob-knuckled hands struggling with the
pot. He imagined himself looking cautiously into her fogged
eyes, half convinced he'd be able, now, to see the immortal
parasite that thrived behind them. And it wouldn't matter.
He'd make the back payments on her recliner anyway.

Horizontal Snow

BECAUSE OF A snag in my thinking I lost interest in both vector analysis and differential equations and had to drop out of college and hitchhike home twelve credits short of graduation. Home was half a continent away and I didn't have a car or bus money and was afraid to ask my folks for help. They had paid my way through three and a half years of engineering school at Platteville, Wisconsin, and I couldn't have said to Dad, for instance, that I wanted to come home because the laws of thermodynamics bored the life out of me. He wouldn't have understood my reasoning.

I didn't have any reasoning. Something down at the underpinnings of reason had given way, and there was no explanation for it. I couldn't even explain it to myself. All I knew was that every time I opened a textbook something numbing, like pain, would stab the back of my head. Or my eyelids would feel thick, as if stuffed with sand. Or I would read the same page over ten, fifteen times and not one word would register.

I kissed my girlfriend goodbye, packed my suitcase, and headed for the highway west. "What's *wrong* with you?" she'd asked, and I had no answer. I'd hurt her, I was aware of that, but my own feelings were in cold storage. I observed her pain in the way a surgeon observes the pain of his patient: with compassion but without involvement or remorse. I was strong and healthy, my appetite was good, I slept well, but nothing interested me. I felt like an animated corpse, moving through a world I had left behind. Greeting myself in the bathroom mirror each morning I would say: Hello, Zombie.

The first ride I hitched was with a family. They dropped me off on the far edge of Minnesota, in the middle of nowhere. It was a lonely stretch of road, and though the weather had been springlike for several weeks, the wind from Canada still had a threat of winter in it. My second ride came minutes before hypothermia set in.

A pickup truck with a homemade camper stuck on the back rolled to a gradual stop ahead of me. The camper was made of scrap wood and had a peaked roof, like a house, covered with tar paper. It looked like an outbuilding of a farm, modified for travel. The man driving said he was going all the way to Bonner's Ferry, Idaho, four hundred miles short of my destination. I hesitated before getting in because the man was so ugly he took my breath away. He may have been the ugliest man in the world. At least I had never seen anyone up to that time as ugly as he was, and I have not seen anyone uglier since. His face was flat as a skillet, even concave. His hammered-down nose was five fingers wide, and his short forehead had prominent supraorbital ridges thick as cables. He looked like something you'd see in an anthropology textbook, as if forty thousand years of evolution had skipped over him. This was 1958, and so much has happened since then that much of what follows seems more like a dream than personal history.

His name was Lot Stoner and he claimed to be a preacher. He drove slowly, under fifty, with both hands on the wheel. He had huge, amply scarred, thick-fingered hands that had seen decades of punishing work. We rode along without speaking for several hours, though now and then he would glance over at me and at the suitcase wedged between my legs. "I specialize in the defeated," he finally said. When I didn't respond to this, he went on to explain that he was a preacher of the gospel. He didn't have a church or a degree from a recognized seminary, but was a self-taught man of God. "You just lost a big tussle, didn't you?" he said. He had yellowing, wide-spaced eyes. They were slightly wall-eyed so that when he looked at you directly it seemed as if he was seeing two of you—one slightly to the right, one slightly to the left. I guessed his age at about sixty, but his hair was bright red and youthful.

Again he waited for my response. I didn't have one. I shrugged and turned my gaze out the side window, where snow-patched fields drifted by.

"I saw defeat in your posture," he said, "while you were standing out there in the elements with your thumb out. I said to myself, 'Lot, there is a young buck who has been in the toilet. There is a boy who hit bottom but did not bounce.' Am I wrong?"

I didn't see myself as that bad off, but he was at least partly right. Articulated, the snag in my thinking went something like this: "The struggle is not worth the reward." It loomed in my mind like a huge door that had just shut, locking itself. I couldn't formulate it in words at the time, but I sensed that it had the clear-cut, irrefutable perfection of Einstein's discovery of the absolute equivalency of matter and energy. I had been an honors student headed for a job in the aerospace industry to help build rockets so that we could catch up to the Russians. Sputnik had been put into orbit the previous fall, and things did not look good for the U.S.A.

"Your hand looked like the hand of a mendicant, upraised for alms," Lot said. "I said to myself, 'Lot, there is a boy who has lost his way.' I am hardly ever off the target about such things."

Lot talked about himself for a while. He said he felt more like a traveling teacher than a pulpit-bound Bible thumper. He said he was too footloose to have his own church, and also that he was too broad-minded and generous with his Biblical interpretations to follow the narrow and self-interested theologies of the fat-cat denominations. He gave examples of his broad-mindedness. "This may astound you, son," he said, "but I can see evidence of divinity in a cow pie, and again in the maggots that devour it." He reached under his seat and pulled out a microphone that had some wires dangling loosely from it. "Ain't that right, Willie?" he shouted into the mike.

A woman's voice crackled over a loudspeaker that was wedged between the seat and the back of the cab. "Ain't *what* right?" she said. She sounded sleepy and annoyed at being disturbed. I figured, correctly, that she was lying in a bunk back in the wood-slat-and-tar-paper camper.

"About me seeing the Almighty Himself in commonplace cow shit," Lot said into his microphone.

"Yeah," said the voice through an unrestrained yawn.

"I can see the Lord in all of it," he said. "In every piece of flotsam and jetsam, in every gnat and mosquito—there He is, doing business like He has every day for twenty billion years. History means nothing to Him. Yours, mine, or that of the damn fool nations."

Lot told me that he'd spent a good part of his life in prison. "I killed a man," he said. "I took his head into my hands and squeezed it until the pressure on his brain became intolerable. There were ruptures under the bone and then the bone itself gave way. He was stone dead before I released him, and the blood from his ears ran in abundance through my fingers. They said later they had to pry my fingers off of him with cold chisels and pliers. I had momentarily lost the sense of myself." He took his right hand off the wheel and showed it to me. The hard, walnut-size knuckles looked like the joints of a machine, the thick wrist timbered with straight shafts of bone.

He picked up his microphone. "Am I sorry? Tell him, Willie, if I am sorry."

"He ain't," Willie said.

"And I'll tell you why," Lot said. "The man deserved what he got. He was worthless. Worthless scum. I know I just told you I can see divinity in flotsam and jetsam. But this man was below that. He was filled to capacity with nothing. He was nothingness incarnate. He was a hole in God's blue air."

"He's getting up steam," Willie's crackling voice warned from the loudspeaker.

We were in the flat rich farm country of central North Dakota, the landscape of boredom itself. A few years later, after having got past my motivational problems, I would be installing Minuteman missiles into this same wheatland for the U.S. Air Force.

"The man I killed was a two-legged lamprey," Lot said. "He attached himself to the helpless underbelly of good-hearted people and sucked their lifeblood from them until they were pale effigies of their former selves. He would fill his nothingness with their somethingness. He was a con artist who had taken my daddy's last dime for an electrical arthritis cure, coupled with painful injections of a useless saline solution. Can you blame me?"

"No," I said.

"And I accept no blame. But while I was up at the state farm I had myself a long time to ponder it. My meditations led me to the light, the holy light, pure and simple. And I am going to reveal this holy light to you, son, free of charge. Spreading the truth is my goal in life. I doff my cap to no sect, denomination, figurehead, or dogma. I do not take my notions from someone else's larder of so-called religious verities."

We passed a small lake and drove through a town where, four years later, I would betray my young wife by going to bed with a farmer's widow named Zola Faye Metkovich. My young wife would leave me, I would leave Zola Faye, but I would stay on at Minot Air Force Base, helping to redesign ICBM parts and support equipment that had failed their stress and endurance tests. I would make a lot of money, drive a big car—an air-conditioned Chrysler Imperial—and have a string of five girlfriends who lived far away from each other in the small isolated towns of North Dakota where people, though born in the United States of America, still spoke with foreign accents, German and Russian. It would be the most exciting time of my life, but of course I did not know it, and could not have imagined it, as I bounced along toward Idaho with Lot Stoner and the unseen woman he called Willie.

Now and then, Lot would take a dried-out sandwich from a paper sack on the floorboards or lift a thermos to his lips. He offered these to me, but I refused. Food from his hand was automatically unappetizing, as if contaminated by his ugliness. He hummed to himself for a while, ate a little more, gazed out at the slow-moving scenery from time to time. It took me a while to realize that he'd quit talking, and that I had been waiting for him to reveal this holy-light business to me, not that I believed in such things or had ever given them much thought. I began to think that he'd just forgotten about it, or had something more pressing on his mind. And then it occurred to me that I was being conned, or that he was self-deluded, maybe even brain-damaged. I leaned my head against the window and pretended to doze off. And then I did doze off.

A crackling electrical scream woke me up. It was Willie, yelling for someone to come back to her.

Lot slowed the truck and pulled off onto the shoulder of the highway. "Go climb into the back and take a look, will you, son?" he said wearily. He crossed his arms on the wheel and rested his knobbed forehead on them. "I'll catch a couple of winks while you're back there."

I got out of the truck into a northern gale. The false spring was over. A new storm from the Arctic was blowing in. In these latitudes you can smell snow in the air. It's not so much a smell as it is a pinching in of your nose, a tightening of the membranes inside. You turn your face into the wind, lift your nose to it, sniff in. "Snow," you say to yourself. "Blizzard."

When I climbed into the camper I saw a narrow-faced woman with Indian cheekbones curled up under a heavy blanket. She had thin, stringy hair, and her hunted eyes looked like those of a trapped wolverine.

"Come here, dammit," she said.

She was lying on a bunk that ran the length of the camper. There was an electric light glowing in the ceiling. The only other light came through the back door, which I left open. She was trying to push herself up on her elbows.

"What's the matter?" I said.

"Lift me up," she said through gritted teeth.

She was young. Maybe twenty, but probably closer to seventeen. I slid a hand behind her back and muscled her forward. "Quit it," she said. "I just needed to get up a little so's I can get set. It's coming."

She scooted forward a little, then lay back down. Her knees were up and her belly was very big. She pulled the blanket aside and her naked belly rose up, tight and shiny.

"You're having a baby," I said.

"You don't say," she said. She spread her knees and screamed, loud and terrible, more rage in it than pain. I stepped back and my head hit the roof. Her microphone was on the floor, next to her bunk. I picked it up.

"She's having a baby, Lot," I said.

"Joy to the world," replied his weary voice from a tiny loudspeaker that had been stuck to the ceiling with electrician's tape.

I put the mike down. Willie was growling between clenched teeth, her head rolling side to side on her pillow. "Is there anything I can do?" I asked.

She waved her arm. It flapped like a broken wing. "Get me that pint-size green bottle out of the icebox," she said. "And don't be an asshole and faint."

We looked at each other for a few seconds. If anything, my heart was beating slower. "Don't worry," I said.

The icebox was a homemade affair with a heavy lid fitted into its top. Among cans of soda and beer and packages of food were a half-dozen pint bottles of gin. I took one of these out and uncapped it. She took a long pull from it, and then I did the same. It was cold in my mouth and warm going down.

"Glory, glory," said Lot, his grainy voice dropping like sand from the ceiling.

"Maybe you ought to be back here with your wife," I said into the microphone.

"We all can't fit back there, son," he said. "There's not that much to do, anyway. You just do what the girl tells you. She ain't new at this."

Wind from Canada mauled the truck. It howled in the wooden slats of the camper. I looked out the door and saw the blizzard, the horizontal snow.

"Give me your hand," Willie said. She squeezed hard enough to make the separate bones touch. The skin of her stomach was pulled so tight I could see my shadowy reflection in it. "Take a look, will you?" she said. "I want to know if he's coming out ass end first. I had two others that did, both stillborns."

She let go of my hand and I moved down to the foot of the bunk and peered between her upraised knees. There, at the dark joining of her thighs, was a little face. It looked like a dried apple. Crimped as it was in those bearded jaws, it looked Chinese and ancient. Its eyes were shut tight, the mouth a stubborn line. The unbreathing nose was flat and wide. The idea occurred to me that this wasn't an infant at all but a tiny old man who had serious second thoughts about the wisdom of leaving the comfortable and nourishing dark for the starved light of North Dakota. The notion made me smile. "Welcome home, chump," I whispered.

"Well?" Willie said. "Is it coming out frontwards of backwards?"

"Frontwards," I said. "Frontwards," I repeated into the mike. "And I think it's got red hair."

"I'm kissing the Good Book," said Lot.

Once the head cleared the birth canal, the rest was easy. Willie leaned forward and took the baby up in her arms, nipped the cord with her teeth, tied it off with a length of nylon fishing line, and wrapped him in the blanket. A small cry—more like the ratchety chirping of a newly hatched bird than that of a baby—came from the blanket. I wiped the sweat off Willie's face with my handkerchief, and she took another swig of gin.

"You're a nice fella," Willie said, smiling up at me.

I thought about that. "I don't think so," I said.

I went back up to the cab. "Fatherhood," Lot said, "is a great responsibility." He gave me a sidelong look of high significance, his off-center eyes splitting me into twins. Then he started the truck and we moved down the white highway.

"You probably ought to get them to a hospital," I said. "Or at least to a doctor."

"We'll stop in Minot," he said. "We'll get some warm food and a place to rest. Doctors aren't important to our thinking. Are they to yours?"

I looked at him, but he was squinting out into the painfully bright air of the storm. "Yes, I think so," I said.

"Someday you'll wake up out of your little nightmare and click your heels, son," he said, shifting down to second as snowdrifts began to collect in the road. He picked up his microphone and said, "What are we going to name him, Willie?"

"Jesus Dakota Stoner," Willie said without hesitating a beat.

"Merry Christmas," Lot hooted into the mike.

"We'll call him J.D. for short," Willie said.

Lot drove even slower as night came on and the blizzard got worse. We stopped in Rugby, an hour or so short of Minot, at an all-night café called Mud and Sinkers. Lot pulled a tobacco can out from under the seat. It was packed with dollar bills. He counted out five, smoothed them out on his thigh. "We'll get us some coffee and doughnuts and sit out this storm.

When it gets light, we'll hit the road again."

We found a booth near the warm kitchen and a waitress brought us coffee and three glazed doughnuts. Willie had Jesus Dakota tucked in a blanket. The dried blood and mucus of his recent birth still mottled his skin, which otherwise would have been a bright saffron-pink, but Willie didn't seem too concerned. She opened her wool shirt and drew out a long thin breast and gave it to the baby. The baby hadn't been crying, but he pulled at his mother with urgent power.

"It'll be good to get home," I said, for conversation's sake, but I said it mostly to myself.

"J.D.'s home already," Lot chuckled. "Home is a warm teat, wherever you happen to be."

"Seattle," I said. "That's home for me."

Lot sipped his coffee, squinted at me through the steam. "Better to be in exile sustained by a dream of home than to endure the disappointments of home itself. Home itself is an idea that never measures up. I speak from experience."

"You're too deep for me, Lot," I said.

"Don't mock him," Willie said. She said it simply, without taking her eyes off her baby.

"You'll find one day that what I said is true," Lot said.

And what good will it do me? I wanted to say, but held back. I was tired and a little fed up with his homespun homilies. I wanted to be back in West Seattle, in my parent's big house overlooking the Sound. I wanted to be in my upstairs room, at my desk, watching the ferryboats at night brilliantly spangled with lights. I wanted to listen to the lonesome call of their foghorns while snuggling deeper and deeper into my old bed.

There were some names etched by knifeblade into the table before me. Rena + Yank. Pete + Vicki. Remember Me, Annette. I concentrated on those names and sipped my coffee, willing the night to pass quickly. I would come back to Mud and Sinkers four years later as a Boeing field engineer, after completing my degree at the University of Washington, the snag in my thinking long gone and forgotten. Carline Minsky from the town of Balfour would be with me, and those carved names would still be here, among half a dozen more. Carline was pregnant and wanted to get married, but I told her I already was married—even though my wife had left several months earlier. Carline broke down, but what could I do? I said I'd pay for the abortion. She took the money, but our little romantic episode ended then and there. Maybe she got the abortion and maybe she didn't. I never found out, nor wanted to.

We'd gotten carried away down in a silo, next to a recently installed Minuteman missile. We were on a service platform, adjacent to the missile's third-stage motor, near the warhead access ramp, and Carline said, "Let's do it, right here." She wasn't supposed to be in this Top Secret area, but there was no one else around within miles who might object. "This motor is fueled by a ton of nitro glycerine, stabilized by cotton filaments," I told her. "It's very dangerous." This was a partial truth, but it made her moan with fear and excitement. We did it standing up, her bending over the rail and leaning out close enough to the Minuteman to kiss the megaton hydrogen warhead. "I'm so hot," she said, and I was too. *Too* hot, it turned out, because we neglected the usual precautions, and she got pregnant, somewhere under North Dakota.

"I saw something else in your posture," Lot said, startling me. He was slumped over on his side in the booth, and I thought he'd been asleep. "I saw something besides defeat, or maybe it wasn't defeat I saw at all. Maybe it was this other thing all along."

I held a picture of blue water and white boats in my mind, so as not to get caught up again in his stagey pronouncements.

"Don't you care to know what I saw?" he said.

Willie stirred. Jesus Dakota turned his face left and right before finding the breast she half-consciously offered him.

"Not especially," I said.

"I'm going to tell you anyway. I saw a dangerous hunger. I saw an unfeedable hunger."

His primitive head, his bright red hair, the fatigue that lined his face—the complete aspect of an outcast and loser. I smiled and shook my head, affecting dismay.

"You were going to tell me something about a holy light. You must have forgotten," I said.

The need for sleep pulled him lower in the booth. He closed his eyes. "I already did. You weren't paying attention, son."

After a while, they were all sound asleep, that odd and aimless family with no future and a harrowing past. Even when a trucker came stomping into the café, kicking snow off his boots, flapping his arms against his chest, and cursing the storm at the top of his lungs, Lot, Willie, and Jesus Dakota didn't wake up. It was 3:00 A.M., and the trucker ordered hot cakes and coffee. He talked constantly at the waitress, and from this I learned that he was on his way to the West Coast. I saw my chance and sat next to him at the counter. He was a tall, thin, nervous man, but he was friendly. He was a talker who was starved for conversation, and so when I asked if I could ride along with him to the Coast, he said "Just don't ask me to stop every fifty miles so you can piss. I've got to make Tacoma by tomorrow afternoon."

I went back to the booth. Willie had scooted over so that my coat was partly under her. I didn't want to wake her up, so I just left it there. It was just an unlined windbreaker anyway. I took one last look at them. I hoped they'd make it to Bonners Ferry, but given what they were it didn't seem to matter much where they wound up. They'd be back on the road again before long, the road being the only place where they would feel welcome.

In the truck, a huge Diamond T hauling double trailers, the driver said, "Who was that ugly fuck and the bony squaw you were with?"

"Just a ride," I said, tossing my suitcase behind the seat.

The trucker poured himself a cup of coffee from a thermos,

shook two white pills from a small envelope. He placed the pills carefully on his tongue, then swallowed them with coffee.

"Got to jump-start my fucking *brain*," he said, winking.

Then we roared out into the blinding storm.

Fidelity

WALT DYER'S WIFE, Loreen, had been abandoned by her lover and she was languishing because of it. Walt brought her some breakfast—poached eggs, toast, tea—but she refused to eat. He set the tray down on the floor next to the bed and rubbed her hand. Loreen, at forty-two, was eighteen years younger than Walt, but now she looked closer to Walt's age. Her hair was graying; it clung to her scalp, thin and lifeless.

"I told you he was a prick, Loreen," Walt said. He didn't say it triumphantly or with a sense of vindication. It was just a simple fact that he'd observed when she started up with the boy, Erik Van Oyens, a twenty-four-year-old poet.

Walt picked up the breakfast tray and carried it back to the kitchen. He ate the eggs and toast but poured the tea into the sink. He was a retired Air Force master sergeant and he kept himself fit with daily exercise. After he cleaned up the dishes, he got dressed. He went back into the bedroom to tell Loreen he was leaving, but she was curled up under the covers and might have been asleep again. She'd been this way for a week. At one point, Walt had asked her to see a doctor so that she could get a prescription for an antidepressant, but she'd refused.

Walt drove across town, across the river to the north side, where small rental houses huddled together protectively as if the builders had anticipated the worst for the prospective tenants. He dug a scrap of paper out of his jacket pocket and squinted at the address he had scrawled on it, then began to check the numbers on the houses.

Erik Van Oyens lived in a paintless house that leaned noticeably to one side. Walt parked the car, got out, and opened the trunk. He rummaged around for a while and found a short stillson wrench. He slipped the wrench into his jacket pocket and went up to the house. He knocked for several minutes before anyone answered.

"I thought you were that Jehovah's Witness dork," Erik Van Oyens said. "He comes by every day around this time."

"I'm Walt Dyer. Loreen's husband."

"Oh, right," Erik Van Oyens said, stepping back and closing the door slightly. "I remember. I saw you once, mowing the lawn, I think."

Walt pushed the door open and walked into the house. He looked around. There was no furniture to speak of. A tired sofa, a bare table littered with papers and books, two chairs. Walt went into the kitchen, the bathroom, and the bedroom. There was a woman sleeping in a narrow bed. He went back into the living room.

"You're a poet," Walt said.

Van Oyens stiffened defensively. "What of it?"

"Nothing of it. You could be a carpet salesman. I'd still be willing to kick the shit out of you."

"Look, man," Van Oyens began, his hands held out, palms up. "Loreen picked *me* up, I didn't—"

"I know she picked you up. You're not the first."

Van Oyens looked confused. "Then what is this?"

"Who's the woman in your bedroom?" Walt said. He took a step toward Van Oyens. "Loreen is in a lot of pain," he said. "She can't take this kind of torment, Erik." He knocked the poet down with a light slap. It was almost a caress.

Van Oyens scrambled to his feet and ran into the bedroom. He began to rummage frantically through his chest of drawers. The woman in the bed stirred. Van Oyens found what he was looking for. He pointed a small revolver at Walt. His aim was shaky and off to the left. Walt kicked him in the knee and Van Oyens fell over, groaning. The woman sat up. She pulled the sheet to her neck.

"Who is this man?" she demanded. "What right does he have coming in here like this?"

Walt noticed that the woman was in her late thirties or early forties.

Walt picked up the short-barreled pistol. "This is a poor excuse for a gun," he said, after examining the weapon. "Where was it made, in Bangladesh?" He broke it open and shook the bullets out. "Twenty-five caliber," he said. "This is a joke." He aimed it at Van Oyens's face. "I'd have to hit you in the eye to do any damage," he said. "Get yourself something decent. This is a bad part of town."

The woman in the bed began making a noise. It was a grating noise—something between a scream and visceral urging. Walt pulled the trigger several times, letting them hear the ratcheting of the cylinder mechanism and the sharp clicks of the hammer. He sat on the bed and touched the woman's hand.

"You're going to have to leave now, ma'am," he said. "You're the real problem here, I think."

Walt pulled Erik to his feet and led him out of the bedroom and into the kitchen. He took two cups from the cupboard and poured coffee into them from a half-full coffee maker.

"I love my wife very much, Erik," he said. He pulled the stillson wrench out of his jacket and laid it on the table. He grinned. "I didn't know what to expect. I didn't get a good look at you that day you came by the house. Some poets are big mean-ass farm boys." Erik looked at the short, ugly wrench and sipped his coffee. "You're her first poet," Walt said. "I suspect you're probably her last."

"It isn't . . . jealousy then?" Erik said cautiously.

Walt shook his head, frowning into his cup. He had been to Korea, to Japan, and had served for a while in Vietnam. He'd spent four years in Germany and had been an adviser to the Egyptian Air Force. He'd seen much of the world and he knew that unhappiness ruled it. The pursuit of happiness was probably mankind's cruelest illusion. Even so, the illusion itself required pursuing, since it was all anybody had. But people, for their own sake, needed to acquire a certain amount of internal flexibility.

"If not jealousy, what then?" Van Oyens said.

"Fidelity, Erik. It's a question of fidelity."

As they were talking, the woman, her clothes pulled on carelessly, walked quickly out of the house. She slammed the door behind her.

Walt put his stillson wrench back into his pocket and carried his cup to the sink. He rinsed it out and set it on the drainboard.

He offered his hand to Erik as they stood together out on the porch. After hesitating a few seconds, Van Oyens accepted the gesture.

"Look, man," Van Oyens said. "It's cool. Loreen and I are finished. It's over."

Walt regarded Van Oyens for a long moment. "No, Erik," he said. "You're missing the point."

Van Oyens scratched his head. He started to smile, then saw Walt's face and stopped himself.

"Do we understand each other, Erik?" Walt said, tightening his grip on the poet's hand.

Erik nodded.

When he got home, Loreen was sitting at the kitchen table staring at a piece of cold toast. Her eyes were red and puffy. Walt stepped behind her and rubbed her neck and shoulders, expertly and with tenderness.

"He's going to be a good boy now," Walt said. "He gave me his word."

Infidelity

PERKINS HAD A sudden intuition that he'd once known the
woman on his doorstep intimately. Perhaps he had loved her
in some small domestic paradise for years even though he
needed to act—against the unreasonable clamoring of his
gullible heart—as if he had never seen her before today, as if
she wasn't the ideal woman he'd imagined for himself since
his adolescence.

"Haven't we met before?" he said, yielding to the impulse.

She was selling something. Possibly a line of personal
grooming articles or cosmetics. But she seemed momentarily
disoriented and confused, and could not begin her pitch.

"I know what you're thinking," Perkins said. "You've
heard that old line of b.s. before. But, hey. I'm serious. You
do look like someone I used to know really *well* but for some
reason can't place."

The woman—fortyish, attractive, slightly overweight, con-
servatively dressed—said, "I'm not offended. In fact, the
same thing occurred to me, Mr . . . ?"

"Flip," he said. "Just call me Flip."

She shook her head as if to regroup her thoughts. "I would
have guessed maybe John or William, not Philip." She giggled nervously.

"I've been reading Shirley MacLaine," Perkins said. This
was a lie. It was true he had read a little of the Shirley Ma-

Laine book on reincarnation, but only while waiting in the checkout line at Safeway. He'd taken it from a paperback rack and had thumbed through it.

"Personally, I think that sort of thing is a dead end," she said. "I mean, it's an obviously attractive idea, but it goes against my principles. I don't think we get off that easily." Her expression darkened; she studied the scuff marks on her brown-and-white spectator shoes. She seemed unaccustomed to high heels and her feet looked painfully swollen.

"Let's talk about it," Perkins said. He swung the door wider. "No one's home but me. Let's have a beer, or a Coke."

She glanced at her watch. "Okay. I can't stay long, but I *would* enjoy iced tea if you have it. It's really baking out here today."

He took her hand—trembling slightly at its familiar feel—and drew her into his house. He saw that her engagement and wedding rings were embedded in the flesh of her heat-swollen finger. "Your husband get laid off or do you *like* outdoor work?" he said, thinking he had made a joke.

"Both," she said, unsmiling.

Perkins led her into the kitchen and pulled a chair away from the dinette table. "I've got a chicken in the oven," he said. "That's why it's so miserable in here."

"Misery is relative," she said.

"But it loves company," he replied, but once again she did not smile.

She fanned herself with her plump, red-splotched hand while he filled two tall glasses with ice cubes. He mixed the tea and brought the glasses to the table. He offered her an envelope of artificial sweetener, which she refused. "Plain sugar, please," she said.

"I *knew* you didn't like the fake stuff. Isn't that proof of something?" he said.

"If you knew, why did you offer it to me?"

"I needed to test my hunch. If I hadn't offered it to you, how could I be sure you'd refuse it?"

She laughed, startling him. She had a low, throaty laugh. It made his heart shudder with a nostalgia that had become frighteningly familiar.

Perkins had been experiencing these warningless assaults of nostalgia lately. An old tune on the radio might call up a scene from high school which would paralyze him for minutes with remorse or longing. Sometimes he would dream about places so familiar and yet so utterly lost that he would wake up with tears on his face, even though the places he dreamed about were nowhere he'd ever been. And now, her laughter evoked in him this identical nostalgia, as if she were a ghost from some recognized but unremembered past, a forgotten lover miraculously returning from the dead.

She covered her mouth and burped. "This is very odd, you know," she said. "Normally I'd never come into a house when only the husband was home. Aside from the fact that it could be dangerous—goodness, just read the newspapers these days!—it's not something *I* would do. It's not me. It's not Helen Langstrom."

"I'm glad to hear that, Helen Langstrom," he said. He enjoyed the texture of her name, how it made his tongue dance lightly on his palate and teeth. But it didn't really suit her, she was more a Sarah, Louise, or maybe an Elizabeth.

"How come *that* name?" he asked.

She wagged a coy finger at him. "You're not allowed to ask that question," she said, "any more than you can ask whose destiny brought me here in the first place, yours or mine."

"Sorry," he said. "Actually, I like your name. It just sounds a bit on the severe side. We had a mean school nurse with a name like that—Helen Sorenson, I think."

She sipped her tea and regarded him with a gray, unwavering gaze that immobilized him. A song ran through his head. "Where or When," an oldy.

"We live in a single layer of eternity, like fossils," she said. "For us there is nothing but this moment. Stop thinking about another time, Flip. We don't have one. The past has its own

presence and the future is old news. You're Flip and I'm
Helen, and that's where it stays. How else can we keep sane?"

"Whoa. That's pretty heavy," he said.

"I majored in philosophy," she said. "That's why this is
the only job I could get. I'm afraid I am an idealist."

They both laughed. Impulsively he picked up her hand and
kissed the swollen knuckles. "Listen," he said, "my wife
won't be home for a couple of hours. Why don't we put on a
record and, uh, dance? You like the oldies?"

She waved her hand in front of her face. "Too hot, Flip,"
she said. "Besides, I'd rather just talk, for the time being
anyway." She reached across the table and ran her fingertips
over his face in the way a blind person would to get an idea of
what someone looked like.

"You weren't Philip. Or Flip," she said, her voice dreamy
now and strange. "No. Not at all. It goes against my principles
to say this, but you were definitely not Philip. I called you
Ben. Big Ben. You worked a team of horses, Ben. Belgians.
Otto and Max, you called them. You'd come in from the field,
dog-tired. I'd fix you dinner—meat and potatoes. You were a
meat-and-potatoes man! And then, after reading the poems of
Whittier and Longfellow for a while, we'd go to bed. Oh my
God, Ben! You were something!" She made a small moan, and
her gaze went distant with a memory of transcendent bliss.

It now occurred to him that Helen was crazy, really bent,
even dangerous, and that he'd been foolish to let her into his
house. And then he thought, *So what?* Hadn't he started all
this with his reincarnation line? Hadn't he believed it himself? Maybe *he* was the crazy one. But who wasn't a little out
of touch these days? Ten minutes of the Evening News and he
wanted to start throwing fragmentation grenades or exchanging his cash for gold bullion. The crooks were in charge of the
world. The savings and loan industry was rotten to the core,
and the commercial banks weren't far behind. The military-
industrial complex had its larcenous hand in everyone's
pocket. Half of Congress was bought and paid for and the

other half was looking for buyers. Highly placed felons didn't go to jail, or if they did go, it was to a pleasant retreat with Jacuzzis and tennis. The president was a self-serving manipulator of public opinion but maladroit, and now, politically impotent. The water was polluted, the air was lethal, and the trees were dying. The poor got poorer, the sick got sicker, the weak got weaker. If someone in this world approached you with a look of tranquil sanity on his face, you were perfectly correct to run the opposite direction at top speed screaming for the police.

But Perkins was a born believer, a congenital sucker. A slick TV evangelist once had him believing that God could express Himself best through electronics. All Perkins had to do to get rid of his depression was put both hands on the big screen and kneel. He held the TV set and begged for relief. And it came. It just didn't last. A week later he was begging his doctor to renew his Prozac prescription. Prozac worked fine, but since he'd been taking it he'd begun to seize up with bouts of immobilizing nostalgia. He'd lost the tension and edge his job required and had been laid off.

He watched Helen slide down a bit in her chair as she continued to make the gasping moans that had been triggered by the "memory" of Big Ben's horsey prowess. Her eyelids were fluttering. He saw the whites of her eyes and became alarmed. He was afraid she might swallow her tongue.

"Are you all right, Helen?" he asked.

She pulled herself together and sat up. "Oh, I'm so sorry. How embarrassing. May I use your bathroom?"

He pointed to a doorway down the hall from the kitchen and she picked up her things and wobbled away from him on her high heels. *That's a first,* Perkins thought, sipping his tea.

When she came back, she said, "Your bathroom is an ugly mess. What do you do all day besides put chickens in the oven? Wad up Kleenex and throw it on the floor? Tell me, Flip—does your wife still love you?"

He was still thinking about what had just happened. And

now he thought about his wife. "It's a good question, Helen. Maybe, in a way, she still loves me."

She sat down at the table and began fanning herself with a plastic place mat. "My husband feels sorry for himself," she said. "He was an engineer for Aero-Tech. Since he got laid off, all he does is mope around the house sailing paper airplanes into a wastebasket."

"You don't love him anymore, then," he said.

"Why do you say that? Yes I love him. Love is a duty, don't you see that? Isn't that what we've been talking about? Love isn't a vapor that comes and goes with every change in the wind!"

Her eyes were angry and wide. She regarded him severely. Perhaps with contempt. Perkins suddenly felt frightened. His mouth went dry. He was a roundish man with a sunken chest and he was desperately out of shape. He tilted his iced tea glass up and drew an ice cube into his mouth. He crunched it, faking nonchalance.

She stood up. "Well, Mr. . . . ."

"Perkins."

"Mr. Perkins." She scoffed a little at the sound of his name. "I must be going. Thank you for the tea."

"I think my wife is going to leave me," he said hoarsely. He'd never said this to anyone and wasn't even sure if it was true. She tilted unsteadily. Her shoe went sideways and she stumbled toward him. He caught her in his arms. He smelled her stiff frosty hair, but it wasn't a familiar smell. She was a stranger after all, aging and half crazy. He tried to kiss her cheek but she ducked away.

He walked her to the door. When she stepped out into the bright afternoon, he said, "Love can't be a duty, Helen. It's a gift." He felt like a complete idiot saying this; it was like one of those encouraging messages he often saw on the marquees of pathetic little churches that exist on the fringes of the great and wealthy denominations. The First Disaffected Methodists. The Uncapitulated Baptists.

Helen stepped quickly and unsteadily down the sidewalk. She looked at Perkins over her shoulder nervously, as if he might have gotten it into his head to follow her. Then he realized that he didn't even know what she was selling.

He raised his hand. He waved frantically, signaling her to come back.

The Whitened Man

I MANAGE SUPERIOR West and am moving up the ladder but don't think I'm on Easy Street yet. Here is what I get for my trouble: a hundred a week plus use of a Park Avenue single-wide. There are two hundred and fifteen single-wide units in Superior. Judge for yourself if it's worth it. If you see it as a rung on the ladder you are climbing then you would say, Yes it's worth it. But you would not say, "Lefort, you've got it made. All you've got to do is collect rent, monitor the tenants, keep things working." That isn't the half of it.

I might get fifty mean phone calls in a week. Any hour, night and day, they don't care. "Mr. Lefort, you said the plumber was coming last week!" "Mr. Lefort, the propane lines are leaking again" "Mr. Lefort, my wife hears dogs. You said no pets allowed, but my wife hears them bark."

They call me Mr. Lefort, as I have asked for simple respect and courtesy, which I allow them in return. "Mr. Lefort, there is a man looking into my windows at night." I am Dion Perry Lefort, and I have left out the gutter language they sometimes use when they call me. I ask for respect but sometimes do not get it. He is strangely white, like the moon. The man who looks into windows, I mean.

I do my best for them, they are my responsibility—I am the manager—but it can be difficult. I carry the Dan Wesson .357 magnum out in the open on my right side. In my Park Avenue

I have a variety of pieces. I have the AK-47, the M-16, two twelve-gauge shotguns—a Winchester pump and an old double-barrel Savage. "Expecting trouble?" I have heard them talking about me. But they are my responsibility. There are fixed video cameras that watch the entrance and a swiveling camera that checks the grounds. I have seen the strangely whitened man who looks into windows at night and I have tracked him out into the fields but I have yet to come close enough to unload a few rounds at that glowing moon-faced peeper.

My unit is next to the gate, but he can scale the fence at any point if he is serious enough. Sometimes on my monitor I see his shadow drift to the ground and move toward the units. I take down the Savage or the Winchester and go right out after him, but Superior is not well lighted and it is easy for him to duck back into the shadows. I cannot fire at the shadows. Innocent people could get hurt.

I also have videocams located in a few of the units, in false-front cabinets, so that I can monitor their needs before they are raised. It is part of the "forward-looking management policy" Superior Properties mentions in letters I get. For example, the time a woman said to her husband, "Louis Smith, I am going to bust this faucet with a hammer if it keeps making that racket." I was over there the next morning replacing washers! It is less expensive to monitor them than to make major repairs. I call them "Smith" for I respect their privacy.

I watch these people come and go in their junkers or on foot. Most work at the cardboard mill. We are between the dump and the sewage-treatment plant. Did I say this was Beverly Hills? But it's how you get started in the business. I am manager today, but soon I will buy a share in Superior Properties. Superior has courts like this in twelve states. This is

Superior West. They own a high-rise in Abilene, Kansas, and several thousand acres of undeveloped properties in West Texas. We are a definite "growth industry," and I will soon be on the ground floor of it. That's why I am willing to put up with the things I have to put up with. I am waiting. I am biding my time. Patience is my saving grace.

Though some will put me to the test. The Bascombes, for instance. Both of them are retards, husband and wife. I try to keep an eye on them but I have two hundred and fifteen units to monitor. I cannot be baby-sitter for all of them. Yet people like the Bascombes have to be watched night and day. For instance, fire. Have you ever seen a mobile home go up in flames? It is a sight that will not be easily erased from your memory. They go up like a fuel depot. Everything in them will burn. The drapes, the carpets, the wallboard. The aluminum shell will burn once it gets hot enough. You have seen aluminum burn on TV. I mean airline disasters. The big jet plane burns white-hot like a star. So does a mobile home. The plastic furniture melts and gives off a killing cyanide gas. Some get themselves trapped inside and head for the shower thinking that cold water will save them but the water comes out steam. Then comes the gas. Imagine the surprised looks on their faces!

I can half-see their surprise as the shower takes off their skin. If the back door is blocked—and most of them have their back doors screwed permanently shut against thieves, or they have the stereo or gun cabinet jammed up against it— then the front door, up by the kitchenette, is the only way out. But that is exactly where ninety percent of the fires start, in the kitchenette, right by the front door. If you are in bed when the propane stove blows you are not going to get out. The windows throughout the unit are narrow and barred with strong louvers, and while you may push your hamster or cat through it, you will not be able to save the baby. I often dream of fires. I have seen the skin sliding off flesh, the flesh crisping up and turning black, the eyes popping like flashbulbs. Oh yes, and the nose-pinching smell of burning hair. I hear them screaming. We lost a unit to fire last winter. They didn't get out. Tanya "Smith" and her two children.

Mr. Bascombe has a simpleton job at the paper mill, sweeping sawdust and hauling trash. He is a stumpy little wart of a man, partly blind, comical in his bottle-bottom glasses, half as tall as his half-wit slut wife Marceline. He calls her Marcy in his mush-mouth fat-tongued way, but she likes "Marceline," the way I pronounce it, so you can hear all the letters. It gives her a little dignity, which is hard for persons like her to come by. Miss Marce*line,* I say, and she looks down, she's so shy, but you can tell she is also pleased. It's a small thing. But the world is made of small things and enough small things done in the right way can help you up the ladder.

Both of them, the Bascombes, come close to normal IQ—if you add them together. The funny thing about it is that Mr. Bascombe is the ugliest toad God ever took the trouble to slap together, while Marceline has got better than average looks except that her eyes cross a little at times. Her body, though, can justify the bikini she parades around in when it's hot. But here's the thing, and you can correct me if I am wrong, a low IQ in common can't be the best reason for getting married. Not that I'm the expert in such things!

Mr. Bascombe comes and goes in his 1956 International. You need to see this truck to believe it. It is solid rust, bumper to bumper. You could tear the fenders in half with your bare hands. You could push a pencil through the doors. The headlights go off in different directions and there is no glass in the side windows. When he starts it, it gives itself a hard shake like an old hound full of mean fleas. It never fails to put a smile on your face watching Mr. Bascombe, who is runty as a dwarf, stare over the steering wheel with his thick-goggled eyes. How does he reach the pedals? Black smoke pours out of the exhaust. His slut wife stands in the cloud, blowing moron kisses.

"Something is going to have to be done about your vehicle," I
said to Marceline once, as Mr. Bascombe rattled down the
road toward the cardboard mill.

She looked at me with those unconscious green eyes, not
understanding word one. *"Ve-*hicle, meaning your truck, Mrs.
Bascombe. It is stinking up the court."

I was not being hard at this point. I was play-acting a little.
I had on my dark glasses and my Dan Wesson was in view. I
laid my hand on the butt of it. I like to look sharp, being
ex-military with honorable discharge. My gabardine slacks
are creased sharp as a bayonet and I change shirts on a daily
basis. I wear a Texas Ranger–style hat which gives me a tall
lean serious look. A manager should look like a manager.

"What stink?" she said.

"Crime-inee, Marce*line,* " I said. "I am talking about your
husband's vehicle."

She looked bewildered. Her lower lip hung down like a
slice of red fruit. Her tongue came out and ran itself along
that lip. She was in her bikini. Since she could not see my
eyes, I took an extra-long gander at her endowments. I swear
to Almighty Jesus that no Hollywood starlet regardless of IQ
ever owned a set of female paraphernalia as milky perfect as
those! Every night the dwarf looked at them, but how could he
appreciate what he had with such a low-watt bulb for a brain?
All I could think of was this: What a waste. Wasted on him,
wasted on the others. It made me want to spit, and so I spit, off
to one side, thinking, You brainless slut!

I cleared my throat. "I have got complaints from your
neighbors, Mrs. Bascombe. They can smell it, since it lingers
long after Mr. Bascombe has shut off the engine. There is a
mechanical malfunction in the exhaust system that will re-
quire immediate professional attention."

Her eyes started to cross, as she could not understand the
words I chose. I sometimes like to use this type of educated
language on her, but only to show her a side of me nobody
thinks is there. I don't mean to make her feel feeble, though

she is, which is why she is so free with it. Which is not especially her fault as the stupid do not understand decent morals.

"My neighbor got a dog!" she said. "You said no dogs, but Mr. Ronny Leeks got Trudy!" She was yelling. One feature of the retarded mind is that it is unable to hold back feelings.

I smiled. "I gather Trudy is a dog?" Sometimes for fun I talk slimy like a Limey. I once said "I am feeling rather blotto" to a complaining crank who wanted his storm door recaulked. "Perhaps in a fortnight, buttfucker," I said. I try to show respect, but this crank did not deserve it as he was abusive. I am a patient man, but I am also human.

I scratched my hair above my right ear. I didn't want her to get too upset, because I needed a haircut, and Mrs. Bascombe, for all her lack of normal brain power, cut hair as good as any barber. And she only charged a dollar, being too dim to charge more.

I put my hand on her shoulder, she was beginning to cry. Retards don't cry right. They are sloppy. Their noses snot up fast. "There, there, Mrs. Bascombe," I said, rocking her a little. "I just want to help you, not hinder. It's probably just the muffler, or the tailpipe." I let my fingers sink into her nice shoulder a little, but it meant nothing to her. She just smiled up at me gratefully, in that brainless good-hearted way such people have, like a dog or an angel. It's a little frustrating how you can hardly ever get a point across to them.

That night I watched them on my monitor as she tried to explain to her husband what I had said. It was comical, because the harder she tried the less able to communicate she would get. Bascombe just sat humped over his bowl of goulash as if the answer was in there, among the noodles. "Your truck smokes too much, you idiot," I said. Of course, they could not hear or see me. He finished his goulash and looked up at her with a worried look. You have seen an ape in the zoo look worried, like he was working out his income taxes. This heard her singing on occasion but I have also heard more than her singing. Now and again a gypsy salesman or those religious boys will come by and Marceline, because she is not completely responsible for what she does, will take the nicer-looking ones into her kitchen for lemonade or soda.

I have seen this on the monitor. You have heard the old saying "One thing leads to another." It's sad but true. I have heard her agree, on the monitor or through the floorboards while lying in the dark under her unit, to *The Book Of Knowledge,* twelve magazine subscriptions for the price of six (she can't even read!), self-cleaning bird cages, German-made coffee mills, dietary supplements even though she has a perfect body (though she's too brain-damaged to realize this), and the prophecies of Joseph Smith or some other offbeat religious celebrity. Mr. Bascombe does not earn enough money for all of this, but Marceline—and here is the problem—never had the word "no" taught to her. It is a very important word, maybe the most important word in Webster's. Oftentimes, while I have been under her unit in the crawl space repairing the plumbing or wiring or plugging holes in the skirting, I have heard her bed skip and hop. Skip and hop. This type of immorality is common among the feeble. They don't know any better. You are no doubt asking yourself, "Why doesn't Manager Lefort put a stop to it then?" My answer is this: It is beyond the authority of the manager.

Nowadays I talk to Mrs. Bascombe but rarely to Mr. Bascombe. This is because Mr. Bascombe and I got into it once. He is short and he is half blind, and, as I have mentioned, backward. But he is as strong as a chimpanzee with arms to match. He got me around the waist and pulled me down from behind as I was attempting to vacate his area. So you see, it wasn't a fair fight at all. Once he had me from behind, with those long monkey arms around my waist, I could not get my wind. I am a tall thin man and a veteran of the Vietnam Era of military service, having been a motor-pool corporal at Fort

was like that, comical. I opened myself a beer and had ;
laugh. Then they went out of the picture and I was left lo
at the table and the rest of the kitchenette. The fauco
dripping. I made a note of that. The TV came on loud
couldn't hear them because of it. I watched the drip
while, then scanned the grounds for the whitened man b
was not there.

"I need to take a look under your skirting," I said to h
meant the trailer skirting, of course, but she took it to r
something else, being stupid. She froze up. She squeezed
arms across her chest as if to hide her female paraphern
"I am referring to your mobile home, Marce*line*," I saic
need to get into the crawl space. I think you have a prob
with a regulator valve." I just made that up on the spot al
the regulator valve as there is no such thing, but I am a qu
thinker and can come up with a good reason for what I
doing without much notice.

"Okay," she said. But she looked doubtful. I have told
more than once what the skirting was but she can't rememb
These units are more than twenty years old and are in co
stant need of minor repairs. They should be replaced w
new units. But Superior Properties watches their pennies.
need to check out the wiring, too," I said, and this was only
half-lie. "I am worried about fires, Marce*line*." Her eyes g
wide, because she knew what a fire here means since we lost
unit in January and the three people who lived in it, as
mentioned earlier.

I have been under her unit often, duct-taping leaks, plug
ging holes in the skirting, and so on. I don't have to ask he
permission, I am the manager, but I like to show courtesy
Show Courtesy and Receive Courtesy. This is my motto.
have lain under her unit in the darkness of many an afternoo
listening to her. Mrs. Bascombe is a secret singer. I have

Lewis, 1963–1965. He locked his monkey arms around me and squashed the wind out of my lungs. I went down to my knees in the decorative gravel. I was looking at black floaters before my eyes thinking, How did all this black gravel get mixed in with the white? The black gravel of course was in my eyeballs, or head, from the lack of oxygen.

I had made a rare off-color remark, this was true. I am sorry for it, since it was against my rule of showing courtesy at all times. It was meant as a joke. People of the mental capacity of people like Mr. Bascombe don't have much of a sense of humor. They will miss the point and you can't explain it to them. They laugh—I have heard them and seen them laugh on my monitor—but it is usually for no reason you can make out. I wouldn't go out of my way to insult a handicapped person like Mrs. Bascombe even though she does not look handicapped in a bikini and she cuts hair as good as any normal barber for one-sixth the fee.

I don't remember the details. Something about her female paraphernalia. I call her endowments "female paraphernalia" because I have a sense of humor, which you need to have if you are the manager. It is said to be a sign of intelligence. The joke I told was something about a gypsy salesman and Mrs. Bascombe's female paraphernalia, him wanting to trade *three* subscriptions for a good long look and maybe a little joyride, Mrs. Bascombe saying "But I only want *two*," when Mr. Bascombe came at me with no warning like a wild pig, low to the ground, and grunting sounds were coming from him, as he bowled me over and took me down to the decorative gravel. He didn't get it.

My arm is still sore at the shoulder, he nearly twisted it loose from the socket. We were down by the skirting, in the decorative gravel. After he squashed the air out of my lungs, he went at my arm. He bent it back and gave it a twist and I wanted to holler but wouldn't let myself. I could have served up an eviction notice then and there. I could have called in the deputies. I didn't because of a forgiving nature. You have to have a forgiving nature if you are the manager. Mrs. Bascombe was on the little steel porch of her unit, sipping soda, her slit green eyes sleepy and faraway as if she was figuring out tomorrow's grocery list, even though she was watching Mr. Bascombe trying to work my arm loose from its socket. I remember, aside from hard breathing—mine and Mr. Bascombe's—a peculiar silence.

I am a fair man. I try to be fair. If you expect to get ahead in this world you need to be fair with people and you expect fair treatment in return. This is a principle I do not stray from, along with courtesy. But though you are fair, you often will not receive fair treatment in return. This always starts me drafting out a revenge, though revenge is against my forgiving nature. But remember I am only human, as I said.

I predict arthritis in this arm when I am a senior citizen thanks to Mr. Bascombe. And though I was joking, I was not lying. The gypsy salesman *did* get at Mrs. Bascombe's female paraphernalia and even the joyride beyond. I did not make it up. I watched part of it on my monitor, and I heard the rest from the crawl space under their unit. The bed would skip and hop. She would sing out. Really! Old love songs. And she would say his name. "Oh, Freddy! Oh, Freddy!" like this stranger had just returned to his home and family after the war. Yet there are times when you need to keep such things to yourself and not make a casual joke out of it. It just makes sense, as it may cause some embarrassment, even though "Laughter Is the Best Medicine," as they say. This happened over a year ago and things are pretty well smoothed over by now, though I haven't forgotten my arm as it still gives me trouble in wet weather. I had reached down for the Dan Wesson but I had neglected to strap it on. I often will not when my visit is informal. I adjusted my clothing and walked back to my unit as if nothing much at all had happened.

Under the unit it is dark and cool. They plumb with cheap copper tubing. The wire is aluminum, which is now illegal. Twenty years ago the war made aluminum cheaper than copper. But it can explode and cause a fire. You have seen this on the news. Ten years ago the power lines east of here exploded and sent aluminum fireballs into the dry grass, causing a wildfire that took out sixty expensive homes. You get what you pay for. One year ago someone replaced their fuses with cheap, nonregulation fuses and their overloaded wiring exploded, causing a fire. Five years ago they hired me as manager.

Everything under the unit is up to code but just barely. You can pull out the plumbing with one hand. You can cut into a water line with your thumbnail. I often have to go underneath with my propane torch and solder. It's not unusual to find me under a unit. I told her I had to check her wiring and her "regulator valve," but there was something else on my mind. I had seen the whitened man the previous night on my monitor in this area of Superior West. My latest theory was that he was getting into the crawl spaces to hide from me. But I needed the evidence. That's why I used the sound-activated tape recorder. It is under their bedroom screwed to the floorboards.

I was under her unit for a while, checking the recorder, which had something interesting on it, and sifting through the dirt and rubble but finding nothing. When I came out I asked Mrs. Bascombe for a soda and a haircut. We went inside and had cold Squirts. She was wearing her red bikini. The thonglike bottom left her hard, milk-white cheeks out for anyone to see and drool over. I imagined the whitened man enjoying himself, coming back for more every night while stupid Bascombe snored. I put my hand on the butt of my Dan Wesson just thinking about this comical scene and how it might turn out if I walked in.

"I need a haircut, Marce*line*," I said.

"Well, I don't know . . ." she said. Her dull eyes crossed a little with doubt. Her female paraphernalia were slick with sweat. The swamp cooler in this unit needed a new pump but I would have to go into town, eight miles away, to get the replacement.

"Look, I have to go into town today to get you a new pump for your cooler. I'd like to look halfway human, if you don't *mind.*"

"One dollar fifty," she said.

It was still cheap at the new price. "Fine," I said. "Let's get to it."

She puts you on an old piano stool after spinning it around so that it's as high as it can get. Then she puts a bed sheet around your neck. She wets down your hair and combs it. She plucks at your neck with her fingers—God knows why. The whole process gives me chills—the good kind—the kind that make you think about what might fall your way. They make me think about the things the whitened man ached to see.

I told her about my Vietnam Era military service, about how me and Sergeant Lester Schmitt used to go into Tacoma for the action. I told her about the time Sergeant Schmitt took on two local boys and stomped on them until they cried. Once Sergeant Schmitt had me flip a coin to see who was going to get a certain blond whore named Gay June. The other one was short and tattooed. Her name was Salina, like the town in Kansas. I won but Sergeant Schmitt said, "We'll flip two out of three for the blond cunt." He said it just like that in front of them! Which was embarrassing. I won again, and he said, three out of five. And so on like that until he got Gay June, the blond cunt, and I got the pig with the tattoos. Sergeant Schmitt was a riot. I laughed, remembering it.

"Pretty funny, right, Marce*line?*"

"What is," she said, flat like that, as if I had been telling her about my collection of historic oatmeal boxes.

Then she nicked my ear. That's the only thing about her that is not like a professional barber. It's almost as if she does it on purpose. You can hear her thinking to herself before the point of the scissors finds your neck or ear. She will suck in her breath a little, stop clipping or shaving for a second or two, you will hear her teeth grinding, then zap, she gets you. I have wondered on more than one occasion if it was just me or was it the same for all her customers. I cuss her when she gets me but she doesn't learn from it. If she draws blood she pours alcohol onto a cotton ball and swabs it. If I yelp, she giggles, which makes me think it wasn't an accident in the first place. But you have to figure, it's only a dollar—make that a dollar and a half now—and your hair looks like a trained graduate of a barber college worked on it.

She is stupid, but she looks so good as she moves around you with her clippers that you can't help toying with yourself under the bed sheet a little while she tells you about things she has heard on TV or from local gossip. Moving the scissors or electrical clippers over your head gets her talking, like any ordinary barber, whereas normally she is shy and unwilling to engage in conversation. It's like another person takes her over, like in those movies about people, usually women, with several personalities under their skin. It's a different version of Marceline Bascombe who clips your hair. Not any smarter, just different.

This hair-cutting version of her deals in gruesome stories. There was a killing recently in the Uptown Apartments, near the railroad depot. A boy had cut up an older man after having shot him through the brains. She said the older man wanted the boy to be his girlfriend. She talked about how hard it is to saw through a grown man's leg or even his neck. She sucked in her breath, stopped the scissors midsnip, then rammed the point into my ear. Christ!

"Goddamm it, Marceline!" I said, jumping up, forgetting for the moment that I had been toying with myself under the bed sheet. I bunched up the sheet around me and sat down again. But she went on with her story as if nothing had interrupted it. She told how the boy switched over to a circular saw because his arms got tired using only pruning tools.

"Bone is harder than wood," she said.

"How very interesting," I said, talking like a slimy Limey. I flinched because I heard her teeth grinding again, but the scissors missed me.

I adjusted my clothes and stood up. I gave her the dollar fifty, then added a quarter, to show there were no hard feelings. I touched the bead of blood on my ear to remind her what it was I didn't have any hard feelings about. I figured she had already forgotten it.

"I say, old girl, don't you think it's about time we got a little friendlier?" I said, speaking English English.

I might as well have spoken Dutch to a boiled egg. The "barber shop" personality had already gone back to its hiding place. "You and me," I said into her unconscious eyes. "You and me need to get together." I wasn't talking English English now. I grabbed myself down below to show her the condition I was in, figuring she could at least figure out sign language if not the spoken word.

I don't think I was out of line. She *was* free with it, you remember. She was a slut. I was not exactly dealing with a schoolgirl studying to be a Bride of Christ. I put my hands on her. I could see she was starting to catch my drift. She finally got the picture! Her eyes got wide. So big and wide I had to take a step backward, the fine hair on my neck stiff.

I felt insulted. What did I do anyway? I am a gentleman, a courteous man. I am a responsible person. I have always treated her with the respect I would show a lady who had a decent set of undamaged brains. Why was I any different than a gypsy salesman? You would think I had come over the fence at night, white-faced, ducking from shadow to shadow. Correct me if I'm wrong, but I believe I was right to feel the injured party in this situation. How would you like to be the *only* man Marceline Bascombe had said "No" to? You wouldn't! Not if you have normal feelings.

I have them. They came on strong. Yes I chased her. I grabbed her. I got her down. The bikini came undone like shoelaces. I was working my pants down when she started to blubber. We were on her bed. She had given up fighting me. There was no reason for her to fight me. She was free with it. I felt the injured party. Yet she was blubbering like a child. This put me off. I had every right, but her blubbering put me off. I knelt over her on the bed with the intention of presenting myself to her in a responsible and gentlemanly way, but she put me off with her blubbering. You have never seen so many tears. Bubbles appeared at her nostrils and I could not present myself to her. To be truthful, I had nothing to present at the moment.

"Forget about it," I said, arranging my clothing. "I thought you were interested."

She quit blubbering. Her eyes were calm now. She appeared to be loafing on her bed, like a normal housewife after having done the floors.

"I'll go," I said. "But I would appreciate it if you would do one thing for me." I lowered my voice, not on purpose, I think. "I would like you to say my name. My name is Dion Perry Lefort. I would like you just to say 'Dion Perry' like you meant it. I have heard you say 'Charles' and 'Freddy' and 'Justin' like you meant it."

"Go fly a kite!" said the simpleton.

Her hand swung back and found the alarm. Her arm whipped forward and the clock bounced off my forehead. I drew my Dan Wesson and nudged her belly with it. "I have the legal authority to put you into detention," I said. It wasn't true, but she did not know what was true or false and never would. She could cut hair, take on gypsy salesmen, and wear a bikini. Period.

I went into the kitchenette and got a Squirt. My hand was shaking. I am a normal man. I have normal feelings. And now they came on strong. Yes, I had grabbed her and I had thrown her down. I had pulled off her bikini, which amounts to hardly anything anyway. But when she blubbered, I could no longer present myself to her in the way a man would if he was not put off. She cried like an infant child, and I have feelings about such things. Some here will make out that I don't, but they are wrong about me.

You should have seen me at my old mom's funeral back in Ohio. I blubbered like a scared baby. The minister had to stop the service for a full minute while I pulled myself together. Hell, I didn't even know my old "mom." She gave me up to the Leforts when I was five. The Leforts always told me how much better off I was with them than with her. She was no good. But in her late years she wanted us to get to know each other. Sorry women like her get like that. Is it too much to ask someone to call you by your name? Be fair in your answer.

Mrs. Bascombe came out of the bedroom with something else to throw. A shoe. It sailed past my ear. I just sipped my Squirt as if nothing at all had happened. I like to give the impression of "complete calm." She didn't look beautiful now, though she was naked as day one. Her back was hunched and her feet looked animal—stumpy and hard. Her hands were knuckled like bird claws and her eyes didn't make sense. I sipped my Squirt casually and moved toward the door, my mouth dry as cotton, my heart taking off.

I took out my wallet and waved a twenty in front of her face. I let it flutter to the ground and then I ducked out the door. I walked back to my unit, my armpits soaked to the beltline and sour.

Sometimes good news follows bad! After I took a long cool shower, the mail came. There was a letter from Superior Properties, postmarked Abilene. "Dear Mr. LaPorte," it said. (Their computer plays games with my name. Once it called me Mr. Leafer. Another time, Mr. Leftoff, for Christ's sakes!)

"Your efficiency coefficient for the previous fiscal year was rated in the tenth percentile of category 'C' once again. We appreciate your hard work and dedication." Someone named Yurkies signed it, if you can trust the computer. Along with the letter was a bumper sticker that said: "I (heart) Superior People." "Our prospects, and consequently *your* prospects, are excellent," wrote this Yurkies, "in that fewer and fewer people will be able to afford middle-class housing as the more traditional two-class system—the working poor and the affluent—becomes the dominant demographic. Quality, affordable, rental units in a controlled and secure environment will be the great need of the next decade. We—and that includes *you*, Mr. LaPorte—of Superior Properties, intend to fulfill that need!"

I felt good enough that night to break the ice with Mr. Bascombe and play an audio tape for him. But I wore my sidearm to show it was not a casual visit. As the songs and calls of Marceline were heard over the thumping bed, Mr. Bascombe began to look like a kid who has dropped his ice cream into the dirt. I felt for him, but after all I am the manager and I am responsible for these people whether they are brain-dead or not, and Mr. Bascombe deserved better than he was getting from the psychotic slut who was in need of some severe discipline.

He listened hard, bending to the little speaker of the tape player. "Birds," he said. "Ocean birds, by the shore," he said in his mush-mouth way.

"That's Marce*line*, you chump," I said. "With a magazine salesman named Freddy."

He shook his oversized head and said, "No, no, it's the seashore and the birds. I been to the seashore and that was the sound of it, Mr. Lefort."

I looked over at Marceline and her green eyes were focused

right on me, in a way so stonelike and calm that for a second you might believe that they were the eyes of a ten-foot-tall museum statue. On the tape her groaning singsong *did* have a birdlike ring to it—I blame that on the poor mike and the little speaker—but how could you explain away the thumping bed and the salesman shouting Jesus! Christ oh Jesus! and her saying Freddy like she meant it unless you include galloping ostriches and trained parrots among the birds of the sea?

"Have it your way, Einstein," I said, snapping off the machine. Not that he would understand the reference.

I stuck the "I (heart) Superior People" onto the front door of my unit, and went back inside. I felt that I had done my level best. The letter from Mr. Yurkies confirmed this. But it was hard not to reflect upon the heavy burden of responsibility I had been dealt. Try managing two hundred and fifteen units by yourself sometime. Daylene couldn't deal with it. She was my wife, gone almost five years. She was no help at all. *Knots Landing* was more of a concern to her than Superior West. You have seen this type of wife before—"The Plague," as I call it, of the working man. They tend to be useless. They enter married life in order to retire at age twenty. Fat and lazy, but smart. She had been to college a year, but was too lazy to stay with it. She married a well-driller named George Bosco who kicked her out after a month. I got her on the first hop but was not as smart as George Bosco. She was lanky-slim with major-league paraphernalia—which I prefer and am sometimes blinded by—but soon she got fat and sloppy, from the ankles up. I told her straight out, By God you are going to earn your keep, Daylene. She said, Adios, you dismal motherfucker! Six months of wasted time and in bed she was meatlocker cold. She didn't want it at all unless she could be "manager," if you get my drift. I hear that she and her dirty mouth are now living with a female preacher. You figure it out!

I have very high personal standards. You need very high personal standards to be a manager for Superior. And yet there are times when you feel nothing you do makes much difference. I felt that way—philosophical—in spite of the cheerful bumper sticker on my front door and the nice letter from Mr. Yurkies. I fixed myself a sandwich but put it down the disposal untouched. I watched TV for a while and when it got dark I checked the monitors. I'd had my fill of the Bascombes for one day but I looked in on them just the same.

They were in the kitchenette, washing dishes. Now and then she would slip an arm around him and he would slip his arm around her. They both had aprons on. Sometimes they hugged though their hands were soapy. "Finish the dishes, you rejects," I said. They would hug and the strength of the hug would take them down to their knees and they would look into each other's face with eyes so alive you could almost make yourself believe they were too dumb to know they were dumb. If that makes sense! "Oh my love," she said. "My dear, my dear," he said. And then they started *crying*.

I made a note of their faucet, which was dripping faster than ever even though I was *sure* she had turned it off properly, as I have trained myself to notice details.

I spent the rest of the night monitoring the grounds. Why don't they give me credit for this? At 3:00 A.M., the whitened man walked straight into the scanner, as if he didn't care about being seen. He was tall and skinny, and his face flared like he had smeared white reflective paint on it. But I think it was just a bad type of skin that is damaged in the sun. Which explains the lack of color and his preference for nighttime activities.

I watched him walk to the "Smiths'" unit and look into the kitchen window. Well, what did he expect to find? People holding on to each other the way people lost at sea hold on to life rafts? I guess he was harmless enough, but I took down my Winchester pump and leveled it at my kitchen window. Just in case.

Wilderness

DAVE COLBERT IS sick of hearing about the geology of the
northern Rockies, but the man driving the car, Marv Trane, is
a relentless know-it-all who never passes up a chance to display his knowledge or to correct Colbert's less encyclopedic
grasp of the earth's crust. The wives of the two men are chat-
ting in the backseat of Trane's Isuzu Trooper. It was Colbert's
wife, Rhea, who suggested the joint week-long trek to Montana. Trane's wife, Freddi—a small, high-strung woman
whose eyelids flutter hysterically when she speaks—had been
bitten on the arms by her husband and had found a sympathetic confidante in Rhea. They had met in Relationship Dy-
namics, a class taught in a local community college's adult
education division. The two men had not met each other until
yesterday morning, and Colbert—who has already had his fill
of Marv Trane—is gloomy with the realization that there is no
way to avoid the six days of misery that lie ahead.

Colbert is afraid of Trane, convinced that the man is dangerous. Now and then Colbert catches Trane glancing at him
with narrowed eyes and sly grin, as if sizing him up. Trane
has done this often enough to keep Colbert on edge. When
they shook hands yesterday, Trane's grip had nearly made
Colbert wince. Then, when Trane smiled, he exposed his teeth
to the back fillings, a trait that Colbert has always associated
with ambition, aggression, and the need to intimidate. People

in the public eye, the great successes of our time, seem to have this mirthless smile, which Colbert has dubbed the Attila Grin.

Trane, however, is not in the public eye. He is an unemployed systems analyst, recently laid off by Lockheed. Rhea has argued that the bites on Freddi's arms were most likely inflicted in the heat of passion, and not intended to cause pain or damage. Nonetheless, Freddi was alarmed enough to seek out Rhea for support.

"He really loves her," Rhea told Colbert, "but he sometimes loses control, especially when he goes off his medication." Trane bit his wife in a Wal-Mart parking lot, during a lightning storm. He wanted to make love, right there in the Isuzu, as the sky convulsed.

"He *forced* her?" Colbert said. "He *attacked* his own wife in a parking lot?"

Rhea frowned, then said, "No. Not really. There was consent, but it *was* a bit surprising, and . . . in retrospect, frightening. Freddi was afraid of what might have happened if she had refused him." Trane, Rhea said, was very upset at losing his job. Being laid off had "unmanned" him somehow. He wanted sex to be random and violent or he didn't want it at all. His consequent mood swings were hard for Freddi to cope with. A psychiatrist had prescribed an antidepressant, then, after further diagnosis and consultation, lithium, but Trane hated the side effects of such drugs and would not take them regularly. Rhea thought a trip into the mountains would be therapeutic. "It will do *us* good, too," she said.

"Up there, above that scree!" Trane shouts suddenly, jolting Colbert out of his troubled reverie. "You can see some outcroppings of Precambrian basement rock!" He rolls down his window and leans out of it, pointing up the sheer slope to the left side of the highway. His face in the wind is Attila: challenging flash of teeth, the warrior's terrain-assessing squint, the taut jut of jaw. The Isuzu drifts over the center line into the oncoming lane of traffic. There is no traffic, luckily, and Colbert, though tempted to grab the wheel, lets the car drift, half hoping it will find its way to the far shoulder of the highway, maybe even roll over into the ditch that borders it. This is the morning of the second day of the trip and Colbert is desperate enough to sacrifice his own safety, and the safety of his wife, if it results in the abrupt end of this "therapeutic" trek.

But just as the car is about to stagger onto the soft shoulder of the opposite lane, the shoulder widens into a scenic turnout and Trane wheels the big Isuzu smartly to a sliding stop next to a rushing cataract, as if this was what he meant to do all along. Trane has his door open before the car stops rolling, setting the parking brake as an afterthought. Colbert leans his head back into the headrest and closes his eyes. *Jesus,* he thinks. *I took five days of emergency sick leave for this?* He turns around to give Rhea a scathing look, but both women are peering out the windows at the cataract that is roaring down a sheer rock wall. "My God, my God," Rhea says, her voice constricted with reverence, a tone that instantly infuriates Colbert.

Colbert is a high school social studies teacher who is in the throes of burnout. He has been in the grip of a fatigue so profound that he has lost his train of thought on several occasions recently while lecturing to his honors class. Each time this has happened, he has excused himself from the room. In the hallway, nearly in tears, he would try to collect his wits. He'd smoke to calm himself, and when he'd return to the classroom he would read aloud from the textbook until the bell rang, giving him reprieve. His honors class—good kids from good middle-class homes—listened to their Walkmans while he read, or they gossiped in small groups. Some of the bolder boys and girls would pair off and make out in the back of the room. Colbert didn't care. He read mechanically from the text, not listening to himself either, fighting the urge to put his head down on his arms and go to sleep.

Rhea, always alert to behavioral aberrations, sent him first to counselors and then to doctors. The diagnoses invariably described him as a candidate for "burnout" even though his physical indicators were quite good—a bit overweight, subpar muscle tone, cholesterol level a few points out of the normal range, blood pressure up a bit, but generally speaking, he was in tolerable good health.

One counselor suggested a career change. But, at forty-two, Colbert is terrified of this option. It isn't an option at all, as far as he's concerned. It's a one-way ticket to chronic unemployment and poverty, and to an even greater lethargy of spirit. He can endure things as they are now for another ten years, when he will be eligible for an early retirement.

Colbert sighs heavily, startling himself. He realizes he has been staring at Trane's wide back, unconsciously curious, and is now abruptly recognizing Trane's posture: legs apart and loose at the knees, elbows out, head bent forward slightly in concentration. In full view of the women, Trane has unzipped his pants and is urinating next to the picturesque waterfall, the hot urine steaming in the cool mountain air. That Trane is relieving himself in front of everyone doesn't surprise Colbert at all, it only adds to his general peevishness. Rhea and Freddi, however, are looking in the opposite direction, squinting at a ridge of snow-capped peaks to the south.

"I *love* this country," Rhea says. "I don't know why we just don't *move* here. My God, imagine waking up every morning to that view!"

"I'm sick of Sunnyvale," Freddi agrees. "I mean, you can't even *see* the coastal mountains anymore because of the smog."

"I could get work making birch-bark canoes," Colbert says. "Rhea could weave baskets from the native grasses and sell them to tourists. We could chew peyote and commune with the mountain spirits."

"David's first response to beauty is cynicism," Rhea says to Freddi. "Depend on it."

"I'm not a cynic," Colbert protests mildly.

"You've got to earn your stripes to be a true cynic," Trane calls over his shoulder as he yanks up his zipper. Colbert is shocked that Trane has heard them. It seems impossible. *The man must have the ears of a bat,* he thinks. Trane leans into the Isuzu. "You've got to understand the system completely before you have the right to doubt it," he says, his teeth exposed in a white challenge that makes Colbert look away.

"Who understands any system completely?" Colbert mumbles.

"I don't mean to pull rank, Davey, but I'm a senior systems analyst, remember? It's my job to understand systems."

An unemployed senior systems analyst who bites his wife and pisses in public, Colbert thinks, and, as if Trane's keen hearing can even pick up thoughts, his smile collapses into a thin sneer and he slaps the side of the Isuzu hard, making the women, and Colbert, jump.

Colbert opens his door and gets out to stretch his legs. He walks to the rear of the car, then beyond it to the edge of the turnout. He hears a diesel truck laboring up the grade, the caw of crows, the rush of wind in the stately Ponderosas. Northern Idaho is more beautiful than he expected and he is momentarily confident that the trip might not be so bad after all. Trane is a bully and a jerk, he knows, but easy to ignore once you stop reacting to his insufferable running commentary and aggressive glances. Colbert fills his lungs with the nippy autumnal air and heads back to the car. For the first time he notices the big red-and-white bumper sticker, glued diagonally—with swashbuckling carelessness—to the back of the Isuzu: "Crisis Doesn't Make Character—It Exhibits It," and Colbert's moment of optimism fades as quickly as it came.

By midday, they are almost in Montana, nearing Lolo Pass. "I've got a surprise for you," Trane says, taking the Trooper off the highway and shifting it into four-wheel drive. Colbert, who has been dozing, is instantly alert. He feels his innards rise, weightless, as the car drops down a steep dirt road that winds through a stand of beautiful old cedars. "There's a natural hot springs down here not very many people know about," Trane says.

"You've been here before?" Colbert asks, alarmed. It occurs to him suddenly that this trip was Trane's idea to begin with and that Rhea was finessed into thinking it was hers. Rhea, for all her night-school classes in pop psychology, could be astonishingly naive. She tended to think that most people were as straightforward and honest as she was, that they meant what they said, and that liars and cheats were their own worst enemies—to be pitied, or rescued by therapy, rather than feared or avoided. She often argued that good therapy could transform the world. She believed that people were basically decent and that civilized behavior was instinctive, not an extrinsic ideal (as Colbert has often jibed) that has teased humanity for ten thousand years like a mirage in the desert.

Trane hesitates, then says, "Oh, sure. I've been here. Years ago, when I was a kid. My dad used to take me to Montana to hunt."

"How wonderful to have a *committed* father," Rhea says. "I mean, I don't approve of hunting per se, but I think a father taking his son on outings and so forth is so . . . *beneficial,* in terms of the son's future stability. I only wish David had had a father like that. A father like that gives his son *permission,* ultimately, to become a man."

"What kind of father *did* you have, Davey?" Trane asks. "Did he give you permission to become a man?"

Colbert ignores Trane's glance, though he can see, out of the corner of his eye, the glare of teeth. "He was a son of a bitch," Colbert says.

Trane releases a single angry bark of laughter and downshifts abruptly, making the Isuzu fishtail. "So was mine," he says. "He gave me permission to get the fuck out of his house."

"Aren't you driving a little too fast for this road, darling?" Freddi says.

"No, actually I'm not, darling," Trane says, mocking his wife's tone. He presses the accelerator to the floor and upshifts, making the car lurch into a nearly broadside skid.

"Please slow down," Rhea says. Her voice is reasonable, but Colbert knows she is terrified. He turns around so that she can see his I-told-you-so smile. Her face is rigid, her eyes are wide.

"Marv knows what he's doing," Colbert says to Rhea. "He's obviously an experienced off-road driver, no need to fret."

Rhea leans her head back and closes her eyes. "Don't take that tone with me, David," she says. "I'm not a child."

"There it is," Trane announces, bringing the Isuzu to a hard stop. They are in a clearing: a bowl with steep granite sides, the high, sky-touching rim of which is screened with thick stands of larch and fir. At the bottom of the bowl is a steaming pool of water about the size of a baseball diamond. The pool is studded with large gray boulders. "Hot springs," Trane says. "This is part of the Lolo batholith."

"Remarkable!" Rhea says, her voice resuming the irritating pitch of reverence Colbert has not heard before today.

"Molten granite magma rose into the earth's crust here about fifty million years ago," Trane says, lecturing again. "What you see all around you is young granite. Now, fractures in the granite and in the Precambrian sediment rock permit rainwater, or the runoff from snowmelt, to circulate deeply enough to get heated by the still-hot batholith before it percolates back up to the surface at the springs."

"Nature's own hot tub," Colbert says.

"Right," Trane says, winking archly. It's a conspiratorial wink that annoys Colbert. *"Better* than a hot tub, in fact," Trane goes on. "The Indians claimed these waters had healing powers. And not just for your usual aches and pains, but for your spirit. Water like this will put your body and soul back into alignment."

Colbert can almost sense the thrill that Rhea is experiencing. It is the sort of thing she needs to believe in, having given up on all the conventional forms of belief.

"Is it safe?" she says. "I mean, can we go in without getting scalded?"

Trane leans into the backseat and puts his hand on Rhea's knee. "A little scalding is just what the medicine man ordered," he says, winking again. He shuts off the engine and the silence moves in on them like a forbidding presence. For a while no one speaks; they even breathe cautiously. Finally, Trane opens his door, and the slight wheeze of dry hinges releases a worm of sound into the body of silence.

Rhea is first to speak. "My God but this is beautiful. Are we allowed to camp here?"

"Who's going to tell us we can't?" Trane says.

The cool, piney air, Colbert notices, has a slight sulfurous stink to it. The disk of blue sky above them seems unhappily far away, an optical illusion generated by the steep granite walls and the tall conifers that grow at the high rim. Trane opens the back doors of the Isuzu and pulls out the camping gear. "I'll set up the tents," he says. "Why don't you ladies try the healing waters? Then we'll have a good lunch."

Colbert starts to undo the ties on one of the bundles, but Trane takes him by the elbow and pulls him aside. "Let me deal with this stuff, Davey," he says. "I've done this a thousand times. You could be a big help by digging the slit trench, off a ways in the trees."

"Slit trench?" Colbert asks, confused. Colbert is not a camper, has always felt uncomfortable in the woods. He prefers picnic grounds with tables and fire rings. He likes to know that convenience stores and telephones are not far away.

"You know—an outdoor crapper," Trane says. "Dig it about a foot wide and about three feet long. Maybe a foot and a half deep." He hands Colbert a short narrow-bladed shovel, then returns to the job of laying out the tents and other equipment.

Even a brief walk into the woods makes Colbert nervous. And these are real woods, the wilderness, not a neighborhood park. The ground is carpeted with pine needles, the scented air is thick and unmoving. Colbert feels that he is being observed by animals he cannot see. Behind a large, privacy-giving, lichen-covered boulder, he starts to dig. The ground is hard and his progress is slow. He has to remove stones of varying sizes from time to time, and the slit trench that gradually takes shape does not have the square dimensions Trane described. It's more of an oblong hole, the size of a steamer trunk. It has taken Colbert an hour to dig it, and his arms and back are burning with fatigue. When he returns to the campsite, the tents are erected side by side with a fire ring made of stones set between them.

"David! David!" Rhea says. "Where have you been? Get *in* here, it's wonderful!" Her voice has a haunting quality, as if it is coming from all directions at once, a voice in a dream.

All three of them are in the water. Colbert sees their heads floating together at the far side of the pool, partly screened by mist. He stares at them for a while, as if he doesn't recognize what he's looking at. "Rhea?" he says.

"Take your clothes off and get in here, honey!" Rhea calls again. Her voice is textured and amplified by the heated water and surrounding granite. He is momentarily transfixed by this vision of the floating heads and by the odd resonance of Rhea's voice.

"Come on, Davey," Trane says, "we'll baptize you. Old Wakantanka lives here." Trane's voice, enlarged and timbered with authority, is double obnoxious to Colbert. He turns his back on them.

"Marv says Wakantanka is the Indian name for the Great Spirit, honey," Rhea calls after him.

"Does he," Colbert says under his breath as he pulls back the flap of a tent. His and Rhea's suitcase is inside, and he rummages through it until he finds his swim trunks. He strips, then pulls on the trunks, a boxer-style pair he bought twenty years ago, imprinted with white sailboats against faded blue. The trunks no longer fit. His pale belly falls over the waistline. Colbert leaves the tent and his skin is immediately assaulted by the cool, humid air, as are his bare feet by the pine-needle loam. When he steps into the misting pool, he chokes back the urge to cry out in pain. The water is *hot,* well over one hundred degrees, but the apparent comfort of the others makes him wade bravely forward against the instinctive urge to recoil. The notion that he is wading not into water but into pure *pain* gives Colbert a moment of giddy panic. He grits his teeth and moves toward the smiling heads resting at the base of a granite boulder the size of a small house.

"David," Rhea says, "those trunks are ridiculous."

"The trunks are fine," Colbert says. "It's the body in them that's gotten ridiculous."

"Don't knock yourself, Davey," Trane says, pulling himself strongly out of the water and onto a shelf in the stone. Colbert tries to hide his dismay at seeing that Trane is naked. He looks quickly at the women, still up to their necks in the opaque water. Their faces, red and finely beaded with sweat, betray no sense of shock or uneasiness.

"Get all the way in, David," Rhea says. "It's more therapeutic that way. It feels fantastic."

Freddi climbs up next to her husband, and Colbert sees that she is also naked. She is even more fragile-looking without clothes. Her small, chalky breasts, webbed with networks of fine blue veins, seem as breakable as china in the early-afternoon sunlight. The Tranes, on the gray rock, look like a posed tableau—Marv, the muscular Roman god; Freddi, the water nymph.

"This place is magical!" Rhea says, apparently unaffected by the casual nudity of the Tranes. She submerges herself suddenly, then springs up pink and laughing, and Colbert— as he has begun to suspect—sees that Rhea is naked, too.

"You'll smooth the kinks out of your system here, Davey," Trane says lazily. He's lying back now, taking the sun, his genitals lolling on his thigh, while Freddi, on her haunches beside him, looks dreamily content, as if water, sun, and the passivity of her husband have conspired to put her into a happy, self-satisfied rapture.

Rhea's large breasts, buoyant and flushed pink in the hot silty water, embarrass Colbert. Colbert is a private and shy man who has always shunned openness in public. Rhea, early in their marriage, would sometimes hug him impulsively, no matter where they were. She'd kiss his cheek or ear, comb loose strands of his hair with her fingers, but Colbert put a stop to it. "I'm sorry, honey," he'd said, on more than one occasion, "but I can't be intimate in public. It's like exposing my private life to an audience of strangers." Rhea said she understood, but often forgot herself, drawing sharp rebukes from Colbert. After their marriage crystallized into routine, the subject never came up again. But now, what the years solidified has become, in one afternoon, loose and undefined, and Colbert feels sick with humiliation; he feels betrayed.

"Take those outrageous trunks off, honey," Rhea laughs, climbing out of the water and stretching out on a rock slab of her own, without any apparent self-consciousness. Colbert regards his large-breasted, wide-hipped wife gleaming in the sun and is suddenly moved to the brink of tears at the mindless generosity of her ample body. The body is so helpless, he thinks—a poor pack animal bent under the crushing weight of a confused, unteachable ghost. This thought depresses Colbert further, and he turns his back on the three glistening bathers. "The trunks stay on," Colbert says, wading away. His heart is pounding hard enough to hear. He is sure the others can hear it, too. He crawls into his tent and puts his clothes back on. Then he goes out and gathers dry sticks for the fire ring, taking Trane's hatchet with him.

Trane, using a high-tech two-burner propane stove, fixes a late-afternoon lunch of wild rice with mushrooms and chicken breasts in wine sauce. He takes a container of prepared asparagus vinaigrette out of an ice chest, and there is a good Sonoma white zinfandel to drink. They sit on folding chairs at a card table draped with a linen tablecloth, and they eat off real china.

"God, I expected to eat Beefaroni off paper plates," Rhea says, delighted. "Whose idea was this?"

"*Mea culpa,*" Trane says. "But I'm glad Davey collected all those twigs anyway. Later on we can make us a little fire and have a sing-along. I brought my twelve-string. How about it, Dave? You remember Dylan? I do passable Dylan."

"David's being a poop," Rhea says. "He's a world-class sulker."

"I'm telling you, Davey," Trane says, "you should have adopted the right attitude out there in the water. A *wicasa wakan*—holy man to you—would have warned you about taking these waters with a bug up your ass. There's probably not a lot of time to get yourself in tune."

"What do you mean by that, Marv?" Rhea asks.

She sounds like a schoolgirl, Colbert thinks.

"I think I'm boring Davey," Trane says.

"Well you're not boring me," Rhea says.

"I just meant," Trane continues, "that according to precepts found not only in Mahayana Buddhism, but in nearly all of the nondualistic religions, including Native American animism—"

"Excuse me," Colbert says, standing up abruptly. "I have to go to the slit trench."

Trane releases a burst of hard laughter that puts Colbert on alert. "That's *funny!*" Trane says. "Davey said something funny." He cups his large hand on Freddi's shoulder and rocks her. "Don't you want to say something funny, too? Show these people that you can say something funny, too, Freddi."

"I can't think," Freddi says, smiling self-consciously.

"Try," Trane says. "Try to think. Who knows, you might get to liking it."

Colbert is awakened out of a dream in which his bare feet are being snuffled by large rodentlike animals. Rising voices have pulled him out of his disturbed sleep, and he lies on his back staring into the close black air of the small tent.

"I don't know why they have to fight," Rhea says.

"I wouldn't call it fighting," Colbert says, yawning.

Trane is talking with the speed and intensity of a manic auctioneer. His rant is punctuated every half minute or so by a whimpering response from Freddi.

"These tents should be farther apart," Colbert says, recalling, wistfully, their widely separated motel rooms of the night before.

"Listen to that," Rhea says, sitting up.

The sound is unmistakable, but Colbert just shrugs.

"He's *striking* her," Rhea says. Freddi is crying softly, begging him to stop. Trane's angry chant has become a barely articulate growl.

"We don't know that," Colbert reasons. "I think it's just a performance for our benefit."

"We'd better do something about this, David," Rhea says.

Colbert lies back down and pulls the sleeping bag over his head. "I didn't bring a revolver," he says.

"I'm *serious.*"

"I know it's hard, but try not to be," Colbert says, rolling over into his sleeping position. The cold, unyielding ground under the tent floor makes his shoulder ache instantly.

Abruptly, the commotion in the Tranes' tent stops. There is a canyon of silence into which Colbert has begun to fall, the dream of rodents nuzzling his feet returning, but before the fall is complete he is pulled back into consciousness by a string of urgent moans.

"They're making love," Rhea, who is still sitting up, says.

"No, it's just sex," Colbert mumbles. "Tarzan's reward."

Rhea sighs. "Everything is a great big joke to you."

Colbert doesn't respond to this. The remark strikes him as not only off the mark but, in light of what he has been going through the past few months, *unfair.*

Then Rhea's searching hand is in his sleeping bag. "Come on," she says. "Let's."

"Rhea, for Christ's sakes."

"It's been a long time, David," she says sternly.

"It's been a week," he says.

"I'm not taking no for answer," she says. Her hoarse voice in the disembodying dark becomes a curiosity, as if it is the voice of a threatening stranger. Colbert imagines startled animals bolting through the forest at the sound of Freddi's eerie vocalizations, as Rhea unzips his bag and presses herself down on top of him, vibrant with a fierce, uncompromising energy.

But Colbert pushes her away. He pulls on his shirt and pants and leaves the tent. He walks to the edge of the hot springs and squats down. A crescent moon suspended in the narrow disk of sky is reflected perfectly in the black water. Colbert takes his shirt and pants off and wades toward the moon, trying not to disturb it. He wades to the far side of the pool and leans back against a wall of granite. He is surprised that he feels comfortable and relaxed, and soon his thoughts drift south, away from the wilderness of Idaho.

He remembers attacking the smug ignorance of his bored honors class shortly before he began to lose interest in them. "Your feelings and ideas, limited and confused as they are, have been *handed down* to you," he told them. "You don't know it, but you're wearing old, mismatched clothes. You think you're wearing originals, you're proud of the ridiculous costume you're wearing. But it's old, *old*, and stinks of the thousand dead bodies who wore it before you!" (*"Gross,* Mr. Colbert," offered Betty Vukovich, a cheerleader, sticking her finger into her mouth as if to induce nausea.) He began to tremble. He had to blink away a shock of burning tears. But the kids just stared at him with drooping interest, like sheep momentarily distracted from their browsing by the irrelevant natterings of a possessed shepherd.

A splash breaks his reverie. Something has entered the water, and Colbert feels his neck hairs bristle. He starts wading stealthily back toward the tents, but he is sure that whatever it was that made the splash is aware of him. A catalogue of wild animals races through his mind, from otters to mountain lions to grizzly bears, and when he reaches the opposite shore, he is breathless with terror. He looks back at the water expecting to see a dark presence leaving a heavy wake, but sees only the rippled moon.

"Hidden in every shaman is a hunter," Trane pontificates. He's been in the water for over an hour and his skin is dangerously pink as he lies on the rock slab, recovering.

"That's it," Colbert says. "I've had it up to here. We're going home. Drive us to Spokane and we'll take the next flight to San Jose."

"Whoa, bud," Trane says, easing himself off his rock with the grace of a sea lion.

Colbert wades away from the group, suddenly fearful. He

hears, behind him, the water parting furiously before Trane's churning thighs.

"You're acting like a spoiled child, David," Rhea says. Her voice is languid, almost disinterested, and this makes Colbert doubly fearful. Something has changed, but he can't decide what it is that has made today different from yesterday. He is aware of his poor physical condition more than ever, how his pale, shapeless legs cannot move with strength and speed through the dense, sulfuric waters.

"Wait up, Davey," Trane says, his voice cajoling now, seductive.

Then Trane's hand is on Colbert's shoulder, stopping his retreat. Colbert turns to face Trane and realizes, for the first time, the true difference in their sizes. His eyes are level with Trane's chin; to meet Trane's gray gaze, he has to look up. Trane's eyes are benevolent and manically intense at the same time and Colbert tries to turn away but Trane has tightened his grip, making escape impossible.

"What do you think you're running away from, Davey?" Trane says. "Remember: Wherever you go, *there you are.*"

"Take your hand off me, you fucking creep," Colbert says, his voice trembling.

But Trane throws his arm around Colbert in a brotherly embrace that makes the stiff bones in his shoulder crackle. Then, with Colbert in tow, Trane starts wading back toward the stones where the naked women lie easy in the sun.

"Let me go, you crazy son of a bitch!" Colbert says, close to tears.

"I've told you, Davey," Trane says, unmoved by Colbert's rage, "you've got to show the right attitude in these waters. This isn't your backyard pool, this is a holy place."

"You goddam phony," Colbert sobs. "Everything you say . . ."

But suddenly Colbert finds himself underwater, held there, unable to wrench himself away from the arm that has him in a headlock, keeping him submerged. The water makes his nose and eyes feel on fire, but the arm will not release him. It occurs to him that Trane intends to drown him, and he begins to fight for his life, but he has no leverage and poor footing, even if he could match Trane's strength.

Then, just as suddenly as he was submerged, he is hauled up out of the water, gasping. He tries to work free of the headlock but Trane tightens his grip. Colbert's face is crushed into Trane's rib cage. He tries to look to the women for help but is unable to lift his eyes to them.

"Baptism, you realize," Trane says blandly, "did not originate with the early Christians. It's a rite as old as mankind itself. Man, very early in his history, realized that he was vulnerable to all sorts of false systems springing from values rooted in the survival instinct—you believe what you *need* to believe—and false *systems* invariably deny the heart's desire to transcend the mundane. Man wants to feel exalted. And so, baptism was seen as the symbolic washing away of the things that clog one's ability to experience straightforward truth."

"Then, it's meaningless to baptize infants," Colbert hears Rhea say. He is astonished that she has maintained her bright and banal sophomoric tone.

"A man like your husband here is unable to experience his own life. He's locked into a totally flawed system. You're right, Rhea. Infants should baptize us."

"Please," Colbert says, his voice muffled. He is becoming vertiginous in the vise of Trane's arm. "Let me go."

"We should *all* be baptized," Rhea says gaily, pushing off her rock and entering the water. "We all need a new start."

"Out with the old, in with the new," Freddi giggles, joining her.

"This, of course, is my point," Trane says, muscling Colbert under the hot water again. This time Trane takes him deeper, and Colbert loses his footing altogether. He feels helplessly buoyant as his boxer-style trunks break the surface and balloon, and though he is terrified, he thinks of how foolish the trunks must look, billowing pneumatically, exaggerating his clownish rump, the faded blue sailboats stretched tight. When he feels he has held his breath as long as possible, he begins to claw at Trane for mercy. And when this fails, he puts his hands flat on the silty bottom and tries to push himself up.

Something moves under his left hand. It is a jagged wedge of granite, roughly the size of a brick. He digs it out of the soft silt and shifts it to his right hand and when Trane finally pulls him into the air, Colbert swings the stone upward with as much force and accuracy as his awkward position will allow and it hits the side of Trane's head, close to the temple. He believes that if he allows Trane to dunk him again, his breath will give out and he will drown, and so as Trane bellows in pain and surprise, his hands now shielding his bleeding head, Colbert drives the heavy stone into Trane's face as hard as he can and this time he hears the wet collapse of cartilage and bone. Trane staggers backward, thrashing the water, trying to stay on his feet. Colbert follows him until Trane slumps down in shallow water. Dimly aware of the screams of the women somewhere behind him, he raises the stone with both hands and hammers it into the top of Trane's skull, and though Trane's eyes are red and blind, he is able to say, "Oh now wait, Dave. Please, Dave, wait," as the water around both men turns flagrantly red.

Colbert, sobbing for breath, wades back to the tents. The bones of his right hand are cramped with pain, as if his hand has suddenly aged and every joint has been frozen with severe arthritis. He looks at his hand and sees that it is still gripping the blood-smeared stone. He tries to will his fingers open but the fingers, white as sun-bleached bone, refuse to comply. He holds his arm out from his side, puzzled, waiting for the rock to drop. He is shaking wildly. His knees unlock, nearly causing him to fall. It is as if all the strength of his body has been concentrated in the hand that holds the stone. He tries to throw it into the trees, but only throws himself off balance, and he falls to all fours, still gripping the wedge of granite.

It is not until he sees Trane's hatchet, leaning against the ice chest, that his hand relaxes. He leaves the stone behind and crawls toward the hatchet. He feels as if he is swimming, his movements slowed but also sustained by water. The hatchet feels good in his hand—it is light and well balanced, and it has kept its edge. It is much superior to a stone. The teacher he once was recalls the dozens of millennia between stone and steel, how the efficient steel blade of progress joyously cut down the astonished enemy.

Colbert feels refreshed and clear-headed as he wades back out to the annoying gabble of voices. He feels as if he's just awakened from ten thousand years of nightmare.

The Voice of America

POP HIT MOM. I heard it, then I heard Mom. She yelled. She started to cry. I unplugged my earphones from my shortwave radio and came out of my room, blinking in the bright light of the kitchen. Mom was sitting at the table and Pop—Wade Eggers—was leaning over her. I went up to him and hammered him. I nailed him. He went down in slow motion, like a swamped boat. I still had my earphones on. I started to kick him but Mom said, *"Don't,* honey," real loud, in that voice of hers that makes you think Jesus is in the next room, watching. So I quit. I had no great hate for him. I had no feeling for any of them. By "them" I mean the men she picked out for herself. I was just sick and tired of it. "It" meaning her life and what she dragged along behind it, me included. If I'd had some dynamite just then I probably would have lit it. In my mind I have burned that house in National City down to the foundation a thousand times, everyone asleep inside. I dreamed of waking up as someone else, in a different place, where things were decent. "Goodbye, forever," I said. I meant it this time.

Mom was drunker than Pop. She got up and went into the living room. I followed her. Blood hung on her lip like a dark red grape. A drop fell onto her carpet. She always said she loved that carpet. It was a fake oriental made in Mexico. "I'm gone," I said. I kicked the television. It was a big cherrywood

car outside some bar in Marquette, Michigan,
exas, Bakersfield, California, or Tijuana, Mex-
about the motel and hotel rooms I had slept in
ting for someone to come for me while a world of
rsed and cried in the hallways and small rooms
below and to all sides. These things are not so
have heard of worse—but they add up after a
you learn to hate them. We had no real home and
f liquor and the noise of their lives was something I
hed to get away from. But leaving isn't easy. There
s you have to think about. Mom married Wade when
irteen. He was her fourth husband, if I have counted
y. None of them was any good. Wade was the worst. I
en him pick up a knife before, though he never had
nough to use it.

ent back into my room. The yellowish glow of the dials
e BC-348 looked like two sour smiles. I plugged my
hones back in and searched around for the Voice of
erica. I loved to listen to the Voice of America. You could
en to all your favorite radio programs as they were broad-
st across the oceans to Communist countries so that the
eople who lived in them could hear how it was to live in the
Land of the Free. *Jack Benny, Duffy's Tavern, Truth or Consequences, Counterspies, The Great Gildersleeve,* and so on. I had
copper wire strung out to the eucalyptus tree in the backyard
for good reception. I found the Voice of America in the thirty-
one-meter band, but they just had Walter Winchell on or
somebody like that with the latest bad news.

"I don't want you to go, baby," Mom said. She had come
into my room. She stood behind me and my radio equipment.
She lifted one earphone away from my head so I could hear
her. Then she put her hands on me. I shook her off. She was
so stupid with booze she didn't know how to act. She hardly
ever knew how to act. Some people just aren't ready for the
world from the time they are born. She is one of them. This
had to be the tenth time she'd begged me not to leave.

Packard Bell with
fell off and broke, b
"I don't want you
honey?"

I picked up the Pa
around for something e
cupboard.

"Stop it!" she yelled. S
"Stop it!" Her fingers trem
could. But I had seen all this b
end to what she could take. Th
act. Everything is an act.

I went back into the kitchen. P
out of a drawer. *That* made me blo
had ever hit anyone. This time he
down. His eyes rolled up showing
tongue hung out. I put my hands aroun
down to him, like he was in a hole. "P
time, I mean it," I said.

To show I was serious I kicked his gut. I
started arching his back and waving his arm
off. I picked him up by his shirt and slammed
on the wall. His head bounced. During all this
earphones on. "Stop it, baby!" Mom yelled.
him!"

In my earphones her yelling sounded like so m
pering music. Let her whimper to Jesus, I thou
drummed the wall with Pop. I thought about all the
when I was younger—how I cried in my bed while s
whatever man she had at the time fought and yelled,
times with strangers they had brought into our house. I w
put on my war-surplus earphones with the big rubber pa
and plug them into my war-surplus BC-348 shortwave r
ceiver and try to pick up the Voice of America. But I could
hear them right through the Voice of America.

I thought, as I slammed Pop, about the many times I had

THE VOICE

sat alone in a
Fort Worth,
ico. I thoug
as a child wa
strangers c
above and
terrible—
while and
the stink
always a
are thin
I was t
correct
had se
guts e
I
on t
ear
Am
lis
ca
p

"I'm going anyway," I said. I was seventeen, almost eighteen, and big. I had talked to a Marine recruiting sergeant. Korea was still going on. They needed men. I lifted weights at my friend Dick Drummond's house. I could military-press two hundred and dead-lift three. I was ready. To leave her behind.

She put her hand on my biceps, which I hardened. "I'd be here alone with him if you went away, honey," she said, squeezing around on my arm as if looking for soft spots.

I took off the earphones and turned around. "That's your problem," I said. "Leave him, if you don't want to take that crap," I said.

"You know I've stayed with him for your sake, baby," she said. "Baby, you *know* that's the only reason I've stuck it out. I wanted you to have a home."

This was too stupid for words. But I had heard it before and was tired of telling her how stupid it was. It was worse than stupid. It was a lie. This was a lie that she believed herself. How people could lie to themselves, and *believe* it, was the miracle of human life as far as I was concerned. I'd seen her do it, I'd seen Wade Eggers do it. I have seen others do it since. If you need to believe something bad enough, you *do.* She sat down on my bed and started crying again. "You could be like Jesus," she said. "Any boy could, if he wants to let it out, if he isn't too scared." This was booze talking. Her Jesus talk made me want to hit her. I got up and left the room.

Pop was puking into the kitchen sink. The kitchen was heavy with the stink of bourbon-puke. She could really pick the winners. I went into their bedroom and took the keys to the Pontiac off the dresser. Then I went out to the car and unlocked it. Pop, at the kitchen window, saw what I was up to. He rapped the glass with a knife. He came stumbling out of the house.

"Don't you dare touch my car," he said.

"Go to hell, you goddam Communist," I said, ramming the gear lever into first and spraying gravel.

I don't know why I called him Communist. He considered

himself self-educated and had a superior attitude. He read books and when he came to a good part he'd read it out loud, no matter who was there or whether or not they cared about the good parts. Pop drove a sandwich and coffee truck and parked it outside the gates of defense plants at lunchtime and at shift changes. That's how he made his living. It gave him a lot of time to read books. Walter Winchell said the Communists were in high places, getting ready to take over the country. They wanted to change how we thought. They had sneaky ways to do this and so you had to keep your guard up. Watch out for those teachers and professors who say things that downgrade our nation. I didn't worry about it. I figured my teachers were too stupid to be Communists. But Pop wasn't stupid. He'd put on is F. W. Woolworth reading glasses and say things like "Jesus Christ was not the son of God. He was just a good magician. He fooled the gullible with sleight-of-hand tricks and with hypnotic spells. Just add him to your list of egomaniac Jews." Mom hated this type of talk, since she was religious, or at least she believed in God and Jesus, and that it was bad luck to bad-mouth them. Pop deviled her for fun.

I drove over to Dick Drummond's house. It was still early enough for him to be up, though his folks were in bed. I honked the horn in his driveway, two longs and two shorts, so he'd know it was me. He came down in about a minute.

"What's happening, Shit-hook," he said. Dick was a wiseass. He got in the car and the first thing he did was switch on the radio. He searched around until he found the L.A. station that played nothing but R and B, which you could not find on a local station. Local DJs thought Johnny Ray was as cool as it got. They thought Les Paul and Mary Ford were hip.

I burned rubber coming out of his driveway and caught a yard of second-gear rubber in the street. Dick whistled, but he was being a wiseass. Dick had this chopped deuce coupe with a full-race '51 Merc engine in it and he could lay a mile of high-gear rubber shifting up from second doing sixty. So a

1949 Pontiac with a low-compression six didn't exactly im-
press him even though I was pretty good at nailing second
with a speed shift.

"Check the mirror, Dad," he said. "I think you left the
transmission in the road." Coming from Dick Drummond this
was a compliment. Dick was tall and lean. He could bench-
press a ton but he couldn't clean-and-jerk worth spit. No legs.

I headed out to the beaches. Dick had the radio turned up
full-blast. Lloyd Price was singing "Mail Man, Mail Man."
We were on a dark street in Pacific Beach. Dick said, "Stop
here a second, Dad." I pulled the car over to the curb. Dick
got out and walked over to a storefront. He raised his foot,
then looked over at me with a comical expression on his face.
Dick could be a bad actor. I knew he could do it if he was in
the mood. He was wearing his engineer boots. I shrugged. He
straightened his leg into the window and it bowed in, then
exploded. Dick danced back from the falling glass. Then he
reached into the window and picked up a suitcase. He carried
it to the car and threw it into the backseat. I popped the
clutch, laid yards of rubber, speed-shifted into second, caught
another yard of rubber. I hit third with another speed shift
but there wasn't any top-end power left and the Pontiac just
wobbled a little and flattened out.

Up in La Jolla where all the bankers and doctors live, Dick
had me drive alongside parked cars, real slow, while he
reached out of his window with a jack handle and knocked off
side mirrors and punched holes into windows. I saw a kid's
bike lying out on a sidewalk. I hopped the curb and mashed it.
Dick laughed.

Back down in Mission Beach we picked up a couple of girls.
They were gang girls who'd been dumped. Their hands were
tattooed. Dick had Julia and I had Inez. We drove up to
Torrey Pines and found a dark spot looking over the moonlit
ocean. On the radio: Earl Bostick playing "Flamingo." It was
real romantic, and Dick had Julia's pants off in half a minute,
but I had too much on my mind for it. Inez said, "What's

wrong, mon? You feeling out of it? *No quieres* nookie, mon?"
She was good-looking enough, but my mood was wrong. I just
didn't feel like it. She was in my lap. Her breath burned my
eyes. I turned the radio dial looking for more L.A. R and B
stations. I found Ray Charles. "Lonely Avenue." This made it
worse.

We drove the girls back to Mission Beach, then headed
home. We didn't talk. We listened to music.

"You okay, Dad?" Dick said when I let him off. "That was
prime muff, man. You missed some choice gash."

I shrugged. I backed out of his driveway and headed home.
Two blocks down the street I caught high-gear rubber by
floorboarding the fat Pontiac for a full three or four seconds
before I popped the clutch. There was a gravel patch on the
street. I slid. The rear fender hit a parked car. This made me
laugh. I drove home laughing, tears on my face, singing like
Lloyd Price.

It was late, almost morning. I let myself in through the
back way and went to my room. I felt ripped, like I'd been
into the wine. I turned on the BC-348 and looked for the
Voice of America. It was lost in static, on every band. Then I
found an American-sounding announcer saying how the Chinese were kicking the Americans out of Korea and how cities
in the U.S.A. were full of crime and how the whites hated the
Negroes. It was Radio Moscow. I shot Radio Moscow the
finger through the glowing dials. Then I went to bed.

"Jesus planned this out," Mom was saying. She was sitting on
my bed. The sun was up. She'd been talking, thinking that I
was awake even though my eyes were closed.

"What?" I said.

"He's gone, honey," she said. "Pop. He left an hour ago.
He's not coming back." She dabbed a tear out of the corner of
her eye. "He was destined to stay four years three months,
and now he's gone. I believe Jesus had this in mind for me."

My hand was sore. I looked at it. It had swollen up and the knuckles were raw and blue. I wondered what he had in store for me. I didn't believe there was anything in store for anyone. People just let themselves believe any bullshit that makes things easier for them. I said it before: This amazes me.

"Oh God, you gave him a terrific wallop, honey," she said.

"He's gone?" I said.

"I've never seen a terrific wallop like that."

"You mean he's not coming home tonight?"

She sneered, and for a second, though everyone always said she was a very pretty woman, she looked ugly. Then she smiled and was pretty again. "Not tonight, not any night. He's gone." She picked up my hand and kissed it. Her lips lingered on each battered knuckle as if to heal it. "I'll make you a nice breakfast, baby," she said.

Breakfast sounded good. It had been a long night. I was hungry.

Insulation

I AM HAUNTED by lightning. When the sky is streaked with jagged blue flame, when the blue-white tongues fork the earth, when the deep-throated anvils or hammerheads drift their weightless tons over my house murmuring my name in the oldest language men know, it is time for me to put insulating miles between myself and the weather or dash quickly to the rubberized shed in the backyard.

Conductivity runs in my family, reliably leapfrogging the generations. My father was not affected by voltage from the sky. My grandfather, however, was lifted out of his Adirondack lawn chair by a furious bolt arcing, literally, out of the blue: no storm, no cloud, no freak manifestation of ionized dust—just naked *a capella* lightning. The empty windless sky gave him false security as he sat reading the papers in the lovely light of an August afternoon. Grandmother was watching him fondly from the kitchen window as she stirred batter for peach cobbler, her specialty. Then the blue shaft, thick as God's middle finger, lifted him out of a satisfied doze as she watched, not in horror, but as one might relive the strangeness of one's dreams.

Shock and horror came later when she found herself in the yard standing at the edge of a burned area in the lawn, Grandfather still smoking at the ears and nose, his head a violent shade of vermilion, his hands clutching with the strength of a strangler his evening *Tribune*. Grandfather had flown up and over the back of the lawn chair, tossed like toy, the vermilion glow fading to something darker, a grim tattoo coarse and ugly, zigzagging from scalp to the conductive center just above the navel—our genetic fault line.

I am not superstitious. Just the opposite. I have degrees in mathematics and physics from a better-than-average university; I have made my living for twenty-two years by analyzing failure rates for the aerospace industry. I along with three colleagues designed the multipurpose Unplanned Event Record, which is now used universally.

But there was a close call last summer, and it changed everything, made me attractive in ways you would not imagine. Now I am preoccupied with insulation. I have had all the tall trees that once surrounded my house cut down. No TV antenna festoons the roof. I wear thick-soled rubber boots, even to church. (The steeple of our church was demolished by lightning a year ago. A char of skeletal beams points skyward, aspiring hope mutilated in a single, heaven-sent stroke.)

This is the truth we live by: A thousand repetitions of an event give you every right to expect the one thousand and first. This is what lies behind the reassuring phrase "Laboratory-Tested." You rely on it. Your warranties would not be worth the paper they are written on if not for such testing. This is why, despite your romantic longings for a less technically suffocating world, you do not believe in ghosts, mental telepathy, synchronicity, healing crystals, New Age music, or the zodiac. Go to two astrologers on the same day and you are likely to have a head-on collision with yourself on the expressway to confusion.

We have a fine new world. It works repeatedly, not in random fits and starts. We have what the ancients only dreamed of: reliability. Chicken guts, crystal balls, tea leaves, tarot cards, *I Ching* sticks, drug- or starvation-induced hallucinations do not produce the reliable and specific data required by jumbo-jet pilots, brain surgeons, market analysts, or, for that matter, wheat farmers. Bypass hard knowledge at your own risk. The "right-brain" enthusiasts, the gurus of intuition, are simply lazy. They want the shortcut that by-passes the difficult road between cause and effect. But no one gets off this road. Superstition remains superstition and it can only lead to the dark side of the mind, where illumination is scant and quirky, and those who travel there soon find themselves lost in the eclipse of reason.

I am haunted by lightning, but I believe in reason. I won't produce convincing evidence here. I am not trying to convince anyone. I am only trying to save my life, my sanity, though it is too late to save Eugenia.

Eugenia had come to fear me. If I reached across the breakfast table to touch her hand, she pulled back, goose bumps spreading up her arms. I would see her counting, though she tried to conceal it. I saw the slight up-and-down ratcheting of her eyes as they numbered the vertical peonies in each panel of wallpaper to distract herself from her fear. A goodbye kiss at the doorstep had become an ordeal for her. Our lips no longer met. We kissed the neutral air. In the bedroom—but I am not one to discuss the bedroom. Suffice it to say that when the forecast was bad, our nights were spent in the stomach-souring dread of distant thunder.

Eugenia had evolved rituals for such times that made the traditional Latin mass seem accessible and abrupt. She made the bed seven times, spraying, again and again, the underside of the blankets and sheets with an antistatic aerosol. She stood on a chair and unscrewed the light bulbs, thinking, foolishly, that by disconnecting them from their source she would safeguard the bedroom. For this same reason, she unplugged the radios, clocks, and television set. She kept crystals under her pillows. Sometimes they found their way into the bedclothes, where they scratched us. But she would not hear my complaints. A sudden breeze with the smell of rain or ozone in it sent her running. She claimed she could see the fine hair along my upper arms rise up as if from sinister sleep when ordinary unmenacing clouds drifted overhead.

She knew—to give her credit—that she was made up of positive and negative charges. We all are. The universe is. There is nothing else. This is the bottom line, perhaps the only line. The play of human events—a phantasmagoria imposed on an electromagnetic field. You knew this, of course. There is nothing more to say about it.

When the electron-hungry clouds—anvils, hammerheads—began to track me down with the same inexorable logic that describes the fall of an apple, Eugenia believed the danger was a consequence of moral fault. She made the sign of the cross before receiving me.

"I am entitled to some affection!" I have cried out on occasion.

"I am giving it to you," she'd remark. "This is it." But she'd wear electrician's gloves with rubber gauntlets that reached her elbows. Gum-soled shoes covered her feet. She coated herself from ankles to earlobes with a nonconductive oil used in the manufacture of electrolytic capacitors that smells vaguely of burning dogwood. I still keep a steel drum of this oil in the garage. The insulation, naturally, also involved the place of intimate connection. The bolt of passion, needless to say, was often neutralized by such rigorous precaution. I won't say more.

I have been to famous clinics. They find my blood, bones, and tissues normal in every way. They find no pockets of ionization, no secret micro lightning rods wired into my femurs or tibiae. My hair has been studied for excesses of copper, zinc, and iron—elements that might seduce electrons out of the sleeping ground. I have been wired to ultrasensitive meters while spinning dynamos were passed over my body, but the indicators did not leap.

The doctors advised psychiatry. They ignored the evidence I offered. One hundred years of empirical proof: grandfather in the lawn chair, *his* grandfather struck down in a pasture, the several attempts on me. My cousin Priscilla was electrocuted by her telephone during a storm. My eldest brother, Paul, his pacemaker dazzled by a faulty microwave oven, causing his heart to wreck itself with fibrillations; my young brother Warden dead on the putting green. And of course there's me: the scalp-tightening sensations whenever a storm gathers, and then the close call of last summer. Evidence. But evidence without theory is noise. I have no theory.

Desperate for a theory, I wrote to Dr. Helper. Helper is a psychologist who writes an advice column in our local paper. I signed my letter "Haunted." "Dear Haunted," he replied. "The abnormal fear of lightning is a well-documented phobia. Like the other common phobias—fear of the marketplace, fear of heights, fear of confinement—it can now be safely attributed to brain-chemistry deficits. Rest assured, you can be cured through appropriate medication. As for your 'evidence'—your 'close call'—please, in the future, do not go fishing in aluminum boats."

I didn't know the boat was aluminum. It was painted dark green and had a woody look to it. The seats were wood, the gunwales were wood, and the oars were wood. I saw wood, I believed wood. It was Ted Lardner's boat. I had checked the weather forecasts and there were no thunderstorms within two hundred miles. I cannot spend my weekends reading technical journals in my rubber shed. I need recreation.

I should have realized the boat was not wood by its action in the water, but Ted had distracted me with the tradition of sky burials in Tibet. The bones of the dead are crushed and mixed with yak butter so that the scavenging birds will eat the remains and carry them, along with the spirit of the deceased, into the sky. Ted teaches comparative culture at the community college and is endlessly fascinating, but even so, I should have been more conscious of the boat.

I caught a fish, then Ted caught a fish. I caught another fish, a trash fish, and then Ted caught a water snake. I saw a terrapin leaving a wake. There were mergansers, fish hawks, and an occasional heron. It was lovely, we had a fine time, and Ted, who makes his own guitars, talked melodiously of how lightning-struck wood is soft and easily worked. It bends cooperatively with applied heat and produces, in the finished product, an incomparable tone. He had his guitar with him, and when we began to believe the fishing would not improve, he strummed and sang. It was idyllic. Even so, I should have been more conscious of the boat.

"My guitar speaks," Ted said. "This is a concert guitar, the back and sides made of struck rosewood, the top of struck cedar."

But there were other voices speaking, and I heard them too late. "Looks like rain," Ted said.

"What?" I gasped. I swiveled about, rocking the boat.

"Boom, boom," Ted said and strummed, and then I heard it too: thunder filtered through trees and hills.

I dropped my pole, heard the gong of metal on metal, and it was then I realized the boat was made of aluminum, not wood. "Jesus, Ted!" I cried out. I picked up the oars, clambered into the rowing seat, and headed the craft back to the dock, which looked to be at least two miles away. Even as I bent to my labor, wind wrinkled the lake.

The first angry white billow appeared at the crest of a hill, and as if announcing its arrival, a basso-profundo roar caromed through the small green valley that held the lake and a few small farms. Unaware of my fear, Ted strummed folk tunes from the 1960s, while drawing peacefully on his pipe.

The last remaining god is weather, someone once said. Clouds are bundles of electrical charges. The earth yearns with free electrons for the upward leap. Overhead the great white muscle of stratocumulus gathered itself toward the lethal flex. The weightless tons drifted silently over us, staining the water dark green. I rowed hard. At last Ted noticed my terror. "Not to worry, old son," he said blandly. "Lightning can't strike twice in the same place, or haven't you heard?"

He held his lightning-struck guitar high and grinned. "We're safe," he said. "Guaranteed."

"There was fire in your mouth," Ted said later. "The water glowed so that you could see huge mackinaw trout eighty feet down. They looked like swimming angels."

All I remember is the taste of sweet onions, the flavor of lightning. You must survive in order to remember it, however. My brother Warden was killed on a golf course. Jean, his wife, was coming up behind, working her way out of a sand trap. It knocked him sideways, off the green, his putter a black wand in his dead fist. Jean said, "I bent down to give him CPR and smelled onions, but he'd only had fruit for lunch."

For some reason, I had my net in my hand as I rowed. The aluminum frame, I am told, turned into a hoop of fire. The oarlocks were welded to their seats. The oars splintered. The fish we caught were instantly cooked. Brass rivets melted and the boat opened. Ted swam, towing me behind. Though I cannot swim, I was extraordinarily calm. I give credit to the strike, which had momentarily reorganized my mental processes. I felt holy in the lake, on my back, Ted's hand gripping my collar, the sky blue and clear again above me as we made our slow way to shore. I believed I was dead and that Charon was towing me across the River Styx.

This mood stayed with me for a long time. I remember it so vividly that sometimes I believe it isn't a memory but an ongoing condition. "Your jacket filled up with light," Ted said. "You were a one-man monster movie." Ted is one of the lucky insulated ones. He can touch exposed house wiring and not feel the thrilling vibration of alternating current. "It was liquid light," he said. "I thought I saw your bones. They were red and alive under your shirt. I saw your heart."

My fillings had melted, burning my mouth. I developed a permanent cramp in the rictus muscles, forcing an engaging

gory. Once you hear the lifters, you begin to hear every-
g—tappets, timing gear, piston slap, the works. You can
r the carbon chipping off the cylinder walls. And then the
ension goes. I mean suspension of disbelief, right down
old grease hole."

efore he became a top romance fiction editor, Cadmus was
echanic. A literate mechanic who got tired of black
rnails, split knuckles, and coveralls. Now he wears laid-
unconstructed double-breasted suits by Ronaldus Sha-
k at a thousand dollars a copy, and gets his nails done
e a week.

hed eggs, bacon, toast, and Jolt—my breakfast. Jolt gets
nica into high gear. A second or third can flips her into
drive. Carlo, my son, says I've ruined my talent and now
killing myself. Carlo won't eat the food I cook. He eats
hed fish for breakfast. Clean protein sources and
ga-3 are his obsessions. He has grown up fearing choles-
and the triglycerides. He belongs to the Overinformed
ration. Educated daily by Donahue, Oprah, the evening
, and weekly by *20/20, 60 Minutes,* and the network
als designed to alarm and depress, the Overinformed
ration know the thousand paths to personal and collec-
atastrophe. They know who is poisoning the air, what
re poisoning it with, and they know the economic down-
f cleanup. They are privy to the timetable for the de-
ion of the ozone layer. They understand the global
ly the elimination of the Brazilian rain forests will pro-
Alzheimer's, AIDS, acid rain, the Greenhouse Effect,
isoning of the aquifers, and the extinction of humpback
s, rhinos, elephants, and the California condor define
uture. Even so, they tend to be a cheerful lot who cling
hopeful notion that we have not floundered past the
f no return, an optimism I don't share.
lo jogs to school wearing a smog mask. He buys expen-

smile on my face I was powerless to remove. Behind my back,
and sometimes to my face, I was called Smiling Jack. At work,
my lead engineer, Phil Stratton, a good man, tried to put a
stop to it but the name stuck nonetheless. Nicknames, however, were the least of my worries. Without warning, I had
become attractive.

In Kmart, car batteries inched toward me until they tee-
tered on their shelves. Computerized cash registers at my
approach gave out tiny electronic screams, losing track of
their sums. The ignition of my car would suffer from confused
timing, often leaving me stranded. My Timex flowed backwards. Eugenia's hairpins, like a caravan of army ants, followed me out of the bathroom.

There is an explanation for everything. This is no idle as-
sertion. It is the philosophy that made the modern world
possible. Next to Newton in my den is a portrait of Einstein.
The thoughtless believe the latter superseded the former. No.
The latter, using the same methods, holding the same belief
in *reason,* and guided by the same faith in the certainty of
explanation, *extended* the former. If you lose your belief in
explanation, you have lost your mind. Your mind is a representation of a five-century-old trend. What is preparing to
replace it offstage, in the wings, grinning in the shadows? I
tremble to think. So should you.

One day I will find an explanation for Eugenia's tragic
death. I could not attend her funeral because of my relentless
smile. Her relatives might have understood, but in my grief I
found it monstrous, a senseless affront. We are electrical. But
shall I declare a conspiracy of electrons? Should I fix blame
on the microcosmic field of positive and negative charges?
Should I say my vulgar smile in the face of my loss was
arranged by an evil jocularity of atoms?

She was insulated. Boots, gloves, electrolytic oil, emotional
distance. Yet the bolt found her. There was no storm. I admit
to anger. A man is entitled to some affection. Yet prolonged
contact frightened her. She ran, stumbling in her boots,

through the house, from imagined danger. I could not help myself: I thundered. I roared. A man is entitled to some affection. I did not feel attractive, though a mob of paper clips, straight pins, tacks, scraps of foil, swarming in the air like gnats when the bright afternoon is cooled by storm clouds, followed me as I roared in pursuit.

I found her in the laundry room, wedged between the dryer and washer. I felt calm, reasonable, prepared to discuss the issue in a rational way, but I knew I was also roaring at her. She looked up at me as if at a bad sky. "Eugenia," I said, but the syllables came out as claps of thunder.

Something kicked her. It reached me as a spent corona, a blue glow that washed over me like a wave, and, like a wave, receded. It came from the 220-volt outlet, domestic lightning, wanting *me*, I believe, but passing through Eugenia en route. I tried to dial 911 but the phones were hot. Storm clouds arrived on the scene, warning me to keep silent, keep insulated, whispering my fate in small cyclones that bent my neighbor's trees and carried spirals of dust into the darkening air.

I have faith that a scientific explanation for these events will soon occur to me.

Her Alabaster Skin

THIS IS MY study, there is my desk, ar
and on the desk is my manuscript, the gr
it, waiting for me, but I am not ready
LaMonica yet. I need one more can of J
through the rooms of my house, one n
myself about my life and the dead end it

I need another fifteen minutes to
Veronica. It is 9:00 A.M., and I need to ge
pages of *Moist Days, Dry Nights* writte
Cadmus Xenedes, is getting nervous abo
ing down, you're losing RPMs, Gregory,
a schedule for Veronica. You are off the

I write three Veronica LaMonicas a y
I've turned in only two. *Heart Murmurs* a
Cadmus sent me a Macintosh to spee
haven't uncrated it yet. Veronica, a tr
understand, or approve of, high techno
need for her understanding or approva
ninety-five thousand copies in six mon
visible to the naked eye in the romantic

"*Rough Hands* has torque," Cadmu
in manuscript. "Torque, and high com
you know? Like you can't hear the va
of these junkers and by God you can

sive, organically grown vegetables with his allowance. He puts a tablespoon of cider vinegar into every glass of water he drinks—water that has been filtered by reverse osmosis—to enhance digestion. He reads excerpts to me from articles in *Organic Living Now,* his favorite magazine. He wants to discourage me away from eggs, red meat, french fries, whole milk, cheese, butter, caffeine, and white bread. Which is to say, my generation's notion of *real food.* He's a bore, but a beautifully healthy bore. His mother moved out a year and a half ago, unable to put up with his organic-living extremism and my sad-sack end-of-the-road pessimism.

Veronica won't come again today. I hope she's only being moody. I fiddle with *Moist Days, Dry Nights* for an hour, trying to trick some life into it while fighting off a caffeine-fueled headache. "Her alabaster skin seemed cool as rare porcelain to Victor Carrenga," I write, trying to get the first love scene into gear. But once in gear, the engine dies. Could be a fuel problem, could be the electrical system. Could be both. Out of gas, out of juice. (Cadmus's lingo is catchy.) "Palpitating in the delirium of anticipation . . ." Jesus. These Latinate multisyllabics are like sugar in the gas tank. The engine gets gummed up and freezes, the plugs fouled with smarm. Carlo comes into my office, eating yogurt. "Stuck, huh, Dad?" he says.

"Aren't you going to be late for yoga practice?" I say. Among other things, Carlo is a kibbitzer. When Veronica is here and cooking I don't mind. But when she's on the rag, dismal in old bathrobe and carpet slippers, hiding from the world, every interference is a major roadblock with no detours.

"Why don't you write a real novel sometime, Dad?" Carlo asks. "I mean, isn't that what you set out to do twenty years ago?"

I swivel around and regard this yogurt-slurping teenaged

hypochondriacal repository of moral wisdom. "You've got a complaint, Carlo? Correct me if I overstate the case, son, but didn't Veronica just buy you a three-year-old Celica? Doesn't she provide you with a steady supply of wheat-germ oil, oat bran, pesticide-free fruits and vegetables, organically grown *rice?* Are you sure you want me to fire Veronica? Do you really want me to join the mainstream of starving writers who drag Integrity around with them like dead whales? 'I'm poor, but I'm clean,' they say. 'Nobody fucks with my dead whale,' they say."

During this speech, Carlo has been scraping the bottom of his yogurt container. "I think you protest too much, Pop," he finally says. "I think there's a real novel in you dying to get out and that's why Veronica is out of town."

"Bull*shit.*"

"Veronica would never use three multisyllable words in one sentence," he says, peering at the page in my ancient Smith Corona. "She may write hog slop but she's still a pro."

"Carlo?"

"What, Dad?"

"Get out."

He ignores me, caresses the uncrated computer. "If you're not going to use this Mac Cadmus sent you, how about giving it to me?"

Two hours later and the first love scene is still parked at the curb. Victor Carrenga is the biggest tongue-tied klutz when it comes to seduction since Miles Standish. "Oh, my dearest Flavia," Vic says, stroking her hand or arm or shoulder. He wraps his sinewed arm around her waist—they are in Flavia's [   ] (plug in: garden, drawing room, studio, etc.), the moon is full and partially shrouded in clouds—night-blooming jasmine wounds the air with sweetness—in the middle distance, the sound of a [   ] (plug in: cello, violin, harp, etc.) can be heard. His arm is steel, her will is weak, her cool alabaster skin in the moonlight stirs his manhood. She feels something move within her, something warm and [   ] (plug in the euphemized bodily secretions).

Where the hell are you, Veronica?

The thunk of mail falling from the slot in the front door gives me an excuse to bail out of my office. A fat letter from Cadmus plus a thin letter from my ex-wife's lawyer.

"Gregory, for Christ's sakes," Cadmus begins, "what is going on here? I read the crankcase sludge you sent me. I'm asking you this—who wrote them for you, Fulton Foulbreath Muffdiver? It reads like something out of the *Journal for the Society of Pudpounders, Dingleberries, and Buttpoppers.* Where did you pick up all those lacy words and pussywhipped sentence structures, from Henry Hollownuts James? Where is my ballsy Veronica? Look, Gregory, I'm telling you as a friend, not just as your editor and spiritual mechanic, this lemon has no *torque.* You've blown your head gaskets, hombre. Also, you're timing gear is stripped. If you had made it to the top of the hill you could coast home, but you're still in the parking lot, kid. Okay, never mind. You'll come through. You always do, don't you? Especially when the mortgage payment comes due. This is just a rough spot in the road. Take a detour, or go back and start over. I like your first sentence. Start from there, throw the other ninety pages into the dumpster. 'Flavia Lockridge decided once and for all to leave Plainfield, New Jersey, and try her luck out west as a landscape photographer.' Now, Greg, old cock, that fucking *drives.* And keep in mind, you are not Emerson. (*Fittapaldi,* I mean; though you're not R. Waldo, either.) Oh, by the way, Veronica is on a tour. She'll be in your B. Dalton's next Saturday. Go buy a book. You ever read the shit you write? It ain't all that bad." A wad of manuscript pages is stapled to the letter, each page heavily scarred with red ink.

The letter from Jasmine's—my ex-wife's—lawyer is blunt. He wants—and will sue to get—a modest increase in the monthly alimony check, having discovered that *Rough Hands* was a modest success. When I get back to my office, Veronica is *there.* I can almost smell her. "Flavia Lockridge decided once and for all to leave Plainfield, New Jersey, and try her luck out west as a landscape photographer. It was just one more thing her husband would object to, but Roger's objections no longer mattered to her." Elated, I jump out of my chair and head for the kitchen for another bolt of Jolt, but when I get back, Veronica's gone again: "Purposefully, and without a modicum of regret," I type, "Flavia envisioned a rehabilitated life-style." I take my hands off the keyboard and look at them, as if they are to blame for this godawful prose. But it's a vapor lock of the brain. I pull onto an off ramp and coast to a dead stop in the middle of nowhere.

Saturday at the mall is like medieval Budapest. A covered street of shops, throngs of shoppers and idlers, street performers—mimes, jugglers, string quartets, beggars in the guise of fund-raisers for worthy causes—becomes a thriving example of human commerce at its cheeriest. I love the damn places, but regret that they have sucked the life out of the city center. But the city is a dinosaur, grown too large and inefficient and dangerous for survival. The mall is the return to safe and colorful village life. Artificial? You bet, like everything else the hairless big-brained congenitally moody bipeds do. The mall is one of our little last gasps, a quaint invention, much like the romance novels of Veronica LaMonica.

"Veronica" is on time, seated at her card table in front of B. Dalton's, a stack of *Rough Hands* in front of her. She is stunning. Literally. I carry a mental image of Veronica that has evolved over the years since her first book. She defined herself gradually for me, moving from the generalities of cliché (tall, willowy, full-breasted, chestnut hair cascading down her splendid Sigourney Weaver shoulders, her alabaster skin seemingly illuminated from the interior by moonlight, and so on) to the specifics that imply an individual (intelligent eyes the gray-green of the sea under a bright overcast, eyes that often have a slightly self-deprecating smile in them; the prominent aquiline nose of old Florentine aristocracy; a generous but not foolish mouth implying a sensuality that is sophisticated yet childlike in its ability to appreciate every experience as new and original). And so when I saw her—the woman hired to play her on this book-signing tour—and saw that she conformed almost exactly to the ghost I'd been carrying around in my head for six years, I *was* stunned. I knew my publisher, Candelabra Romances Inc., had been sending surrogate Veronicas out on signing tours for several years, but I'd never been interested enough in the scheme to go check one of them out.

"Hi," I say, approaching her card table and picking up one of the gaudily illustrated paperbacks. "Selling many books?"

She smiles up at me, and her Veronica LaMonica teeth are just as I had envisioned them. "Oh, yes. Quite a few, in fact. *Rough Hands* has been one of my most successful efforts."

For her sake, I don't want to let this go too far. "Look," I say. "I'm Gregory Pastori."

She gives me a blank look, her smile still in place, and I realize that she hasn't been told who writes these trashy teasers. "I'm the real . . ."

But I'm cut off by a customer, a women in her forties, hausfrau all the way, who sweeps up an armload of the luridly illustrated paperbacks and says, "I'm getting six for some friends, and another one for me. I'm afraid my copy is worn out—I've read it at least a dozen times!" The woman, humble and tongue-tied before celebrity, is silent as the books are signed. She practically genuflects when she leaves. "Veronica" looks up at me with those incomparable eyes and says, "I'm sorry, you were saying?"

"I was just going to say that I'm a writer, too."

This doesn't interest her. Her eyes become horizon-gray.

"I'm sorry," she says. "I am unable to help you."

"I . . ." My jaw hangs agape. I hadn't expected *pity*. It's as if I'd told her I had some incurable skin fungus.

"Writing is a difficult, solitary profession," she says, touching my wrist, a nurselike gesture. "Most fail. I do not recommend it. On the other hand, if you feel you must write, then, by all means, write. But do not ask other writers to provide shortcuts for you. If you have real talent, then your work will eventually be published. And even then you may find your work does not appeal to a large audience. No, it is a difficult, solitary profession, and I do not recommend it."

She has not only learned her speech well, she has the acting ability to give it authenticity. She looks world-weary and jaded now, as she lights up a Pall Mall and blows smoke into my chest. The cigarette is a prop—she doesn't inhale and she stubs it out after two more frowning puffs. "Well," I say, "I only do it as a hobby. I hardly ever send my little stories out to publishers and such."

"There are more satisfying hobbies," she says, "than cooping yourself up in a little room typing prose fiction all day long. Why don't you take up golf or fly fishing? It's much healthier."

It's easy for writers to be cruel. We live in a constant state of self-doubt. We carry an unborn twin next to our spleens, a sneering monster who lets us know how elegantly or comically we fail. Sometimes we can let this monster twin speak for us. I'm a little surprised that Candelabra Romances Inc. coached her in that little-known peculiarity of the trade.

"Though I regard writing as my hobby, I *am* a published author," I let my snotty twin say, his words friendly as honed steel. "I've had work in *Over the Edge* and in *New Age Cannibal.*"

"Really?" she says, her writerly veneer mottling. "I didn't realize, Mr. . . . I'm sorry, I didn't catch your . . ." She's all goofy and out of synch. I can hear her valve lifters kissing her rocker arms. She's losing manifold pressure.

"Pastori," I say, extending a coolly elegant but forgiving hand. "Gregory Pastori."

"It is always a pleasant surprise to encounter another published author while out in the field," she says, reading her invisible cue card.

"Isn't it?" I say. I decide to strike while her timing gear has jumped its grooves. "How about lunch, Miss LaMonica?"

For an instant I can see behind the mask—the cool, evaluating eyes, the full lips pursed in judgment. She could be an executive secretary at Candelabra, which would make her a boss without portfolio or the power to kick ass. Responsibility without authority. One of the civilized world's best-kept secrets is that nothing in it works without executive secretaries or administrative assistants, also known as Girl Fridays back in the primitive days of unashamed sexism. "Why not?" she says gamely. "I've just got one condition—no shoptalk, okay?"

"There's a great Thai joint upstairs," I say. "My treat."

"The signing is over at three. How about an early supper?" she says, her sea-gray eyes pulling me in like a friendly riptide.

The magicians who keep Candelabra Inc. at the top of the pulp-romance field know what they are doing. "Veronica" not only looks the part, she has the qualities of mind and heart of someone who might have written *Firestorms in the Blood* (Veronica's first effort, written with the innocent joy of a beginner), and we hit it off instantly. After our early supper we get slightly bombed at a place that hires old gray-haired rhythm-and-blues artists of the forties and fifties. We dance to the mellower numbers, the Ivory Joe Hunter–style tunes, and even though our era was the sixties, we get sentimental and misty-eyed and we hold that mood all the way home to my bed, where [   ]

Plug in one of the following:

(1) Her alabaster skin, in the soft glow of moonlight that fell through the casement, inspired his urgent manhood to complete the bonding of kindred souls.

2) He hadn't felt this hot for a woman since the night his ex got loose on Pernod and wanted to do it standing up in a Parisian pissoir, front to rear.

(3) His crankshaft never knew such RPMs. His super-charged turbine was a tornado of power. She opened her throttle wide and her engine roared, putting out almost more torque than he could handle.

(4) All of the above.

I wake up alone the next day and am tempted to believe the worst: schizophrenic breakdown. Daylight dreaming in 3D. Brain-cell fission. The Veronica I have been piecing together all these years has reached critical mass and has come to life, a Frankenstein creature of the half-real world of psychotic delusion. I pull the blanket over my head to shield myself from this line of thought, then I hear her voice, laughing in the kitchen.

Veronica and Carlo are having a breakfast of sliced mango and yogurt. Carlo is enjoying himself immensely. The sappy grin on his face is not typical. Usually, at this time of the morning, he's brooding over the newspaper, collecting more evidence of mankind's dark fate.

"Dad!" he says. "Veronica's terrific!"

"I know," I mumble, exchanging a quick glance with Veronica, who is wearing—appropriately for an alter ego—a pair of my pajamas.

If Carlo picks up my meaning, he's playing innocent. "She's into organics," he says. "Not just superficially, either. She knows her nutrient chemistry!"

"I know," I mumble again, the taste of her chemistry still with me.

Veronica pushes a bowl of yogurt-buried mangoes in front

of me. "Have some of this," she says. "It will start to clear your system."

"I believe my system is clear, thank you," I say significantly. "I'd rather have eggs and bacon, if it won't make you two gag."

"That's the sort of diet that will guarantee you'll be spending the last ten years or so of your life in and out of hospitals," she says. "Eating properly won't necessarily extend your life, but it will improve its quality. You'll die healthy."

"I've got no complaints about quality," I mumble.

Veronica excuses herself then from the table to get dressed. She has to catch a ten-o'clock plane. When she's gone, Carlo leans toward me and whispers, "Dad, she's *sensational*. Are you going to marry her?"

It is not a recommended feature of quality parenting to tell your teenage son that he has his head up his ass. I dip into my yogurt, giving myself time to restructure my response. "Carlo, do you know who she is?"

"Sure, Dad! She told me. She's Veronica LaMonica, the *real* one. I mean, the fake real one. The public one. The one that *doesn't* write soft porn, and you've got to give her credit for that."

"Did you tell her, wiseass, that *I* am Veronica LaMonica?"

"No way! You can do that later. But that's no big deal. No one takes that garbage seriously anyway. What difference could it make to her, or to anyone, who actually *writes* the fluff? The whole series could be done by a computer. Why do you think Cadmus sent you the Mac? They've probably got software now that can do three-quarters of the work."

In spite of my own misgivings about what I do for a living, Carlo's little demonstration of ingratitude annoys me. "I am an artist," I say, mustering dignity. "Oh, not a great artist, not even a mediocre one, but I am an artist just the same. Words, Carlo, don't come that easy, even the old worn-out ones."

Carlo, by way of apology, waves an impatient hand across

the table a few times. "Okay, okay. But think of the advantages, Dad. I mean, you could write the books, and Veronica—or whatever her real name is—as your wife could do the interviews and signings and such. You guys could get supercoordinated."

I head for the fridge for my morning can of Jolt. My brain isn't working fast enough to keep up with Carlo's hyperactive nervous system, which he must have inherited from his mother. Why is he suddenly playing the marriage broker? Because she knows her nutrient chemistry?

"Are you feeling all right, son?" I say.

"Dad, I *like* her. She's the neatest lady you've brought home since you and Mom split." His impassioned, clear-eyed face makes me wonder if I, as a child, ever had such intensity, such belief. I decide, no, nothing approaching Carlo's directness and honesty ever troubled my sly, trouble-dodging path through life. I am a professional taker of the Easy Way, and have been ever since I learned that my parents, my teachers, and most adults gave you what you wanted once you gave them what they wanted. This matured into a Philosophy of Life. Some call it Pragmatism, such as our current leaders. It is sold to the world, these days, as Virtue. Why else did I allow myself to become Veronica? Why did I give up my small but impractical dream of writing from the heart? The sigh I release has more meaning in it than I want Carlo to grasp, and I cover it with a phlegmy fit of romantically tubercular coughing.

"Well, hell, I like her too, Carlo—"

"Besides, Dad," he says, blurting out the secret of his attraction, "she's a professional *accupressurist!* She's actually studied holistic healing techniques. You'd never have a caffeine headache again! And don't tell me you don't get them. You've got one right now."

I am relieved as well as saddened by this. Carlo's budding pragmatism will diminish him a bit, but it will also secure the quality of his life just as effectively as nutritive responsibility.

"Jesus, Carlo," I say. "What did you do, *interview* her for the job?"

"Talking about me?" Veronica says, dressed and stunning in the doorway.

"Dad has a caffeine headache," Carlo announces.

"Poor baby," Veronica says. She stands behind me and touches my temples with her fingertips. She finds the hard, choppy pulse there, and applies a slowly rotating pressure that seems to siphon off pain instantly. She slides her fingertips to the back of my skull, then down my neck to my shoulders, the dull ache trailing after them like the brats of Hamlin after the Piper. She picks up my hand and squeezes the pad of flesh between thumb and forefinger and a bolt of pure pleasure passes through me, as if all my endorphins have been dumped into my bloodstream. Orgasm without friction, sweat, sticky residue, or romance. There might be a market for it.

"Don't stop, Veronica," I beg, without shame, when she returns my hand to my lap.

"I've got to get to the airport," she says. "I've got a signing and a couple of personal appearances in L.A. tomorrow. This may surprise you two, but it isn't easy being Veronica LaMonica."

Not much surprises me these days. The nation is shocked to learn that the captains of oil tankers will lie drunk in their cabins as their ships drift toward the gutting reef, or that airline crews often get hammered in an airport bar before takeoff. But the suicidal irresponsibility of those charged with guiding our delicately structured world seems entirely reasonable to me. Oh, our postmodern devices are indeed the wonders the technocrats make them out to be. Unfortunately, the hairless, big-brained, congenitally moody biped is always *behind the wheel*—drunk, below or above deck, distracted, poorly trained, recently divorced or two-timed, underfucked, overdrawn, doped, delusional, or just sleepy. Eventually, in one way or another, he'll allow the front tires to hit the soft shoulder and we'll all go screaming over the cliff.

I want to be wrong about this. But the caveman who invented the ax probably dropped his first redwood on his family. When I think of Carlo and his Overinformed Generation, I get mildly optimistic. Generally inept as parents, we have nonetheless raised a generation of kids—with excellent surrogate parenting from Donahue, Oprah, Geraldo, *60 Minutes*, *20/20*, etc.—who are too *scared* to go to sleep at the wheel. I would trust Carlo at the helm of the *Exxon Valdez*, or in front of the control panel at Three Mile Island. I just don't want to sit in a bar with him for the greater part of an afternoon.

Carlo is behind the wheel *now* in fact, taking me to the airport. I don't know whether he talked me into this or whether I'm just escaping his nonstop, logically impeccable harangue, which has gone on now for two days.

"I can't just go to L.A.," I told him. "I don't even know her itinerary."

"Call up Cadmus, he'll know," he said, not missing a beat.

"You wily devil," Cadmus said, when I asked for "Veronica's" schedule. "Mr. Goodwrench to the rescue, eh? You won't regret it, Gregory. The lady—Paula Voorhees—has great torque, even in overdrive. Measurable in foot-pounds, buddy. That's what they say around the shop. Fantastic gear ratios. And if that isn't enough, she's also got the classic lines of an XKE Jag. But listen, you'd better keep both hands on the wheel with one eye on the tachometer and the other eye on the road, if you follow me."

I didn't follow him at all, but then I hardly ever did. Cadmus can be as arcane as a Zimbabwean diviner of chicken entrails. Besides, I wasn't looking for anything that needed a lot of long-range planning, Carlo's arguments notwithstanding. Even with a thing as predictable as a romance novel, I advance the plot one day at a time, hoping for little surprises that make the morning's work fun in spite of the fact that I'm following a road map. You take what you get, and sometimes what you get is not a poke in the eye with a sharp stick. Which is my humble hope for the world.

Carlo wants to carry my bag into the terminal—to make sure I get on the plane—but I tell him, "Don't worry, be happy, we're all going to fall off the edge of the world anyway," which makes him frown because he knows better than I do how close we are to the brink. I give him a bear hug and a kiss, for he is my son and I love him more than Donahue and Oprah do and he needs to know it. He wants me and the planet to have a second chance. And a second chance is the sweetest blessing any of us can hope for.

Rudderless Fiction: Lesson 1
(A Correspondence Course)

STARTING OUT: Decide on a version of yourself you can live with. (Sweet, rank, deluded, wise, thick, brassy, naive, monstrous—this will be your point-of-view character.) Notice we didn't say, Decide on what your story will be about. Let's put that on the back burner. On the front burner: character. Your first assignment—wear the clothes, for one full week, your father (if female, substitute "mother") would approve of. Now note, in detail, how you feel about your life achievement to date. Do you fear you will be found out? Some say this fear is an essential quality of the writer's personality. Entertain, for the moment, the child's awful notion of Mother and Father in primal embrace. Play with the red fiber of your soul in the titillating way a cat strings out the internal organs of a bird, then pretend you are dealing with a character whose name is, for instance, Don, Barb, or the Loner.

Say Don's life is a mess. Say his wife just walked, preferring a young buck with artistic sensitivity named Stu. Or say Barb's husband, Helmut, decides to move into his secretary's apartment and then, a week later, Barb's sweet retriever, Love Me Do, dies of a twisted intestine. You get the idea. We call this "The Rack" (Lesson 2). I got on the bus in Phoenix, hoping never to see that town again. Or, I was on the bus to Albuquerque when this loner sitting next to me decides to get friendly. "Tell me true, Bud," he says, "you hate me, don't you? And you don't even know me, right? This's been going on all my life." In each of the above, the writer has "Hit The Ground Running" (Lesson 3).

Are we going to have a knuckle-biting stroll through the troubled thickets of family, or a ball-busting adventure among the wrongheaded and disoriented? These are the two categories we recommend. (Some have combined the two with rewarding results.) Which one you choose will reflect your life to date, and what you've been able to make of it. Have you been through the mill and *still* not gotten wise to the "Setup" (Lesson 11), or are there cracks of light beginning to leak through? Story will help you decide. If nothing else, story is a "teacher."

Story. Defining "story" is like trying to define "food." You know what food is, but there is such a huge variety you know that one cuisine will seem utterly alien or absurd to habitués of another. You need training in the cuisines, you need training in the microbiology of organic matter, the chemistry of nutrition. You need to be able to discuss the compounds found in various food groups as if they were old friends. A story, as food, is a snack, a good meal, or a feast—depending on what you've got stashed in your "Deep Freeze" (Lesson 35). We feed on the lives of those who are starving.

You know, I was young once, too. I'll never forget the first time I tasted *Homard à l'absinthe.* You're no bargain, my first wife had said. I was twenty-six years old but still wet behind the ears. She had a great influence on me, Bunny did. She was from New York—Yonkers—and I had come east out of the hills of South Dakota. I was the typical farm boy, complete with ankle-high brogans, drawl, and double-breasted suit in a single-breasted era. Educated but ignorant. I thought "missionary position" had something to do with church politics. I had a good job and supported her and our three little tykes quite well. Soon I became in charge of the Venturi Design Unit of Mikkelson Carburetors. You're no bargain, she said. I honestly believed I was a bargain. Honey, you're no bargain

either, I said. You're a *steal*. But charm doesn't work. She
jabbed a thrusting finger into her yawning mouth. I stormed
out of the house—by that time we were living in Piscata-
way—and got drunk at La Maison de la Lune. In the lounge, I
met Ardith Sorrentina (Lesson 6). "Let's eat some of that
homard," I said. Why do I bring this up? Let us just say, for
the moment, that art must hold the mirror up to life. Not the
flat mirror. Avoid the flat mirror at all costs. Remember the
fun-house mirrors of your youth? Convex, concave, rippled,
cracked. The thin man looks fat, the fat man looks murder-
ously lean, the dependable man looks multiple and deranged.
Each of us has but one mirror. If yours is flat, take our course
in Architectural Drafting.

I am on the bus to Albuquerque and this old boy gets on at
Las Cruces. He's wearing a beat-up canvas backpack that
issues puffs of mold spore every time he shifts his weight. His
greasy gray hair is long and snaky. I worry he is going to sit
next to me, but he takes a seat next to this little old lady two
rows up. The guy starts talking to her. She tries to ignore him.
She takes up her knitting or crochet work, and leans toward
the window. But he's hard to ignore. He's on a mission of wild
truth-seeking. He thinks he can solve his life if he keeps
telling it. You can hear him over the roar of the diesel engine,
you can hear him over the wind of travel, you can hear him
over the crackle of collapsing cells inside your beleaguered
brain. He's droning on about how even his mother did not like
him:

She barred him from her breast.

She put him up for adoption but there were no takers.

In school he applied for the role of Outcast and was unani-
mously accepted.

He was the cooperative butt of playground pranks.

He became a masturbatory loner who found work as an
appliance repairman.

He pretended to be lame once, to attract the pity of strangers. He retains the limp of this ploy, even though it got him nothing.

He married a woman less attractive in most ways than himself, and yet it was *she* who grew to despise *him.*

(The woman he is telling this to is calling to the driver for assistance. The driver warns the man to shut up or he'll put him off the bus right here, ten miles from Socorro.)

A man and a woman are having lunch in Tucson, say. It doesn't matter where. Writers who worry themselves about "where" want a safety net under their aerialists as if local flora and fauna, established gentries, social blight, family, the various institutions that give a world its purpose and shape, were a base reality that persists with some sort of metaphysical integrity beneath our squandered lives. Forget about it. There is no such net. The aerialists are balanced on thin wires above pure abyss. At its best, "where" is an *emblem* of pure abyss. Underscore this, too: We live in a context of unbroken ignorance. God will love you if you take this to heart. This is the one constant you can rely on (though the propaganda that convinces you otherwise is growing more sophisticated daily). It is the single, timeless truth that informs (paradoxically) your work. Your assignment now is to go out and study the paintings of Edward Hopper, all the time repeating to yourself: We are the aerialists. We are the abyss. Between each of us there is no net. My home, my town, my nation—they will not catch me when I fall.

I felt myself falling through black bottomless space. You're no bargain, she said. You're no bargain either, I said later that evening, meaning it now, which more or less completed the rift. How did it begin? Let me count the ways. *Mea culpa:* I was less attentive after Denise was born. Why did we name our children Dennis, Denise, and Daniella and then *re*name them Perry, Penny, and Patsy? There is no overestimating human frivolity. If one day we are replaced by supercomputers with robotic features, I would be last to complain. (We are halfway there, now that quantum theory has given us the 85-nanometer chip. Chips smaller—but more reliable—than brain cells will soon be on the market.) Are you finished? she would ask, cool and immobile as marble. Stung, I would withdraw from her, angry but spent. (When writing about sex, it is best to understate; Lesson 12.) Is there a happiness that does *not* collapse like withered flesh into desiccated bone? Do not show me a fictional denial. Do not produce the latest Burning Bush Romance as proof positive that love triumphs over all. Assignment: Go out and get half shit-faced and think about this.

Let's return to the couple in the restaurant that may or may not be in Tucson, Arizona. What is going on between them is partly submerged in an "Artistry of Gestures" (Lesson 5). Everything in life has a signboard on it, but it's invariably the *wrong* signboard. (Be alert: The world is painted with splendid lies.) Think of the iceberg's sea-hidden five-sixths. The loner on the bus is the narrator's iceberg. Don Bremerton stirred his coffee even though he had not used the cream or sugar. "I feel so displaced, Angela—it's as if you've restructured your thinking about us," he said. Don took pride in his ability to put nervous strangers at ease. He had perfected mannerisms and verbal techniques to defuse their paranoia, stomach pains, and even boredom. But none of his methods seemed to have an effect on Angela. Angela looked at him over the elegant, enamel-hard menu. "I'm sorry?" she said, a distracted Gioconda smile moving her lips imperceptibly. Don swallowed with difficulty. He knew that smile, how it made him feel as useless as a canceled stamp. . . .

Here is embryonic melodrama *in situ.* This is like a silver wind chime touched by the first gusts of a storm, whereas another proto-story might bring to mind an alley full of garbage cans being knocked around by feral dogs.

I saw a woman in a restaurant drink twenty containers of

nondairy creamer as if they were thimbles of good whiskey: incident. Incident: A large blond man in a good suit asked me for spare change. He was hungry, he said. I said, The hell you are, you're just greedy for abuse. But incidents are not stories. There is no story in a bothersome old man getting kicked off a bus. There is no story in Don saying, Have it your way, Angie baby, and then strutting out of the restaurant, flipping off the world. He can't pull the Gordian tangle out of his own brain as if it were a slipknot. We *need* dependencies. We need to see how the cranky and spurious are really the "Universal in Costume" (Lesson 46). This is how we recognize our common lot. These writers will die for your sins, which are also their sins. They will give you all they know and much more. The great poets have it: "Give the initiative to the word." "Death is the mother of beauty." "We think by feeling. What is there to know?" "Don't claim it and the sea belongs to you." "People possess four things that are no good at sea: anchor, rudder, oars, and the fear of going down." And, of course, "Were beth they biforen us weren?" These are your basic articles of faith. Repeat them as you once repeated, in the darkness of childhood, the Lord's Prayer.

I found myself going down alone: My rudder and anchor were the bottle. I say, "Thank Jesus for the bottle, even though it led to my professional ruin" (Lesson 49). I could not direct the dozen young engineers who needed my guidance. I no longer cared about venturi design. I went on the road, discovered Beth Zanknor. She liked to fuck and drink and argue. She had a husband somewhere in the Far East, repairing short-range radar sets for the army. Beth liked to say, "Clyde, the future is the future but the past is what you make it." She called all men Clyde. She had long skinny toes and was able to pick up magazines with her feet without tearing or wrinkling the pages. "You've had three months of Beth Zanknor," she said, "and I've had three months of you, Clyde. Whaddya say we call it an afternoon while we're ahead?"

Life is not a perfect grid, marked off, leveled, easy to look at, predictable. Hold the mirror up. But first, make sure your mirror has an *honest* bend in it: It must always reflect more, and sometimes less, than is "out there." Don't bend it to be "Fashionable" (Lesson 50). Your next assignment: Check-out-your-mirror. Examine it. Be sure you can abide its irregular shapes. Can you stand to have people whose respect you'd like to court call you Liar? Lunatic? Dipshit? Fraud?

"The hairy truth lives coarse and timeless under the bald lie." I think T. S. Eliot said that. Fiction is a lie (since *we* are) and poetry is the supreme fiction. You must find your ounce of poetry in the bus to Albuquerque, even if you wind up hopelessly entangled with the confused ramblings of unredeemable bores. Don married Angela on a bright afternoon in Tucson. He was young and dazzled by his own prospects. Over the years they've had four children and now Don finds himself locked into a hateful job sorting through stacks of legal papers for a government agency that oversees federal loans to new businesses involved in aerospace subcontracting. How did he get into this? Don is thirty-five, Angela is thirty-one, and both of them are lonely. Maybe Angela believes her beauty is beginning to fade and she associates this with the idea of Lost Opportunities. Known for her calmness in the face of domestic calamity, she is now visited by panic attacks. These usually afflict her in the early hours of the morning, 3:00 A.M. say, the hour of the wolf, as the poet so aptly called it. Her pills, powerful as they are, merely dull the beast. Her behavior becomes intriguingly unpredictable. Where are your sympathies here? With Don, with Angela, or with Stu Stormovik, the landscape painter Angela has started an affair with? Your sympathies had better be everywhere; they had better be with Don, Angela, Barb, Stu, Helmut, Love Me Do, and with the hateful old loner, who may or may not be a child molester.

Are you sure you want to go through with this? We will be happy to refund your initial payment—minus a twenty-five percent penalty to cover our costs. Nowhere in our prospectus do we say that writing is easy, enjoyable, or a pleasant way to make one's living in the privacy of one's own home without a time clock to punch or a boss's rosy ass to kiss. You may wind up like the loner on the bus: boring, despicable, repetitive, unoriginal, telling your stories out of habit and ugly impulse rather than out of the simple virtue of serving a communal need. Troubador, bard, skald, campfire ghost-story teller. Raconteur. If you cannot see yourself in this light, then how *can* you see yourself? Others may see you as narcissistic, self-obsessed, guilt-ridden, and bent on exposing your squalid but rather ordinary and nonexemplary life to "connoisseurs" of the "arts." Give it up *now*. They may be right about you.

And now we come to the hard part: You must know when a tale comes to its natural conclusion. In story-writing you don't begin with meaning, you end with it. But don't ask what is meant by meaning. You were told to keep this on the back burner. Now you are being told to keep it there. In fact, let's turn off the gas. A story should not mean; at best it should be meant. You didn't plan on it, but Helmut wins all the marbles. Let him. Who wins and who loses is always beside the point. Imagine yourself scuba diving off the California coast, out by the continental shelf. You're in comfortable green water, the sandy reassuring bottom in view, when suddenly you glimpse the vast black trench beyond the lip of the shelf. Make yourself linger there a moment. Oh God! Now write: The End.

Every story is a detective story. The murder goes unsolved even after the killer has been gassed, hanged, injected, or gunned down by the SWAT team. Philip Marlowe sits in his office knocking back straight shots of blended whiskey when reason tells us he should be thinking about raising a family in the law-abiding valley. The story is over, he has triumphed, but he's still puzzling it out. The detective story is a metaphor for every other kind of story (Lesson 22). The Heart of the Matter is the Heart of Darkness. The heart is also a lonely hunter.

Why do you think we actively seek the pain we knew as children? *Nostalgia?* If you don't think you do, quit now.

After Don Bremerton has killed his wife and her lover, and is tracked down and caught, he goes to the gas chamber with absolute calm. What can Marlowe do about that inexplicable Absolute Calm? (Lesson 80). What can you do about it? Where do we go from here? (Lessons 81–82).

I kicked him in the balls but not hard enough. He threw me down on the pool table, a cue stick against my throat. Go ahead kill me you fruit, I said, which was, in retrospect, unwise. I see this as the "Apex of My Self-Destructive Era" (Lesson 51). Out of catastrophe comes progress, reads a certain hexagram in the *Book of Changes*. He brought the thick end of the cue across my face, moving my nose over an inch. I woke up in an alley. The doctor who put my nose back, after hearing about my life odyssey from highly respected engineer to bottom-feeding drunk, said, "You know, Bud, if I were a writer, I'd write about you." That put the idea in my head for the School. Natalie O'Naillovich helped me with the organizational work, she also backed the enterprise with her divorce settlement. We got married and function, to this day, as a team. Sex life: Hey, not too bad for a couple of carved-up gray-heads with a list of physical complaints long as your forearm! We share a house in Connecticut but have separate bedrooms. My snoring—her night sweats. My small bladder—her teeth grinding.

How to Know When You've Reached the Stopping Point: When you've finished, your "Emptiness" (Lesson 13) will collide with the barrier of white space at the end of the last sentence. The collision should make a haunting sound. You will hear it. The untended vacuum between where the writer leaves off and the reader begins must chime. Or be bridged by thunder, or by that incendiary laughter that authorities fear. This is the place in the story where the aerialists realize there is no net and never has been. We watch them in horror as they try the impossible stunt—or we watch them in shame and embarrassment as they refuse to attempt the easiest trick of balance. Sometimes we leak furious tears as they—so beautiful, so brave—lose their grip on the slender bar that suspends them above all that "Inviting Nothingness" (Lesson 59). Oh yes, we are lost. But we are lost together.

Important! Send your next payment, or your request for partial refund, to the School before the first of the month. This will expedite the paperwork.